Under False Flags

Under False Flags

A Novel

Steve Anderson

YUCCA
Publishing

"I always thought everyone was against war until I found out there are those who are all for it, especially those who do not have to go there."

—Erich Maria Remarque, author and wounded WWI veteran

LETT, WENDELL, 21

Corporal Wendell Lett and his buddies spent most of the time crouched or prone, breathing dust and bitter black smoke, the passing NCOs screaming instructions so fast that they ended up asking each other just what the orders were. Hand signals they had down pat in training only confused. Was that halt or quick time, take cover or commence fire? They did what the others did. They didn't even know where the hell they were.

Lett's rifle platoon was heading inland from Utah Beach on the afternoon of June 6, 1944, advancing through Normandy farmlands and orchards. The thumps and cracks of artillery and firefights threw them off. Near or far? Hostile or friendly? Just by hearing, Lett caught on that all these guns, however precise and controlled in training, could prove so unruly and disloyal in the real world of fighting. Then a sergeant passed the word that enemy snipers were picking off anyone from majors to privates, some from just yards away. Another platoon had lost three guys in two hours and another their lieutenant. Lett only saw the first dead from a distance. Six or seven had been lined up along a dry dirt road and tagged for graves registration, looking so immaterial like a supply of olive drab packs and bedrolls. A lone German sniper could play a lot of god, apparently. Yet Lett didn't know one guy who had died. Some of his buddies even started crowing that they had been spared the worst of it. One joker from his squad, Private Tower, showed off the dent in his helmet where he'd caught a ricochet.

One sniper turned out to be a woman, a French civilian with a German rifle. She was up in a tree. Lett and his squad watched another team pull her down. She wore a black beret. She had bright red lipstick and a tomboy scowl, like some wayward bobby-soxer grounded from going out. What were they supposed to do with a prisoner like that? Some argued she was a spy since she was out of uniform, but in her own country? They sent her on back to the POW cage.

Already the front was looking so different from what a man was led to believe, from what a boy wanted to imagine. Before this first day, Lett couldn't help but see his company marching in step toward the enemy in vast formation and full gear, bayonets high and chins up, sworn draftees all of the Army of the United States. The whole company alert, steeled. Like most young GIs, he had seen too many movies back home. And then their Normandy landing had turned out to be a cakewalk. His platoon had strode onto Utah Beach right from an LST, their troop transport ship. Sure, the salt air carried the reek of that black smoke, and of gunpowders, but the latter only reminded him of exploding holiday fireworks. He could hack this, he told himself. He was hoping to make assistant squad leader. For now though, he had to stay in the middle of the twelve-man pack and keep moving like they were told. He still had a teenage face even at twenty-one, with curly hair that clung to his forehead and a quiet tone to his voice. It didn't exactly make a sergeant or lieutenant take much notice, not yet. He knew that.

They dug in for their first night on the line. Lett shoveled away with his foxhole buddy, Sheridan, the two flipping dirt at each other like boys on a camping trip, then cursing when they hit roots and rocks. At that point Lett could still claim he wanted to make a difference. The morals looked clear-cut: Hitler and Tojo were the aggressors, and the free nations of this earth had to defend themselves somehow. A deeper motive had become clear to Lett once the drill instructors and trainers stopped shouting at him and began to show him the ropes. It sounded corny to tell it, but Army life gave him a kind of structure. He had been raised an orphan. His father was an alcoholic moonlighting as a salesman. His mother died from overwork. Dad finally killed himself after Black Monday, 1929. The head nun had revealed all this to him at an early age if only to show him how good he had it raised in a Mennonite orphanage, where the aging nuns clung to a strange old German dialect. He didn't talk about his upbringing much, since these Mennonites spoke the enemy's language and were one of the sects, like the Amish, that raised their own to be noncombatants—conscientious objectors, the War Department called them. As a boy he had dreamed of running off to Spain to fight the fascists like one older orphan did. Yet the Mennonite elders had warned them: "It takes far more grit to swear off arms than it does to bear them." Even when Pearl Harbor hit, they had preached conscientious objection. Lett might have leaned that way too if the mission didn't look so clear. Besides, anything beat toiling away on his own in Columbus stuck in a boarding house and working three two-bit jobs, saving money for night school even though real jobs were still scarce. So he had volunteered before the draft found him. He hadn't done it out of pure patriotism. He knew few who had. He thought it would give him a leg up. And he was sure to meet a girl that way, somehow.

Lett and Sheridan's digging took them till dusk. They settled down inside their two-man foxhole, Lett's muscles aching and his sinuses tickling, the earth fresh around them, showing wiggly worms. Their line edged a field and a low hill beyond, but they couldn't see it anymore. When full darkness came, the platoon sergeant passed by to check on them and the rest. Then it was just he and Sheridan. Sheridan didn't talk much, wasn't always ribbing or boasting like other guys. Lett could appreciate that. But Sheridan had been getting quieter. He gazed around with bulging eyes as if he still couldn't believe this was all happening to them. They listened to far-off shelling and pops of gunfire.

"For the duration plus six," Sheridan said. "That's what we signed up for. It will be like this every night. You know that, don't you? It's just a chain gang, Wendell."

Lett didn't answer. He pretended he was asleep. He told himself Sheridan was weak. He would show Sheridan otherwise.

Early the next morning, Lett volunteered to join a team of five from another platoon going to check out a farmhouse on their left flank. The company S-2—the intelligence officer—had heard about enemy activity in the area, and Lett's lieutenant wanted him to fetch their platoon water while there. Already some canteens were running out.

The house was the standard gray block built of uneven stones, been there since before America. Lett didn't know the GIs in his team. Their sergeant led them to the house using caution and checking windows, which were shuttered. Lett lugged along an empty jerry can.

They kicked open a door. Screams met them. A family stood at a table in candlelight, all having jumped from their seats. The balding father looked about thirty-five and his wife was fuming, shielding a skinny boy no more than ten years old. The sergeant asked in broken French if they'd seen any Germans here. They hadn't. Pointing downward, the father said something about the family living in the cellar now. The sergeant sent two down to check it out, and took another along to check out the upstairs. This left Lett to watch the family. The front door had swung shut, bringing dimness, and the candles' tiny but sparkling flames mixed with slices of morning coming through the shutters. They stared at him a moment and went back to eating, tearing at their bread and slicing off hunks of a soft white cheese. The aromas made the room smell like a deli. Lett shouldered his M1 Garand rifle, sat on his jerry can, and pushed his helmet back off his forehead. He imagined himself plunking down and digging in, maybe learning a few words of French. This was his first real contact with locals.

Times like this, he had told himself, would only reaffirm why he was doing this.

He shared smiles with them, including *maman*, but they didn't offer a bite. He thought about trading some of his K-ration packet for some of that smelly cheese.

They heard a faint "whump-bang," and another. Enemy artillery. Lett had already learned to recognize this sound as the dreaded 88 mm gun; those veteran GIs who'd survived North Africa lowered their voices whenever they spoke of 88s.

A shell landed, not far, enough to jingle the windows behind their shutters.

The father rushed to a shutter and listened.

Another shell soared in, rattling the shutters and simple open china hutch.

The father glared at Lett. "You fool!" he shouted in English. "You breeng on us!"

The two GIs rushed from the cellar, the others back down upstairs. "Move it!" the sergeant shouted and ran out the door, leaving it to bang against the wall.

The family started to file back downstairs to their cellar, the youngest boy first. Lett waved hands at them. "No. Come with us!"

Shells landed closer, making chairs hop.

"*Non!*" shouted the wife, heading down.

"Dammit, come on!" Lett shouted.

The father scowled at Lett from the cellar stairs.

"I don't think it's safe," Lett muttered in English.

"It is safer than you," the father said. He ducked his head and stepped down, pulling the cellar door shut behind him.

The 88 shells pounded at the earth, shifting the whole house. Lett lunged and tumbled out the front door as another explosion spewed dirt in his face. He gritted his teeth, expecting shrapnel. He ran around craters and slipped on something—intestines had scattered from a torso, ripped open. He passed a severed foot white as porcelain, a helmet glistening red. Explosions rocked the ground. He sprinted for a wooden fence. The sergeant cowered there, his back to the shelling. Lett grabbed him by his web belt but the sergeant clawed at the fence. Lett let go and pressed down as low as he could, his helmet rim digging into earth, forcing himself into the weeds and dirt with toes and knees, elbows and hands like some crazed upside-down snow angel.

The shelling stopped. Lett stood, his legs wobbling. The fence was scattered, its pickets bloodied. The sergeant was gone, as if evaporated. Lett couldn't hear. A pressure had filled his ears and head, surging with a sharp ringing sound.

His legs found his feet. They carried him back to the house. There a heap of charred stones and blackened timbers smoldered, the embers popping and burning in little spots. One wall still stood, with a shuttered window. Lett stepped onto the heap. The center was a crater of churned earth. He looked down in, his eyesight suddenly sharp. He could make out every detail, from the scorched woodgrain shiny like fish scales to the smallest shard of china. Stones and earth had collapsed into the cellar. He counted three hands protruding, two bloody feet—not together, and the chalky bone of what looked like a hip.

He shuffled back toward his platoon, stunned and wooden like a marionette being dragged along. Cow carcasses lay among more craters, some butchered into shreds of flesh, others whole with legs stiff and straight out. A dog sprinted by as if crazed, heading who knew where.

A tent held their command post, just inside an orchard. A fold-up desk stood outside the CP. Platoon lieutenant Reardon sat shouting into a field telephone. No one seemed to notice Lett. He slumped down on a pile of packs and gear a few yards away, leaning on his M1. A medic came and looked him over, patted him on the shoulder and headed off. He sat there a long time. He relived the scene and a hot shudder seized him, as if his skin had been ripped off and his heart hung out in the air, raw from the exposure. He couldn't breathe. He started gasping. The medic came back and pressed a pill into his hand.

"I didn't get the water," Lett muttered. "I don't even have the can."

"You got a canteen," the medic said, but pressed his own canteen to Lett's lips.

Some time later, the medic was walking him along. "You got to get back to your hole," the medic said. "It's heating up. We're staying put for now."

"Okay," Lett said.

Lett made it back to the line, to his hole. To Sheridan. Sheridan would listen, Lett thought. The truth was, he'd tell old Sheridan, the only thing they'd done by checking out that house was let the German spotters zero in on them there. S-2 had no idea. He climbed into his foxhole, crouching next to Sheridan. Sheridan had his head resting against the dirt wall. Lett thought he was sleeping. Then he saw the hole where Sheridan's nose had been, and the blood and the blue, gray and pink of brains oozing out from the back of his helmet, down his collar. A sniper? Shrapnel? Lett sunk down, his chest seeming to expand and contract at the same time, squeezing at his organs.

The shelling returned, more 88s pummeling their line. Its thunder-wake left men screaming and wailing, the medics and squad leaders rushing around to quiet and brace them for the assault that could come. Only more shelling came. Lett had compressed into a ball down in his hole. He spent the afternoon this way, sharing the hole with Sheridan, the smoke dimming the sun and the shock waves slowly sending soot and mire down onto the poor bastard, first a dusting, then a covering, a brown shroud.

Days became weeks. Lieutenant Reardon died, and two sergeants, and five more grunts after Sheridan. They advanced into what locals called the *bocage*—hedgerow country. For miles inland

Normandy was laced with little fields, each sharing four to eight-foot-high ridges overgrown with centuries-old hedges, bushes and thick roots, all loaded up with frantic krauts itching to cut down Lett's buddies from every direction, camouflaged and firing everything from sniper rifles to rocket launchers to cannons. Hedgerow country combined labyrinth and slaughter. A man entering a field got hit from all sides. A man hugging a hedgerow for cover got a barrel pressed into his temple or buried alive as a German tank came charging through.

They were never rested, never taken off the line. It was march, attack, take casualties, seize the objective or pull back. It was pick 'em and put 'em down, dig in for every night. Secure vulnerable open land with mines and booby traps of wires strung with grenades. Lay down the "commo"—phone lines running three hundred yards back to the CP. Dig forward outposts for sentries who trembled through their two hours' watch in the dark, listening for Germans all around them, some of those sick bastards even trying to chat them up from across the line. Huddle in a hole. Dream of sleep. Worry about doing it all again. Next day, move out and attack and lose men and gain or give up ground, never really knowing what had transpired or if any real military objective had been won; then pick 'em and put 'em down . . .

As they slogged onward they learned to lighten their loads, tossing any gear they didn't need. Lett reduced his mess kit to just a spoon he kept in his trouser pocket, polished by the wool. The only reason he kept his thick little GI bible in his left breast pocket was for the added protection it was supposed to give. Men even ditched their toothbrushes. Some turned inward, and selfish in their worry. They stole others' blankets and half tents, shovels and the extra underwear they themselves had just tossed to lighten their load. The selfishness waned after the first few weeks, and stopped cold once each had faced death. Then the superstitions and talismans appeared, everything from rabbits' feet to coins to murmuring incantations before an assault or a good pounding. If a GI thought the simplest saying or routine was keeping him alive, he would keep repeating the ritual—until it didn't. Lett heard everything from epic poems to math equations, saw men tap their helmets to their own codes, stand on their heads, chew on dirty grasses like tired cows.

Lett had gotten another foxhole buddy, the joker Tower, from New Mexico. Tower stepped on a mine less than a week later, a Bouncing Betty mine. The Germans designed Bouncing Betty to launch a couple feet up before detonating. Bouncing Betty blew off a man's bottom half. In no time she was making men plead with the ground under their feet whenever they traversed new terrain, making promises, cajoling, sobbing, anything to convince the ground to favor them. Lett had watched from afar as medics made POWs haul away Tower on a litter, covered with a blanket, just pale-green arms hanging out. Next to Sheridan, Tower had been his best buddy. They went all the way back to the Army reception center. They had hit dance halls together in the states and pubs in England, and Tower got all the girls just like the swell guy in the picture.

On the morning of the day he died, Tower had told Lett that no amount of superstition was going to help them. The truth was, it was a numbers game when a GI looked at it rationally. Tower had said: "How many times can a man toss a quarter, and have it just land on tails?"

FRINGS, HOLGER, 36

0150 Uhr, 19. Juni 1944: In the moments before impact, Holger Frings of the German War Navy always imagined his wife, daughters and family and all their fears. Frings steered his S-boat as if they themselves rode aboard, huddled together below deck, the night sea pounding at their wooden hull, and only his helmsmanship could protect them. He could sense the flutters of their hearts in his fingertips on the wheel. Now he felt the hull shudder from the two torpedoes just launched, fired from each side simultaneously to keep the bow from listing, the killer eels cutting through dark water toward the enemy ship cruising into their path about 400 meters away. The faint silhouette had looked like a troop transport, what the Allies called an LST, nearly 5,000 tonnage. Frings had piloted for the ship as ordered, speeding at a right angle toward its portside, grasping at the handles of his wheel in the cramped wheelhouse with walls blackened for better night vision, their radioman Hahn at his left shoulder trying not to breathe down his neck and engine telegraph man Kammel on his right shoulder doing just that.

The ship flashed and erupted with a colossal crack. Direct hit!

A red flare soared up from the ship but its searchlights sputtered, overwhelmed by flame.

Captain Hanssen shouted orders through the voice tube: "Now go! All full ahead, rudder hard to port!"

Frings steered them sharply aport as Kammel telegraphed the captain's throttle-up order to the engine operators below. They roared away at close to forty knots behind the lead S-boat before them, its wake foaming up, its bow rising high, a mirror image of their own boat in two-by-two *Rotte* formation—Frings' boat following as the "slave boat."

All deck crew scanned the sky, the horizon. Frings peered out the double-glass windows, his heart thumping, his life vest pressing at the wheel handles. The rest of the English Channel remained dark and void of silhouettes, rising and falling, surging and swelling. Frings didn't miss seeing the Cliffs of Dover tonight. After so many hell runs that white wall had come to remind him of a hull-busting glacier, that or some freezing tidal wave never to be outrun.

The ship behind them burned. Shock waves pulsated the water under their boat, from the splitting, bursting hull, imploding steel and men.

As captain, *Oberleutnant zur See* Hanssen conned from the open bridge right on top of Frings' wheelhouse. "It's a bloody miracle, make no mistake, we're blessed tonight," Hanssen was panting through the voice tube. Two in the morning neared along the Southeast English coast near Dover, a dim night, cloudy, the wind from the northwest. Even before they had reached their assigned quadrant, no enemy had come to tear holes in them. Such fortune was as rare as could be. For the last couple years the Tommies had seemed to know where they lurked even before they did themselves, and the S-boats had become the sitting ducks like the convoys they used to prey on. The Normandy invasion of June 6 had only tightened the vice, plunging them into a meat grinder. Frings had seen America and what it could reap straight off the assembly line. This now was the big harvest. The invasion fleet kept coming, flowing from England across to France, the peaks and shapes of so many ships like a city skyline, as if London and New York themselves were being stretched across the Channel. The Allies defended it all with an iron perimeter of patrol ships and boats, mines and air cover and intensified radar, always the radar. Over the last couple weeks Frings' fellow S-boats had kept pricking this giant. It only got more of them killed. They were on track to lose at least twenty boats by the end of the month, more than the previous year total and almost half of this year's. Between four flotillas alone, only 13 of 31 S-boats running at the invasion had remained afloat. Finally the *FdS*, the S-boat flotillas' Commander-in-Chief, had sent them back north—here to their old stomping grounds along Southeast England. At least they had a chance here.

The lead boat began turning back around. "Rudder starboard ten, new course three-fifty," Hanssen shouted down to Frings, ordering him to follow suit. "It seems we're going to take a look."

Frings circled around to face the flaming wreck as it submerged, bow first. The wheel gave him different vibrations now, shudders, creaks and cracks, drones and groans. He couldn't hear the screams but he felt the familiar ache in his chest. Next time it might be them sucked under in such a fury, swallowing sea and getting swallowed up forever. They had twenty seamen aboard his S-boat—short for *Schnellboot*, the War Navy's fast torpedo craft. He was the "Number One," also called *Schmadding*, the nickname for the longest-serving, most experienced ranking seaman. His actual rank was *Obermaat*, a Petty Officer. The varieties of S-boat differed slightly but their boat was a retrofitted mishmash—just short of 35 meters long and five at beam, top speed nearly forty knots, torpedo tubes enclosed in the raised forecastle, with two extra eels on deck midships. They had a new armored bridge, a "skull cap" made of a special alloy called Wotan, and did they ever need it. For mine-laying sorties, bulky mines replaced their extra eels and launched off the stern. 2cm guns midships, fore and aft. Daimler-Benz diesel engines. She was patched up and cobbled back together, defying the odds that had demoted other worn boats to training flotillas or the scrap dock but had sent most to the bottom.

The lead and slave S-boats sat about five hundred meters apart. The sea burned before them, a mammoth bonfire reflecting off the oil on the waves, expanding and illuminating like a sun surfacing from underwater.

"All slow ahead," Hanssen said, following the lead boat. Frings and Kammel made the boat ease forward, the diesels whirring below. As a craft the S-boat was long and narrow, but she could lumber and flounder in the wrong hands—or when following a careless lead boat. Conning the lead boat as always were their flotilla chief, *Kapitän-leutnant* Schirakow, and its captain, Baum. Now it appeared Baum and Schirakow were going to have them check for survivors. This wasn't the policy. Late in 1942 Grand Admiral Dönitz had ordered that no enemy would be saved, responding to an incident in the Mediterranean whereby a German U-boat tried to collect the survivors of RMS Laconia, an armed merchant cruiser also carrying civilians and German prisoners of war. In the chaos, American planes had attacked. Losses were heavy all around. Younger officers like Hanssen welcomed the admiral's policy, for Allied planes were also bombing German cities and with little regard for civilians. Hanssen had lost two sisters and a grandfather in Hamburg air attacks. Most on board had lost someone back home, not to mention on the front. German bombers had hit Allied cities too, but that wasn't the point. Frings had to agree with Hanssen. Seeking out survivors like this was only inviting another trip through the meat grinder.

The sea fire burned so bright that Frings donned sunglasses. They crept forward.

"Survivors spotted," radioman Hahn said, relaying the word coming over their ultra-short wave set. The sighting had come from Baum's boat, but Schirakow hadn't given further orders.

Hanssen kept Frings on a steady course. Black forms appeared against the blinding conflagration. Life rafts. Loads of them, their silhouettes crowding the heaving crests of sea.

"Germans!?" Kammel shouted—Baum himself was on the radio, so loud the little speaker crackled: "We think we hear German survivors out there," Baum was saying.

German POWs? If this was a troop transport, it was entirely possible.

"Lead boat wants to check it out," Hanssen said. "Hold on tight."

"Shit," Frings muttered, and felt Hahn and Kammel tense up behind him. "Easy, boys," he said, giving them the hard eye of the Number One.

Hanssen ordered, "rudder starboard ten." They drifted toward the life rafts coming at them. On Frings portside, Baum's boat was doing the same. They did have some support—two other pairs of boats from their flotilla lurked less than a nautical mile away, searching for more of the convoy.

The bow rose and fell as they idled along. Frings felt the heat of fire through the double-glass, the heat stretching the skin on his cheeks, and smelled the black smoke passing over their boats. The life rafts neared. Frings heard shouts and felt stomping above on the open bridge—Hanssen and the watch officer were moving around to all sides, directing the crew to ready safety lines and ladders. Frings peeked out windows and through the hatch to the starboard bridge wing skirting the wheelhouse. All deck crew wore rifles and machine guns slung, bulky figures in their denims and oilskins, life-jackets and helmets. Their three double-two guns were manned and ready.

The ship's flame died as the vessel went under, bringing a veil of darkness like a sack pulled over their heads. Their searchlights and flashlights arced and flicked around.

Over at Baum's boat the life rafts clustered at the hull, the survivors' faces ashen. More swam up. They neared Frings' boat too, the rafts' rubber slapping and sloshing at their hull. Frings saw soldiers in the rafts. Their uniforms were American. *Amis.*

Up above him Hanssen had the megaphone: "Any Germans here?" he shouted in German to the rafts.

"Help us!" men shouted back in English, the accents American. "Take us aboard!"

"I say, any Germans out there?"

Frings heard a survivor scream: "What does it matter, you kraut bastard—" Other survivors silenced the man.

He looked over to Baum's boat. The silhouettes of the crew and those of the rescued Americans mixed and fluttered on deck, as if in a crazed dance. Some men fell back overboard into their life rafts, the water churning and frothing, the men flailing away. Others swam up, grabbing at life rafts and lines and ladders.

Pops of gunfire flashed on Baum's boat, so unreal it looked like firecrackers, sparklers. Men wrestled each other on deck. One survivor had a weapon. The man fired at the bridge from midships. Return shots sent him tumbling over the portside railing.

Frings pivoted around, checking his windows, hatches. Survivors had made it aboard his boat now, all enemy, Americans. Some dropped to the deck in exhaustion. Others fought with his crew, hand to hand. A man went overboard, then another.

A survivor rushed into the wheelhouse screaming. He rushed Kammel and Hahn, plowing them into the corner. Frings locked arms with the intruder, so close Frings could smell his fear, a gamy sweat. Frings kicked him back out the hatch and pinned him to the bridge armor. A seaman grabbed the man and heaved him overboard.

Hanssen shouted orders from the bridge while the enemy survivors shouted at their own to stop. But life rafts kept coming. Men fought out in the water, some in life jackets and some not, arms pinned on one another in ghastly wrestling matches, holding each other under, strangling each other, screaming. Oil on the water reignited, consuming them.

"Warning shots!" Hanssen shouted to all gunners. "Fire at will!"

Both boats fired. The salvos pounded like giant hammers, flashing flame from bow, midships, stern, rocking their boat. Shots hit life rafts and men out in the water.

"Cease fire!"

Dead men bobbed, body parts floated. A few men groaned out in the water, dead already. The burning sea oil crept toward them, engulfing them too.

Another survivor showed in the wheelhouse hatch, sopping with oil. The man had a knife. "You butchers," he hissed. Kammel had grabbed an MP 40. He fired so close the flame spewed right into the man, who flew back, bounced off metal and rolled away down the deck as ricochets pinged around.

Hanssen shouted: "Number One! The wheel!"

The oil fire neared them, the blazing water gurgling with debris and air pockets. They drifted toward Baum's boat. Frings grabbed the handles, correcting, spinning the wheel.

Reds and greens lit up the sky—enemy flares. Searchlights hit them. Yellow darts shot past, tracers of bullets. British MTBs— motor torpedo boats—charged for them portside at right angles. The fast boats kept firing and salvos hit them like massive chains crashing against the boat.

Baum's boat headed off, pumping out diversionary smoke from its stern canisters.

"All full ahead! Rudder starboard ten, new course one-fifty!" Hanssen shouted and, "Smoke now, smoke now!" and the fake fog gushed out behind them, rolling across the waves.

The MTBs turned and followed.

"Return fire, all fire!" Frings heard Hanssen screaming at their gunners. Baum's boat fired away, his bow high, the surging wake reflecting flashes. Spray lashed at the windows as Frings wheeled into a zigzag pattern on Hanssen's command, the smoke laying down a wall of fog behind them. The MTBs couldn't keep track. Their salvos flickered from within the fog but dimmed, withered.

Baum sped onward, Frings falling in line astern. He clenched the handles and let out a scream, bearing his teeth.

0400 *Uhr:* Two hours later. Somehow the two S-boats had evaded the Tommies. The rest of the flotilla only found them for the return march after having lost them to radio static. They had taken too many hits and holes again. Both boats had some rust, and rust did not like hot bullets. They cruised along at slow ahead while the specialists below made sure nothing more was about to burst or conk out. Frings' boat had lost one man, a new assistant gunner—a round had ripped through the sailor but his oilskins had somehow kept his shredded chest inside the thick leather. A few seamen had wounds and contusions and were brought below where the salt mist couldn't sting in their wounds, but they had to keep the dead sailor on deck because the mess was simply too much. Meanwhile, any dead *Amis* had gone off their open-ended stern.

Three survivors remained on Frings' boat, all Americans. The *Amis* were wounded severely, their bodies blackened with smoke and oil. Two were too exhausted to speak. Because of his English, Frings had the job of interrogating the one able to speak. Two seamen hauled the man, a young soldier, to the wheelhouse hatch. Frings shouted from his wheel at the American, which made Kammel and Hahn snap their heads his way—few crew knew Frings had been on merchant ships speaking English. The *Ami* was too shocked to curse them. He said their LST was packed with troops and jeeps—they were replacement soldiers, infantry. And the man passed out. Hanssen ordered the three survivors kept around the main compass mounted amidships behind the wheelhouse, had blankets brought up for them, then a tarp over that when it began to rain. He posted a seaman to train an MP 40 on them.

Baum's boat had two men killed and their wheelhouse was shot up, their engine sputtering. The flotilla had lost another boat from a mine, fire on board, three dead, two burned so bad the partner-boat radioman could hear them screaming through the short wave.

Engine telegraph Kammel and radioman Hahn had apologized for getting caught off guard, and Frings told them: "If I ever catch you two mucking up like that again, you'll be scraping rust in the North Sea," but he wouldn't report it. All had seized up at some point. "Besides, you made up for it," he told Kammel. "Just watch those goddamn ricochets."

Frings held the wheel tight and peered into the darkness, trusting the water, the lookouts, Captain Hanssen, and the lead boat only because he had no choice. He slid his pipe between his lips, wanting to light it. And shivered. June had turned cold, but that wasn't what made him shudder. The water had taught him many rules in life, yet in the last four years those rules were under constant attack. He did all he could to make some kind of order out of it. On an S-boat, the Number One supervised all the seaman duties—there were watches to manage, cleaning and restoring, disputes, and discipline, and morale, right down to picking a lineup for a football match when a patch of bad weather kept them in their pens. Meanwhile, the specialists below deck dealt with the motors and fuel, the torpedoes and the grub (their cook was also a torpedo-man, in fact). Frings hadn't expected to become a Navy sailor, yet he had been left with little choice. He had done a good ten years in the merchant marine, but by 1940 the merchant work had all but dried up for Germans. War meant he'd be drafted sooner than later, so why end up in the mountain corps, an airplane or a trench? He could survive on the water. He'd grown up in Cologne on the Rhine River like his father and his father's father. He had helmed a river tug for the first time before he was twelve. In what was renamed the *Kriegsmarine*—the War Navy, a sailor could choose a technical career path or serve as a regular seaman. He chose the latter; he would do his time, then get back home.

If he survived at all. Those first trying months on an S-boat seemed like a happy stroll now. Back then it was simple. Flotilla command would send them to a quadrant, say, near the mouth of the Thames or close to the Dover coast. There they sat in *Rotten*, in pairs ready to prey. Back in 1940, they sunk French and British destroyers off of Dunkirk. He remembered summer nights speckled with endless stars, like confectioner's sugar sprinkled over the world. Not that simple meant easy. In winter, the sea spray was so cold it froze right on deck, railings, glass, all. Torpedoes malfunctioned. They had to grease every moving part exposed to air and water. Whether in summer or winter, their engines could conk out, or boats collided, or were rammed on a run. They never had enough boats, but they always had a chance. In about 1941, the enemy started knowing exactly where they ran. Radar was to blame. Radar changed everything. Radar let the Brits pinpoint them but they, in turn, could not know if the Beefs knew. It made the most routine stroll terrifying. The enemy always had a bead on them, sometimes reaching their positions before they did. Things only got worse into '42, '43. Some improvements came. They had dampeners for their exhaust. They had the armored bridges that could stop light flak rounds but little else. They had bigger guns, supercharged engines, so-called smart torpedoes that only crapped out on them. They tried out new tactics but these were based on unreliable radio monitoring or haphazard Luftwaffe sightings. The Luftwaffe's lame warnings had become a pantomime farce, while the enemy spotters seemed to have a direct phone line to every bomber pilot. And still the radar never came. Even when German technicians developed their own *Funkmess* radar devices, the S-boats never got them. They were all like helpless little forest creatures—untold beasts of prey swooped down on them whenever they dared pop their heads out of their burrows. By '44 they were losing boats faster than new ones arrived or the repaired ones came back. Replacement sailors got younger, greener. Captains and flotilla chiefs pleaded for radar. The Allies were now intercepting their radio transmissions, and had surely figured out their secret codes. Yet no one up high would consider the possibility, Hanssen had told Frings. Meanwhile the enemy had become an iron boot, crushing them into particles. And now the Allied invaders were sure to break out of Normandy soon and charge east as their bombers kept pounding German cities.

Frings could only do so much from his wheelhouse. Captain Hanssen up on the open bridge above called all the shots, aided by the watch officer, lookout and signal man. Hanssen ordered Frings when to steer and how. Hanssen ordered engine telegraph man Kammel to relay speeds to the engine operator below deck. But even Hanssen himself could only do so much. He could only follow whatever the ranking Schirakow commanded from the lead S-boat, which captain Baum conned though he was only an *Obersteuermann*, a Master Chief Petty Officer. Yet Baum had more sea hours than Hanssen, was a rare 1937 vintage trained on the first S-boats, and had the flotilla chief on his open bridge.

Frings manned the wheel, but he had no real control. As helmsman he had to stay on the wheel, always in the wheelhouse, in all combat situations and dangerous sorties. He was an implement; he was implemented by orders. He was just one gear in the engine. He was only another link in the chain. The order of this machinelike system used to give him comfort, a feeling of freedom even. Now he only saw it as a curse that kept a man helpless. One break anywhere in the chain, and the whole machine broke.

The formula had become the problem. The powerlessness had been eating away at his thoughts, keeping him awake. How could he survive to care for his family if his wheel gave him no control? How could he keep them safe so far away in Cologne? They were so exposed, all the cities were. There he had his parents, his kid sister, his wife Christiane and two daughters, Elisa and Kristina, four and five. When he thought of his little girls, he still saw them as the toddlers they were when he'd seen them last. They expected him to survive. He had promised them.

He had to stay above water; he had to keep them from going under.

He grasped at the wheel, wrenching at the handles. His chest burned raw as if his skin had been ripped right off, exposing his organs and heart to the salt air. The night's sortie had only showed him how easily the chain could break, and what men did to each other when pushed to the limit. It made Cologne and his family seem so much farther away. It made him fear the breakable chain even more. What part of it would finally snap, and when?

He leaned into the wheel and wheezed, swallowing back down the burn of vomit rising in his throat. He shivered again. He found his feet and lit his pipe, breaking his own no-flame rule.

The eastern sky thinned to purple on the horizon. A fog obscured the coastline where their base at Boulogne opened up to them. Once moored back inside their S-boat pen, Frings finally was able to leave his wheelhouse. It was six a.m., but the thick concrete bunker blocked most all of the morning breaking outside. As he always did, he touched their boat's talisman mounted on the wheelhouse, a small double-sided axe atop a log slice—one stroke for each dull blade. Two bullet holes had come within centimeters of it this time, but none had ever hit it.

He made his way around the boat, taking stock, sizing up damage, asking questions, calming men down. The sentry came up to him, shoulders sagging, his MP 40 slung.

"Why aren't you watching the *Amis?*" Frings said.

"They're all dead, *Schmadding*. First the two, then the one. They just . . . gave it up."

Frings shook his head, fighting another burn in his chest. He climbed below. The motors were giving off a nasty diesel smell, on the verge of burning, enough to make the seamen below sick. He heard patters and snorts coming down the narrow passageway as their compact little black and brown hunting terrier strode up, sniffing at him with care as if checking for wounds. Frings gave their sea dog Vigo a rub on his head, which earned Frings a few licks. Vigo was no fool. In the old days, Vigo had often found his way up on deck during a run and snuggled the main compass midships, the calmest spot on the boat. Vigo hadn't ridden up there for far too long, choosing to hide out below deck, and who could blame him?

Up in the forecastle, Frings passed the tiny captain's quarters that was the Hotel Adlon compared to the sailors' shared bunks in the stern. As *Kommandant*, Hanssen had a bed that folded up into a table and leather bench, complete with a little bar built into the wood-paneled wall. Hanssen had plopped down on the bench, the leather squeaking like a fart. The captain looked smaller when he wasn't up on the open bridge leaning over the range finder and gritting his teeth in frustration like he did, his peaked captain's cap far back atop his pale, narrow face with droopy eyes and long forehead, all combined in a surprisingly handsome way. The man was all of twenty-six. He had come a long way since stepping aboard in late 1942. He was Frings' third CO. The man had stayed alive longer than any of them. He was a naval legacy, his father a battleship officer in the Great War, and as such had gone to Mürwik Naval Academy of course. He spoke High German while Frings did his best not to confuse others with his Cologne dialect. While Hanssen looked the newsreel and magazine version of a boat captain, Frings was the boulevard tabloid version of a carnival strongman with his block of a head and thick reddish-brown hair. He had let his outdated large mustache grow into a beard, and on board he often wore a brown civilian sweater and blue-white checkered kerchief under his oilskins or denim. Yet every sailor saw he was a Number One and in case anyone doubted his know-how, Frings' uniform bore the rare S-boat War Badge—an oval of gold wreaths topped with that all-pervasive Nazi war eagle and a silver S-boat speeding out from the center, its bow up high.

"Number One," Hanssen said. "Do you want to know something? There were no Germans on those rafts. None at all. How do you like that?"

What could Frings say? He could not protest that their flotilla chief Schirakow and lead boat captain Baum were reckless if not contradicting general orders, and Hanssen wouldn't hear of it. It suggested someone's court martial, if not his own. Old hands like Schirakow and Baum certainly knew how to whitewash action reports. Yet Hanssen wanted to know what Frings was thinking. Since their recent slaughters battling the invasion fleet, Schirakow and Baum had been acting more rash in the lead.

"That is unfortunate, *Herr Oberleutnant*," Frings said.

Hanssen grinned and wagged a finger. "Remember this: Reckless is good. I applaud it. But it has to work to our advantage, instead of us wasting our lives to save those dead already. You know this war is a new sort of war. It is not my father's, or your dad's. So when our boat gets its good chance, we won't go and waste it."

0700 hours: The flotilla had its billet in a brightly painted country house a few kilometers up the coast in Wimereux. They had a couple tables set out on the front lawn, and after a return march crews would gather there and wind down despite the morning coolness. Frings rode back in an open truck with a group from the other boats, Number Ones and NCOs mostly, swapping stories, ruing mistakes and working out in their heads just what the devil would want in their reports this time. Their uniforms hung off them, suddenly heavy, as if sizes bigger.

At the billet a young *Matrose* stood on the front steps, facing Frings. He held a telegram. The others slapped Frings on the back and wandered out to the tables. Frings took the envelope, and something in the seaman's eyes told Frings to look at the telegram somewhere alone. He stomped through the front grass, around to the side of the house. He ripped open the envelope:

From Cologne:
From Your Christiane:
Horrible air raids. Your father, mother and sister lost. Heavy damage.
Your daughters and I are safe. Stay safe. Here we feel much sorrow.

Lost? Lost meant dead. Frings' chest seemed to have filled with concrete. His boots sinking into the sodden earth. He wasn't sure how long he stayed there, but at some point his mates had huddled around him, and he had curled up with his back to the stone wall.

He couldn't speak, but he heard their talk. They had gotten orders from the *FdS*—they were heading back out that night. A large convoy was reported. Someone said: "The *Schmadding* here can't go out, not with death in his family. It's standard procedure—"

"No!" Frings shot up, pushing off the stone wall, staggering to his feet. "I'm going out," he growled. "I'm going out tonight and every goddamned night we can."

***

Wendell Lett was changing. He knew he was. His senses had intensified from all the caution. Every sparkle, color, edge and curve took on a gleam that imprinted in his memory, except the awe was reserved only for things he had to fear. He saw no pretty green fields or picturesque medieval towns—he saw sniper hidey-holes, machine gun nests, 88 haunts. Caution became his particular talisman, and learning from mistakes in the field his obsession. It helped him get a grip on the constant, grinding terror that he and all of them felt to the marrow, in their every waking and sleeping moment. Before an assault they had to pee from it, or shit, which many did in their trousers or foxholes and often. They had little appetite and used to blame it on their rations, right down to the powdered lemonade. Meanwhile, real sleep had become a distant dream. If Lett ever slept lying down for more than a couple hours it was like coming out of a coma, like smoke had filled his head and he had a horrible taste in the mouth, a tongue like dirt. They learned they could find some sleep while footslogging in file, and Lett probably got more shut-eye on the march than in his hole. Their nickname for this was easy: "marching dead."

In July, Lett's battalion finally broke out of Normandy. He was pulling his weight. He had an archaic sort of German, from growing up among the Mennonites. He had mentioned this at his reception center and again in training and an instructor had written it down, but no one brought it up again. Now it was finally proving useful. He offered it up whenever the platoon or company needed a question answered from a POW. It helped them dodge ambushes and shit creek. He knew his name went into after-action reports, but the S-2 intelligence officers at battalion or higher had never come asking for him. They had their own translators. Why would they need a dogface? Dogfaces dug in. Dogfaces killed.

He had his first up-close kill. He had killed before but it had always been from cover, from a hole or behind a stone wall firing away at a position with the rest of the squad. He had seen the enemy drop. He had seen their ripped-apart, leaking, oozing bodies contorted when his squad marched on by. Face to face was another matter. It happened in a town. In a foyer of a house. A German had tripped on steps trying to flee upstairs. The man fumbled for his rifle but it clattered down the steps, right down to Lett. Lett had him covered. The German had a simple, broad face, with longer hair showing from under his helmet like they had. "*Hände hoch!*" Lett shouted. The German raised his hands. Lett heard footsteps upstairs shuffling his way. So he fired. It laid the man out on his back, filling the stairway, the blood trickling down the edges of the steps. A team had rushed in other doors. They captured two snipers upstairs. They shot them on the spot, and all was clear. Lett had wandered back out the building. His squad was taking a break, not saying much and slumped on a stoop, leaning into one another. Lett sat next to a couple would-be old timers like him, Mancuso from a California farm and Bartley a Detroit suburb. They didn't console Lett. In the last week they had lost five, two of them from snipers. Lett wanted to feel something, even a brief warmth of vengeance done, but in the moment he didn't feel a damn thing. He wanted to throw up and ball and seize up like guys did. But he felt nothing. He wanted it now. If it came and found him later, who knew when it would end?

Mancuso died the next week. Mortar burst. Bartley was Lett's foxhole buddy. He went the same week, but he didn't die. He had bolted from Lett's foxhole during a shelling. They found him a day later, wandering the rear line, naked and covered in mud, muttering in Latin. No one had even known he spoke the language.

At this point, Lett felt a secret relief when others bought it and not he. He imagined others felt that way, but who would ever say it? They had been knitted too close now. It was like saying you wish you'd never had your child. The company was losing guys faster than there were days. Every original sergeant Lett had known was dead. Most of the officers in Lett's company were gone within a month—many dead, some injured horribly, a good few cracked up, a couple simply went missing; and others were taken off the line for incompetence that got so many men maimed and killed it couldn't be ignored. Lett's platoon went through two lieutenants after Reardon. A certain Lieutenant Hannity passed all orders through the platoon sergeant and never made the rounds. Hannity preferred to spend his time kissing up to the company CP. A sniper got him doing that. The next one, Lett didn't even remember his name. He fancied himself some kind of two-bit Patton, complete with the chickenshit insistence on rear-line formality, wanting them to wear ties—as if they had any. He stepped on a mine looking for a place to have them dig a shitting hole. Good riddance.

Then came Tom Godfrey. The Second Lieutenant looked like another 90-day wonder straight out of OCS. He wore one of those windcheater tankers jackets the officers liked, a mustache fit for a publicity officer, face handsome in a common way. He smiled too much for the front. This one wouldn't last long, they figured.

Sergeant Krebs had been leading things meanwhile. Godfrey listened to Krebs, and to all of them. He asked for opinions. He made the rounds at night when they were dug in. He remembered to whisper up on the line. He let Krebs talk him out of another dodgy night patrol ordered down from the deaf men at battalion, telling company they had done the job and all was well. He did send out a patrol when it was light, but he led it himself. When one Joe cracked up, he sent the man to a rear-line depot to pick up goods, all so the man could have a little time to put himself back together. He even shared his officers' liquor ration with them.

The first direct thing Godfrey said to Lett was after dark. The looie had crawled out to their observation post, and crouched with Lett in the vulnerable forward foxhole. It had been a fubar day, fucked up beyond all recognition. They had lost two old hands on a patrol that division itself had demanded. "I tell you," Godfrey whispered, "if any beings from space ever bother to visit this old planet, I doubt they'll look at us humans as the best thing that's ever happened to it."

"We're more like its plague," Lett whispered back, and Godfrey patted him on the shoulder before moving on.

In August they pressed on toward Paris but never got to see the joyous old capitol. They slogged through small towns and down country lanes in the heat, heading east. Lett's feet were so calloused he could light a match off them. One evening they finally got a brief rest, in a little wood outside a village. Word had come down that they wouldn't have to dig in that night. They wouldn't move either. Division needed more of the rear line to catch up. This was like announcing a guy had won the lottery. To celebrate, Godfrey took a team into the village to scare up booze and food. They came back with burning strong brandy and hard cheese but no bread. Somehow a mailbag had gotten through, and guys sat around reading, sharing stories from home. Almost every GI had loads of mail and wrote almost just as much. Lett got fewer mail than anyone. Distant relatives wrote to him, most out of a sense of obligation, he reckoned, and he had little desire to write them back. He had gotten one letter from an aunt, and another from a fellow orphan now on a ship in the Pacific. They might as well have been someone else's letters by mistake. He was used to this. As an orphan most of his life, he didn't think about it much. A man almost grew accustomed to the rootlessness. He knew it gave others an uncomfortable feeling. Krebs wanted to get him into a card game, but Lett was fine just leaning against a tree, smelling the breeze that came through the leaves with a sweeter scent, looking out at the blue sky going dim for the night and void of tracers for once. He didn't even need any of that cheese, especially not without bread. This might have been the first time he couldn't hear battle for well over two months, including nighttime. He got to thinking about how he would meet a girl if he ever made it through this, if it could ever end. It didn't matter where, or how—it would be the start of something stable. Then he extinguished the thought by summoning that raspy coughing fit he couldn't shake. Such thoughts had faded in the last month and probably should, he thought. The odds were just too poor.

Godfrey made the rounds and poured brandy into canteen cups, an unlit Lucky Strike flapping on his lips. Most Joes only got Pall Malls and Raleighs. So Godfrey passed out his Luckies, and when they ran out, he somehow came up with Camels. He ended up kneeling beside Lett. Lett wasn't smoking. He had quit cold turkey during a night of horrid shelling, another superstition. Where absurd horrors loomed, ad hoc superstition reigned.

Godfrey's teeth shined in the dusk light, and he lit up. He shared the view with Lett a while. "All these guys reading mail, playing cards, who needs it, am I right?" he said finally.

"Keeps em going, though," Lett said.

"Sure. Listen. I got word from a local, there's a nice woman in town looking to entertain a real American hero."

Lett threw an eye on the platoon lounging around them. He shook his head. "Better check with quartermaster, see if they got any left," he said, showing Godfrey a smile. Some guys had made it in this or that town. It wasn't that the thought didn't interest Lett. But the combat, the drudgery, the marching and constant shelling squealing inside his head all sucked away such urges. It sapped a man. Besides, his field jacket was torn, his trousers stained from the urine and shit not to mention the blood; and only the dirt helped to hide some of it. His constant stubble had become a beard, and he wouldn't have been surprised to see it gray. He must have smelled like the inside of a cattle car. "Thanks. Really. But I'm not interested in sharing," he added.

"That's just the thing. No one knows about her." Godfrey smiled and placed a hand on his heart, but then his smile dropped away, leaving glossy, longing eyes.

"Ah, why not," Lett said.

Godfrey perked up. "There you go."

Lett pulled himself to his feet, brushed off a top layer of dirt, slung his rifle and hung his helmet on his belt. He didn't bother cleaning up any more than that. What could it help? He didn't even have his toothbrush any more. "Should I bring something, a bottle?"

Godfrey smiled. "Oh, no. God, no. She's got you covered. Just, head for the north edge of the village, look for a little *rue* leading along the creek. It's a cottage. Red shutters. Can't miss it."

Lett tipped an imaginary hat, and walked off for the village.

Her name was Véronica. Her two-room cabin smelled like perfumed candles, as if to cover GI-stink maybe, and Lett didn't ask. She had high eyebrows, painted on. They drank a glass of red wine. She said she hated brandy and hoped the Americans drank it all. Her English was excellent. She looked to be about forty. She had to be a pariah in this village, Lett thought, unless she had brought some manner of fading fame with her. She wore a dark thin sweater with pink peter pan collar and a long skirt, looking like a schoolmistress.

She sat him in a wooden chair near the table. She unbuttoned his field jacket, and her rouge lips seemed to enlarge twice their size as she leaned toward him. Her large breasts brushed against him, he could smell a little underarm odor on her, and it only made him want to give in more. He didn't move to touch her. He didn't want to soil any of this with what he had become.

He closed his eyes. He imagined her pulling up her dress and working her way onto him, her flesh stroking his and melding with his as he sank his face into her breasts . . .

He smelled something, meaty rich like dark chicken and salty fat like bacon. It popped his eyes open. She had returned with a plate, fetched from the tiled corner oven, and gestured for him to pull up to the table. His mouth hung open. The plate held a heap of legs and breast, crispy potato slices, cooked cabbage.

"It's duck. A confit," she said.

Lett dove in. The chair creaked and banged at the floorboards as he ate. He finished without a peep, just his mouth hanging open again, and to his surprise Véronica kissed it.

She loaded him up another plate.

"France thanks you," she said when he finished. "We shall not clean you up though, not yet. They shall only make you dirty again."

"Ain't that the truth." Lett had to shake his head. "You didn't have to do this. I didn't even want to talk. I just wanted to sit. In a chair. In a house with four walls. I would have been happy just watching you drink wine."

She gave him a playful slap on the forehead. Keeping him in the chair, she gave him a neck message that made his mouth hang open one more time.

"You shall make one girl a most wonderful husband someday," she said.

"Thanks," he said, but he had a hard time imagining it, seeing it. He didn't tell her that part. There were those odds again.

He didn't know what Véronica was, and he didn't ask. He left her two packs of Raleighs because he wanted to. She shrugged at them, and kissed him on the cheek as he left.

As Lett made his way back in the dark, he wondered what this world would be like if women ran it. People would still die, but surely they would not be slaughtered by the shipload.

A few Joes smoking made it easier to find the platoon in the dark—Godfrey and Krebs were evidently letting the boys light up at will, considering. Someone was snoring. A couple others trembled in their sleep, and many uttered muted squeals from those nightmares that they all had. It was strange to see them like this at night, above ground and out in the open, and getting harder still for Lett to imagine living as he had before, in peace. The card game was peaking, complete with drunken whispers. But most men just lay stretched out in the open air, such a rare luxury that may never happen again. Lett felt for an open spot, plopped down and lay on his back, and sighed with ease for the first time he could remember. He found the stars in the sky, so many they crowded out the darkness in places. He didn't know where Godfrey was in that moment, but he knew the lieutenant was keeping an eye on him from somewhere in the dark. He knew another thing, as he started to doze straight off: They would not be shelled here that night.

That one carefree eve was the last true rest they got, one of the first since Normandy. Another month had passed, someone said, but it might have been ten years or ten minutes. Lett had turned twenty-two years old and didn't realize it until two days later. All sense of time was lost to a guy like Lett. They had crossed the Marne and Seine Rivers. They passed through Paris but couldn't stop and enjoy it. They over-stretched their lines out of the brass hats' eagerness, which left them even longer without their supply of chow, gear, mail and more. They had more uneasy patrols, faced more scrappy flanking attacks. Lett had killed four Germans face-to-face total, if he bothered to count, and many more from a distance. The close ones were never like in the movies. Usually they would just run into each other. He saw their faces most nights, in his nightmares. They were floating in a dingy together, on rapid water, just the four of them. Sometimes Lett drowned them, holding their heads underwater if he had to, one by one, bubble after last bubble. Other times they drowned him. The people at home would never know what killing was. They'd never know that he had killed pigs. On a patrol they had checked out a farm after a battle. Bodies lay everywhere, American and German. Ten or so pigs must have gotten free, and had gorged out the stomachs and chest cavities of the corpses. The beasts circled and paced the scene and rolled in mud and blood. So Lett shot the swine, one by one, and left them where they lay. Someone else could go and cut the pork out of them.

They got a break from marching while the advance into North-eastern France kicked into high gear. They hitched rides on trucks and tanks and crammed into local cars they marked up with US Army stars. Allied aircraft ruled the skies, yet friendly strafing was com-mon. They fought using far more replacements now, many of them college kids that had once been spared for the stateside Army Spe-cialized Training Program, the ASTP, but the War Department had to abandon keeping the smart kids at home because front-line units were losing too damn many. They came from the repple depple at the rear—the replacement depot, a kind of orphanage for the damned, the way Lett saw it. In Lett's company, the casualty rate was reaching well over 150 percent, which didn't seem possible until one counted all the replacements who bought it and often within days. There were too many reasons for this. The replacements' training wasn't as good, seeing how they were rushed into duty. Many got hit freezing up and bunching when trouble started. Under fire, the veteran GIs knew never to cluster—that only gave the krauts a bigger target. Under fire, the old Joes always kept their heads up and eyes open and legs moving. They could tell incoming German shells and outgoing American, and didn't hit the deck every time they heard artillery or saw a bomber up high. Of course they shuddered and tightened up though when hearing the clatter of a Tiger tank, the rapid rattle-belch of heavy German machine guns, like industrial sewing machines running out of control, or the shrill howls of *Nebelwerfer* rocket launchers. All of those made their assholes eat underwear. The homefolks and rear-liners figured the veteran got less scared as he slogged along, but it didn't work out that way. Lett had dizziness, nausea, stomach cramps, sweating, headaches, rapid and irregular heartbeat, insomnia, and those nightmares. They all did. Their fear was a confining pit of a cell. Part of the problem was they felt so alone once any action started. GIs lost contact with one another. Americans were talkers normally, but under battle pressure they clammed up more than Germans or Brits. Then there was the relentless fatigue. Dogfaces weren't bums or goldbrickers or sad sacks but they did look somewhat like hobos, meaning laborers on the move, and felt and behaved like them too. These were dejected, stooped, weary men. Hands trembled, heads jerked at unknown sounds, guys stared into space and truly didn't know where they were. One man thought he was back in the *bocage* for a whole week. He saw imaginary dense hedgerows along every open road.

A doctor visiting from the rear had revealed, after Tom Godfrey plied him with whisky, that GIs with little or no relief from combat ceased being effective soldiers at about 200 days, on average. The War Department had been doing studies and was learning the truth from their guinea pigs on the line. Yet even those findings were laughable, the doctor admitted. All it took was one nasty shelling. Lett himself saw that far fewer than thirty days took many guys down. For one ninety-day period, Lett's unit was off the forward line for about ten days tops before he stopped counting. The Brits rested units after about two weeks, they were hearing, but GIs stayed up on the line for sixty days or more without real relief? They weren't even guinea pigs. They might as well have been rats. It wasn't about the weak or strong, cowardly or brave. Every man had his breaking point. How a GI broke was different for each Joe. Even a rest only helped so much. Some originals who had been injured had come back, with limited duty. Lett had assumed they'd be rested and ready. They only seemed more jittery and vacant, hollow, haunted.

They entered Belgium, one step closer to Germany. Sergeant Krebs was killed, mortar round, direct hit. That left less than ten in the platoon from before Normandy, maybe forty in the whole company. They made another old timer platoon leader, a Sergeant Charles, and Lett got his sergeant stripes. Sooner than later they'd make him platoon leader. This would only make him stand out for good, Lett knew. And once the Grim Reaper took notice, the bastard never let go.

***

Holger Frings' father Peter had a withered right leg from World War One. When war had broken out, Frings' grandfather Siegfried had expected his son Peter to join the Imperial Navy. The Frings were all men of the water. As a young man, though, Peter thought it a rebellious act to volunteer for the Army. In any case the big war would be over so fast, everyone had said.

Peter's rebellion put him in trenches along the Belgian border with France for three years, the dirt walls packed with the body parts of men ripped apart and churned back into the earth by shelling. Eventually this got Peter gassed, which gave him a life of breathing troubles, then a leg mangled by shrapnel after his regiment was ordered to hold a defensive line increasingly indefensible under so much shelling and mustard gas and the new British tanks, but it had hardly looked that way to the deaf and blind generals back in their villas, as Peter called them. Peter's leg hobbled him but didn't keep him from returning to the Rhine to work alongside his father, Siegfried, for the Frings men were boat pilots and river guides and Peter would always be too.

Holger Frings had always thought his father a stupid man for becoming a *Landser*. How could he not have known that the water was the only freedom from all the curses of the land?

Now the sea war brought its own curse. The only thing Frings wanted after hearing of the air raids that took his father, mother and sister—his only sibling—was to keep going out and sink ships, destroy the enemy, kill their sailors, help exploit any advantage the S-boats could find. Flotilla command would make him take a leave. It was mandatory. Three days. But even that had to wait. The Normandy invasion routes had to be tested before it was too late. So the flotilla continued to poke at the Allies' defensive perimeter, laying mines and harassing the patrolling corvettes and MTBs.

After one nighttime sortie, Hanssen's boat had sighted an unexpected target: A Royal Navy rescue tug had gone astray, drifting, an hour before daybreak—one stack, two token flak guns. The little goose hadn't moved. It might have had engine trouble. They still had two torpedoes and they were on their own, free from Schirakow and Baum and the rest of the flotilla. Captain Hanssen did just what Frings hoped. They set upon the hapless tug. They charged it going twice full ahead, guns firing, both torpedoes away. The tug exploded like a toy volcano. It went under within minutes. And they sped back for base, Frings steering them safe along the French shoreline. In that moment before impact, he had sensed no fluttering hearts in his fingers on the wheel, no, not any more. He had shouldered the true reality of things. This war was a new kind of war. Hanssen was right—they needed to be more reckless. It was the only way to get this goddamn job done. It was the only way back to his Christiane, to his daughters, and any life he still had left.

He finally took his leave on August 5. He had wanted to come to Cologne, but Christiane talked him out of it. Seeing the city in total ruin would only sap his spirit, she wrote. Besides, his family's bodies couldn't be found, and the funeral had been put off. So they would meet in Brussels, halfway. Christiane refused to bring the girls. She said Belgium was too close to the savage invading Allied armies with their gum-chewing black Americans and the corrupt, Imperialist English. The girls had to stay safe with her sister Hedwig in the country, and Frings couldn't argue with that.

He had wanted a quaint hotel away from any sign of war or occupation, believing Christiane would prefer it. He also didn't want to stomach seeing all those rear-line staff types with their *Druckposten*, those "stress posts" that pained them so by keeping them from the front lines where they really wanted to be, or so they proclaimed. Yet Christiane had insisted on a main hotel, the Metropole, that was requisitioned for German officers and NCOs. It stood in the Old Town near the Grand Place square, surrounded by majestic buildings.

Frings wore his Navy undress blues; he had tried his civilian clothes but felt like an impostor so he changed back, telling Christiane he didn't like the way his civvies fit after losing so much weight. They met in the lobby, hugged, kissed, and went up to the room. They sat at either side of the polished Biedermeier table by the window like two traveling businessmen come to meet about acquiring a new machine lathe. Back home, he learned, Christiane now helped out with the Winter Relief and worked with a caterers who did party events for the golden pheasants of the Rhineland Nazi party. She made cakes, served champagne. He didn't care for that but what could he do? War required work. The catering job had turned into a permanent position, which meant she had to join the Nazi party. War work demanding blind loyalty. This was another reason he had gone for the Navy: Members of the German *Kriegsmarine* could not be forced to become a member of any political party, including the Nazi party. This had been a long naval tradition, and they had somehow held on to it despite Hitler's grip on all institutions. So they had few brownshirts or screwhead types mucking up the Navy ranks, at least not on board.

She had felt at her lapel a few times. Frings' seaman's eyes could make out a tiny hole there where she normally wore a Nazi party pin. It was all he could do not to nag her about it. They would discuss her party membership when he returned.

Her brown fur coat looked new as did the structured dark blue dress and jacket she wore with a yellow blouse, somewhat like a naval staff officers' uniform. She had even gained some weight, apparently one of the few Germans to do so. It suited her, complementing her natural curves. He concluded that it had to be all that catering.

"War becomes you," he said, hoping she still appreciated his sense of humor.

She laughed. "You're not doing poorly either." She reached across the table and touched his S-boat badge.

"Just a little tinsel. Earned it though, I can say that. I don't have chest disease like all your rear-line stallions."

Her smile faded. "'Chest disease'? What is that? Some sort of sailor slang?"

"You could call it that. Just means, the ones who started this mess, who are running it now, they're obsessed with hoarding all the medals they can. So they're sick for it, see?"

"Well, of course you are not," Christiane said, stabbing out her cigarette.

She used a cigarette holder now, and more makeup, and her hair was shorter. She kept finding herself in the vanity mirror, but not in a narcissistic way. It was more surreal, as if she was checking to see if she was still here. As if watching her outside herself. Frings knew what she felt. Grief had a lot to do with it, he told himself.

His pipe hung from his mouth, unlit. He was on this third *Jenever*, an homage to captain Hanssen out there in the shit somewhere. Hanssen liked the Dutch gin. She drank mineral water, with bubbles.

"I do like your beard," she said, but in the same blank way she had commented on the gilded steep facades of Brussels' Old Town. Quaint, but still foreign.

He toasted her. He downed his gin. He told her how his father Peter had returned from the last war changed forever. Sometimes the man would just stare off, or break down crying. He had seen bombing. Shelling. Dead friends. The horrors still visited the old man. No one could imagine, he had told his son. Frings had never stopped trying to make Christiane understand why he had gone into the Navy. If he had to fight for his country, it could not be on land. That was where men went to die, or were changed forever at the least. He was not going to be changed. They had everything—a proper apartment, two beautiful daughters. When back in Cologne, he was going to get a good boat job on the river. He hoped Christiane still believed it, because she was scared. He could tell. Her eyes pinched where they used to glow.

"About Cologne," she said, lighting another cigarette. "I should tell you what I know. It's why we're here stewing like this, isn't it?" She told him how the bombing attacks killed his family. His father Peter had been on the Rhine, aboard a tug boat working as an inspector. British fighter-bombers strafed the river before sundown. At that point, Frings' mother Ursula had only known that her man had gone missing aboard a tug in a river attack. She had gone to bed that way, if she slept at all, and it wasn't clear if she'd even tried to go to the air raid shelter. It was supposed to be safer where they had moved, still on the left bank but south of their long-damaged family apartment in the old St. Martin's Quarter. It was never safe enough for Frings. Two years ago, he had made Christiane and the girls move farther out, across the river to Dietz. The heavy bombers came in later that night. Frings' sister Ingrid had been with her mother, comforting her instead of returning home to her own street. Christiane said: "I found out later—in the chaos, the tug your father was on had been left to burn, until the river took it. The bodies aboard have not been found."

"Wait a moment. A tug? He was on a tug?" Frings' brain seemed to boil, stinging his eyeballs. He squeezed his eyes shut and pressed his fists to the table. He saw that enemy tug blazing, erupting, descending.

"It's my fault," he muttered.

"What? No, it is most certainly not."

"What do you know about it? Eh? What?" He pounded at the table.

Christiane shuddered, as if doused with icy water. She glared at him. A tear rolled down her face. She went to wipe it, but touched the wrong side. It was that mirror again. She wiped it on the third try. Of course she would be sad, Frings thought. Then again, it wasn't her parents who had died. Hers lived safe on an estate in Brandenburg, well east of Berlin—not as owners but the caretakers, though it was hard to tell the difference. Like her sister Hedwig she had come to Cologne to be a nurse, which she promptly gave up once they were married. He wondered why she never returned to the hospital once the war started. Certainly dressing wounds did more good than baking cakes for warmongers.

"And where were you? Just where were you?" Frings said.

"Where do you think? We were safe over in wretched Dietz just like you wanted."

Floundering around in this room was like being in a fucking hospital. All Frings wanted to do here was get drunk. He just wanted to get back out and sink ships.

"I would have liked to see my two little girls," he said.

"But, I fear for them so," she said. "The enemy is coming. They will come to our door. Then we will stop them, Germany will," she added, as reciting the words of a song.

"Sure, certainly," Frings said, lying. Calming down. The last thing he needed to do was smash the table. He lit his pipe.

There was just one thing he didn't understand. "It's strange that your sister Hedwig has taken in the girls," he said. "She never liked other children besides her own."

"Well, she does now," Christiane said. "It's amazing how war changes people, Holger."

"I suppose."

They sat in silence, drinking, smoking.

"You must know: I'm moving the kids farther away," Christiane said. "Far from the city. The right bank is not safe. Dietz isn't good enough."

It hit Frings low in the gut, making him gasp. "What? Why? No. Our street hasn't been hit. We have a solid shelter."

"Your mother had a solid shelter."

"No, I won't allow it."

"It's decided," Christiane said, her voice so firm he had to look up at her. He even looked in the mirror at her. Her jaw had set hard.

He grunted. "So, it's off east to the Brandenburg estate. Is that it?"

"No. They will be close to Cologne. But out of town."

"Your sister's, then."

"Yes," she blurted as if he'd won a guessing game. She had practically spitted it out.

What could he do? He loved his daughters dearly, but Christiane and they were the ones who had to put up with the fear of bombings all the time. He understood that. He poured another. He bit down on his pipe, wanting to snap it. He muttered, "If these goddamn bronze bigwigs would only give us the right tools to fight. So we can get this over with."

"They are trying, our leaders. Quit calling them names, all these bad words. They love Germany." She rolled her eyes at him. She never rolled her eyes. Where had she learned that?

He said: "Tell me something: What did you mean, 'we'?"

"What? I never know what you're saying."

"In the telegram you sent. You wrote, 'here we feel much sorrow.'"

Christiane checked the mirror. "It's just an expression, isn't it?"

And they sat in silence again, slumped, hands limp on their laps.

"I'm going back," Frings blurted.

"I know that. You have to."

"No. You don't understand. I'm going back early. Tonight."

"Why? What are you talking about?"

"I have to. My boat's a bucket full of holes without me."

"I see." Christiane took a deep breath. She nodded. She stood and straightened her jacket like someone about to give a speech. "Well, if you must. It is your duty."

She told him: If he was going back early, so was she. There was a train to Cologne that night. He watched her pack, the Dutch gin getting on top of him, making him sink down in a plush corner armchair. He didn't even know if he had a way back, a train or a truck or what.

She was the first to leave. She stood in the doorway, suitcase in one hand, a bag slung neatly on the other shoulder like an officer's map case. Tears rolled down her face.

"I can't take it," she said. "I need to be secure. You understand? I need them safe."

"I know," he said. "Write soon. All right?"

"I will."

He kissed her on the cheek, and the lips, but they were dry. He needed moisture. He sunk his tongue in, and she let him. He held her by the back of her head, cradling it, and then held her face in his rough fingers. She smiled. Her tears had already dried.

"Tell me something," she said.

"Anything."

"Have you killed anyone?"

He took a step back, scanning the carpet for the right answer.

"Well? Have you or haven't you?"

He nodded. "Of course, yes, I have."

"Good. Then keep doing it. And do much of it. Before they do it to you." Her eyes lit up, as if she heard a voice speaking the words to her, nothing at all like the way her eyes used to glow. She held onto the doorway and smiled, bearing teeth, and it looked more like a grimace. "You must hold on. You must have faith. Soon we will have our Wonder Weapons, Holger. Our Wonder Weapons will turn the dark tide. Everything will change. You will see. Those degenerate murderers! They will all see the truth of our power!"

Frings hitched rides back to his latest base in Ostende, Belgium, ending up in a troop truck full of boy soldiers, replacements rapt at the sight of a fighting sailor. They peppered him with questions about the heroic war at sea.

What could he say? Tell them what they wanted to hear? Confirm the pap in the newsreels? The truth would break their hearts, or at least turn this truck into a prison. So Frings told them:

"I'll be dead soon, and so will you. You are all going to die, boys. And it's going to be worse for you when it comes for you, because you are fighting on land." He gestured with his pipe as if telling a campfire story. Their faces had directed downward, facing the muddied planks of the truck bed. One boy was already sobbing. "Meantime? You will not even recognize the home that means so much to you, and it will not recognize you. Yet you'll keep fighting to get back to it. Then that's gone too. My father, my mother, my sister are all dead. My wife believes in Wonder Weapons that will save us. But nothing will save us. Nothing will save you."

***

Wendell Lett, trembling, eyed Tom Godfrey as he passed around his officer's liquor ration, pouring right into their open canteen cups. Godfrey was giving them more than usual. He wouldn't look Lett in the eye. He had gathered all old hands around to the platoon CP that evening, no matter rank or duty. The moldy old barn they'd set up in smelled like bullshit, but it wasn't from the stalls. Godfrey had just been called to battalion and had to hear the so-called logic behind the magical feat they were to pull off next. They were going to take the Belgian town up the road in the morning: Mettcourt. Artillery would soften it up. They could call in tanks and fighter-bombers if they had to, battalion said, which usually meant they could not in time. This one would be tough.

The retreating Germans were turning desperate, crazed, nasty. When they decided to hold a town, they meant it. Their own recon wasn't helping. They had a captured German combat medic who'd gotten lost behind their lines, and Godfrey had Lett interrogate. Waffen-SS were holed up everywhere in Mettcourt, the medic told Lett, wanting to save lives, any lives. But battalion wasn't listening, because division was not listening. It was almost making Godfrey retch. He kept swallowing hard, like he had cotton stuck in his throat.

"They're like factory owners," he told Lett. "They have no right idea what happens on their assembly line. Up on the front line. Never seen the terrain, let alone the enemy position. It's all radio and telephones and remote control, that's the real horror of it. Just links, more detached the longer and higher the links go. And up there they never get replaced because they never get killed like the rest of us. They find a good billet and cozy up. The new brass rotating in? It's all go-getters and high flyers with big plans but the problem is, those plans are meant for us."

In the morning, September 7, their artillery stopped far too early, Lett thought, his hands jittering as he slung his rifle talking to himself, lips chapped, sticky. He had abandoned his bulky M1 Garand for the smaller and lighter M1 carbine, and the change had been troubling him extra for days. Now the fear of extra trouble hit him hard. His stomach clenched up, and rolled. He pulled his pants down right outside the barn. A kid just in from repple depple saw him and stopped and gaped at the sight of his bearded, twitching, shitting new sergeant.

The platoons approached the town without much resistance. Some blocks were smoldering but not enough. Nearing the center of town, they found a street intact. Lett's squad broke into teams, to clear blocks of buildings down one side of the street. Godfrey had his own squad on the other side; he wasn't about to hang back on a dirty job like this, he had told them. Most of Lett's squad knew the ropes, Lett had made sure of it. People called it street fighting. It was more like breaking into homes with TNT. They started upstairs if they could, moving downward. Take the first house, rush up the stairs to the top floor. Blow a hole in the adjoining wall with a bazooka or explosive charge, move through to the top floor of the next room or building, and work back down, up, do it again, back down. Hallways, stairways, rooftops, basements. Hustle on, don't stop, keep it moving, squint and don't breathe in. Enemy snipers would try to wait it out and stay hidden. If a team stopped it was stuck on defense. It was dangerous as hell, a floor could give way or stairs or a place could be booby-trapped, but anything was better than open street. The street was for the loony, the rear-line commandos, the newbies. Out there the kraut machine guns and snipers told a guy his fortune. Ricochets doubled the danger, and the Germans gunning from the top floors knew it and tried for them. Lett was as comfortable as could be taking a street this way, which meant his insides boiled and froze, seized and churned up. But by now he worked like an automaton in low gear, going at it mechanically, deliberately, cautiously. And if he bought it? He bought it. It wasn't going to be from anything he'd caused. It would happen because of someone's mistake or just dumb bad luck, something that reeked but he couldn't smell.

They toiled their way through the buildings, up and down, down and up, to the end of a main street. They'd found one sniper, downed him with one shot, and found three others defending a kitchen. All SS. The three gave up, but Lett's team were here clearing houses, so what were they supposed to do with them? Their BAR man shot them. The smoke and dust clogged their sight, their breathing, muffling the sounds of the same shit-storm Godfrey's squad was creating across the street. Lett tried not to think about Godfrey's squad. Godfrey had a green bunch with him.

Lett's squad reached the last building on his block, overlooking a small, tight square. A group of civilians had fled here, huddled together on the ground floor, children among them. Lett had a team check the cellar. Was it sturdy? It was, they said. They had to be sure. He needed them to be. They were. So Lett told the civilians to get down there and stay there.

Lett's team spread out on the ground floor, scouting the scene from windows and doorways, panting and sweating, veins buzzing, the bazooka and BAR men hugging their heavy shooters. Lett's head pounded. His stomach burned with cramp. Water streamed out his eyes from the smoke. His hands had clawed up and stiffened, as if from a living man's rigor mortis if there was such a sick thing. He pressed his fingers back around the wood of his carbine.

Decoy smoke was thrown out back down the middle of the block—a GI had crossed the street for a powwow. It was Corporal Baines. Baines huddled with Lett. Godfrey's squad were having a rough go of it, Baines said. They had reached the end of the building but hadn't been able to clear out all the Germans. "They're everywhere, just everywhere like rats and more rats, above and below and behind us," Baines rattled on, gasping for breath. Sweat and tears streamed down his jaw, neck.

"Get a hold of yourself. All right? Take a moment," Lett said.

"Okay, okay, but . . . the looie's doing his best but odds aren't good, aren't good at all."

"Listen. Listen to me. Backup is on the way."

Two more squads were coming up through each block in support, but it wouldn't be enough. Lett would have to send for more. He had looked across and saw the play. At the nearest edge of the square was a fountain, between the ends of the two blocks. The square was tight enough, the fountain broad and squat, but it would not be easy.

Lett looked across to Godfrey's building again. Smoke poured out various windows. Far back down the street, two medics were rushing into Godfrey's building.

Godfrey showed in the doorway opposite Lett, huddled with a demolition team, BAR men. His face was a pale mask. The huddle was going on without him. He stared out. Finally, Lett made eye contact. It seemed to snap Godfrey out of it. He gave a thumbs up.

It was something. Lett had Baines toss out a smoke grenade.

"Go! Go!"

They headed out in teams of two, crouching, aiming, boot toes scuffing on cobblestone. Wind swirled the smoke and pulled it away. Baines fell, blood splashing on the stones. A bazooka man took one in the face, his metal tube bouncing away clanging. The rest got pinned down before leaving the doorway.

Lett had made it to the fountain. He signaled for the rest to cover him only now, send a getaway man back, get more medics. The smoke had shifted back. He couldn't see Godfrey through it, but he heard the burps of German machine guns and saw the glow of a flamethrower through the blur.

They didn't have a flame team here.

"Fuck, fuck," Lett whispered, clicking in a new magazine.

The smoke cleared, bringing wisps of a black residue and the reek of fuel, like tires afire. Lett looked over to Godfrey. The flame had expired, but the doorway was torched.

Godfrey appeared, on his haunches. He gaped as if he was screaming, but no sound came out. He clenched at air, as if climbing a ladder. His Thompson gun lay next to him.

Another team drew fire so Lett bolted across to Godfrey, hurtling into the doorway. Godfrey was blackened. Half his face and upper lip were a bright glowing red, wanting to blister. His helmet had fallen back and his hair stood up, singed. He kept clenching at air, screaming in silence. Lett touched his shoulder. He looked right through Lett, crying now, and curled up, seeming to shrink to boy size. Lett held him there, at his hip. He smelled a stench of burnt flesh, but it wasn't Godfrey. Deeper inside the building stood a black mass, what looked like a stump for cutting wood. A charred man. Only the GI helmet nearby told Lett whose side it was.

"We're going back," Lett said. He dragged Godfrey through the buildings on Godfrey's side, up and down, finding the holes they had blasted through, stepping over bodies. Bullets whizzed at them through blown-out windows.

The squads had pulled back. Lett heard footsteps, German voices. They kept going.

They reached the end of the building where Godfrey's squad had come in. Frantic covering teams waved them through, back toward the edge of town.

Somewhere on the way out of town, Lett handed Godfrey off to a medic. That was the last logical thing Lett remembered. His reasoning had reformed into something else. He only remembered moments. It was like piecing together a bender blackout. Despite the smoke and stench he had never breathed so clearly, felt his muscles so strong, had so much energy. He charged back into town.

He reentered buildings but couldn't recall which. He might have gone deeper in, beyond the fountain. He must have looked like a man busted out of an asylum. He remembered the hot urine down his legs, soaking his trousers. He recalled a scowl on his face, a sick rictus of gusto. He kicked in doors, rushed up stairs, lunged through blown-out walls. He snatched up a Thompson gun, ammo magazines. He shot at corpses. He found four SS crouched in a bathroom among glossy shards of porcelain tile and bathtub, SS men but they were all cracked, hands up high, fingers pinched together waving imaginary white hankies. "*Kamerad!* Surrender," they shrieked. Lett laughed and fired into them but the Tommy gun only clicked and clicked, empty. Grimacing, he stood over them and reloaded. The soldiers squealed and cried, hands over faces, eyes, ears, monkey see, monkey do. Lett moved on. In an attic he came up behind a sniper in a dormer. He kicked the bastard right out the window.

At some point he sat on a carpeted floor in the remains of a living room, holding a soldier in his arms, cradling him. They were both crying. The other was a German, no more than 15. Then it was only Lett crying. His trench knife stuck out of the teenager's underarm, up high in it, the blood dumping out like a faucet. The boy's muscles relaxed, his frame went limp, and it was like Lett was holding a sack of sand and rocks. "Sleep well, sleep well," he muttered in German into the teen boy's ear. And Lett slumped against a wall, suddenly dead tired. He just wanted the air attacks to come, to bring the roof right down on him. Get it over with, speed this up.

The air attacks never came. No one came. He made it back outside. Daylight was fading fast. He saw the fountain, and he stopped and listened. No one fired at him. Had the SS pulled out? He was so goddamn tired, his legs quivered like noodles. His lungs had flattened. His scowl had dropped away. He wandered back, right down the middle of the open street.

He found the platoon outside town on the edge of the wood, already digging in, feverish and wheezing, hissing whispers at each other like convicts on the lam. Someone was leading Lett along. It was the replacement who'd watched him shit by the barn. The kid had his arm around Lett's waist. He carried Lett's carbine, but there was no Tommy gun now.

"They done pulled out," the kid was saying, "the krauts, they high-tailed er. Everone figgered you done fer."

Lett tried to speak, but it didn't work. It must have sounded like a squawk. He swallowed, tried again: "Where's Godfrey? Where is Tom?"

Lett's company lost ten before the Germans pulled out of Mettcourt, including Sergeant Charles and another medic. The replacement kid who'd walked Lett back was killed by artillery the next day—friendly fire. Lett never knew his name. Lett wondered why they couldn't have just bypassed Mettcourt. Then he heard another division had pinpointed the town as a headquarters complete with staff brass, which meant the place would be off limits to enlisted men.

The aid station had sent Tom Godfrey to the rear for treatment, and that was the last Lett heard of it. Mettcourt left Lett as the last original Joe in his platoon and yet luckily, horribly, another looie was ordered to take over, Rossini. Lieutenant Rossini had experience going back to North Africa, but Rossini had been off the line injured so long he might as well be green. He had the highly tuned fear of the doggie. He deferred to Lett's opinion on most decisions, which was just about right. Lett would be named platoon CO in due time. They might even make him lieutenant with a field commission. And that would be that. He was too tired to care. He was walking dead and knew it. His nerves had no sting in them. His skin felt like a thick covering he'd pulled over himself, dull to the touch and rubbery. He always had a sometimes briny, sometimes metallic taste in his mouth and the harshest country brandy couldn't wash it out. His stomach was a knot that turned into snakes, writhing. At rest, his eyes only saw things as blurs. Every town was gray, every field green. It seemed like his whole body was filled with a sand slowly hardening into concrete. Sometimes, didn't matter day or night, he saw dead guys he knew sitting next to him, or nuns and kids from the orphanage, and he found himself talking to them. Odd memories popped into his head from as far back as his few years with mom and dad—a happy dinner, on a drive in the country, and the episodes were so real they would jolt him up, making him stand and pace around, even in his hole. He had stopped asking the name of whatever puppyface he shared holes with, even after they had slept hugging each other all night for warmth. No one really wanted to be his foxhole buddy, because legend had it that the ones who did kept dying off the quickest.

He had seen guys reach this point. When they started getting visitors, when their very presence signified death? A man didn't need an abacus to do the math. Lett thought about it openly now. When he did go, provided his face was left intact, his skin would go off-green and a little shiny like wax. Maybe his mouth would stay open a little. Or his eyes. He hoped not. Things could crawl in there, or crawl out. But then again, what would he care?

It was all too true what Sheridan had predicted—this really was just a chain gang. It all haunted Lett. Godfrey coming apart, more dead kids, his lunatic spree in Mettcourt. The latter preyed on him. Why hadn't he gone to find those civilians down in that cellar, protect them, lead them out if he had to? Those people hadn't occurred to him, not even the children. He had become a mindless ogre, a murdering troll about to be murdered. He would never kill himself like his deluded and dipso father, but wasn't this what he was doing to himself? What they were doing to him? If nothing else he would let himself be overworked to death, like his mother. And no amount of killing could quench the demand on him.

It was the only way out, the one-way street. The men in charge gave them no rest, and if they did they would only send them back out, the rest they got being the only thing worse—taunting a guy with a taste of living again. And when they were done in the ETO they would only ship off to Japan for more, or maybe keep advancing into Russia, to fight Joe Stalin. Sure, they would. It would go on forever. The new war was a total war and the whole world to come would know nothing else.

***

Holger Frings could not find Vigo the sea dog anywhere on board. Their little hunting terrier had the whole crew searching for him after they had survived a wild sortie up the mouth of the Thames dodging searchlights and mines and coastal artillery. Vigo had stayed below but had been shaking and howling more than usual. Then he was gone, missing in action. The only answer was, Vigo had found a way off the boat. Their clever Vigo had chosen to take his chances in the surging cold dark water. Hanssen called crew together to discuss getting another sea dog. Frings insisted they did not. It was too goddamn deadly even for *Hunde* now.

Frings' flotilla had pulled back again, northeast to the S-boat pens in Ijmuiden, Holland. It was September 1944. On land, all along the broad Western front, the invasion could not be stopped. Allied forces were charging across Northeastern France after trapping untold thousands of German troops in the Falaise Gap and saturation-bombing them into shreds, shock and madness, ants in a sandbox trampled by schoolboys.

He had written a brief letter to Christiane's sister, Hedwig, asking about his girls. Hedwig wrote back that she hadn't heard from Christiane for months. His girls had never visited. Hedwig's man was missing in Russia and she had her hands full with her own children. Once she had offered to take his girls in, but Christiane had declined.

On the morning of September 10, Frings stayed aboard their boat inside its concrete pen while the crew went back to the billet hotel. He was doing this more these days. He had already gotten word they were going out again that night, so why not? There was too much to get done. He fell asleep on a seaman's bunk, down in the stern.

When he woke, an envelope lay next to his head. A sailor had left it for him. He sat up on the bunk, trying to shake the cobwebs from his head. It was from Christiane. The postmark was from Königswinter, a charming village along the Rhine and a magnet for tourists and Nazis on holiday. He ripped open the envelope and scanned the letter:

> I'm staying here permanently, with our girls . . .
> It's safe here, so far from the war. Dearest Holger, I wish you could know just how much I have suffered too. I have been so scared, so frightened all the time that I thought I was losing my mind . . .
> The girls are so happy here. They've made fast friends in the local League of German Girls . . .
> There is another man. I can tell you know. If you must know, his name is Werner Scherenberg. He's the former Nazi Party Gauleiter—

Frings had heard of Scherenberg—guru of Golden Pheasants and bronze bigwigs party-wide. They didn't get any browner or more smeared with shit. The type who liked to have his portrait photos taken in profile, peaked uniform cap and all. The former regional Nazi party leader had become a rich factory owner, it was said, using forced labor to produce winter clothing for the Eastern Front.

> Herr Scherenberg has a villa here. It is our fortress. He will keep us secure until we win the war . . .
> I'm sorry it has to be like this. Herr Scherenberg has friends who

are excellent lawyers. They will file divorce papers. We would like you to have a certain sum of money to keep you well, should you ever return from our heroic war at sea.

Please do not write. You will not receive a response . . .

Best of luck to you. You're a brave soldier for Germany . . .

***

Wendell Lett had a rattling cough and constant diarrhea and spastic tremors when he wasn't muttering to himself or just staring into vacant nothingness. The thousand-yard stare or the goony bird look, they called it. Speaking in dogface tongues. He had red, leaking eyes. He had long fingernails, which served him well as tools, and his beard had become matted. He had long ago quit bitching about rations or not getting hot food. He only ate for fuel now.

Lett had become the platoon CO de facto. As expected Lieutenant Rossini had proved a wreck, childlike in his worries. The unknowing bystander would never have thought Lett capable of leading. He may have looked and sounded cracked, but when it came to the job at hand the fundamentals kicked in, like someone winding up a key in his back. He insisted that the company keep a warm, preferably lighted dugout or building for any patrols or sentries going out or coming in. They were risking their butts and deserved it. They could take their time there, with hot coffee if possible. A man could field strip or just dry out his weapon if he wanted. Like a coach, Lett would go around explaining the mission to each man, telling the latest replacements exactly what made them dead fast. He wanted to lead the patrols by this point, anything to escape waiting to be shelled again.

In late September, Lett's company approached the border of Germany. They faced the *Hürtgenwald*, a dense wooded area to the south of the nearest German city of Aachen. The Hürtgen Forest contained the *Westwall* border fortifications, which war correspondents were calling the Siegfried Line. Company had Lett send out patrol after patrol in the forest, day after day, like logging crews filling a cut quota.

They got into few firefights, not many. They found out little. Usually they came back with the eerie feeling the Germans were just lying in wait, watching them. To most, the German forest looked the same as the forest on the Belgian side. Most were fools. This was the Germans' country at stake now. Who knew what they had in that dark forest? And it was getting colder, fast. Over the summer and into fall Lett and his now-dead friends had spent their share of nights in the rain, but those nights were warm and summery. Wet was one thing. Damp and chilling was another. Then there was snow. If this was to be anything like Ohio, they didn't have the gear or clothing and supply was nowhere near catching up to them.

Lett knew the big play. All those patrols told him. Soon they were going to clear out the Hürtgen, for as long as it took, and the Siegfried Line with its pillboxes and bunkers and death traps. Then Rossini, Lett and the other platoon leaders were hearing just that from company, who got it from battalion, and division, and up and up the chain went the links.

They pushed deeper inside the Hürtgen but had to dig in. The forest here was like nothing Lett had ever seen, something out of a bleak folk tale foresworn in the Middle Ages. It teemed with fir trees one hundred foot high, the trees choking all sunlight, their dark and thick branches hanging low and intertwining with those from other trees, so low the men had to stoop to make it past, the rain, dew and melting frost trickling down from on high to pick up speed and dump on them, the drops slapping at their helmets and shoulders and gushing cold down their necks. They trekked over hill after forested hill. The only roads were narrow, with little passage for armored support, and the few firebreaks mined or booby-trapped. Yes, this one was infantry's show. On the first night of rain, their holes filled with a foot or more of water and mud. In the mornings, guys were starting to rise from their holes with numb feet. Trench foot would hit fast.

Then came the artillery. Like evil scientists, the Germans had studied the forest and asked a question: How could they turn all those close-packed trunks and branches, stories and canopies and the very earth itself into weapons in themselves?

Tree bursts, they called it. The Germans fused their artillery shells to explode above them, inside the treetops. Impacts and craters, concussions and searing shrapnel had been bad enough. Now the trees—the canopy sky above—rained giant and sharp wood shreds and splinters and hot metal. When not in their holes, GIs had been trained to hit the earth. With tree bursts, this only offered a man to the tree burst gods. Men lying prone got hamburgered, liquefied. So GIs figured it out. No more hitting the deck. Now men hugged tree trunks. It was the only way to get clear. The shrieks of incoming and the cracking and splitting of branches sent whole squads hugging trunks, sometimes a few men deep, which made the outer ring a bulwark that didn't always survive. The dead would simply drop away, slashed and ripped apart from above and down the back.

Guys covered their foxholes with logs, earth, rocks, anything they had. The wood-metal storm found them if they weren't protected, and sometimes when they were. The last original from another platoon bought it that way, a splinter the size of a lamppost hammering down through him like a huge nail. Maclean was that guy's name. The burly redhead had seven kids back home in Oregon, where he had been a logger of all things. Then Lieutenant Rossini bought it by tree burst. The medic had to pick him up in pieces and place him in a soggy basket for handing off to graves registration.

On October 2, a Monday, Lett took out a squad of eight to patrol a small ridge. It had started raining hard before dawn as Lett huddled with the team in the CP tent, the gusts ripping through the branches above sounding like beach waves crashing against the canvas. Their tent lantern went out and wouldn't relight so Lett poured some gasoline on the dirt floor and lit the patch, just to give the guys the impression of warmth. He had finally scored the new double-buckle boots with high leather cuff and Goodyear rubber soles. Not even these would stand a chance in this weather, and that worried him more than anything.

He glared at the newest replacements, making each look him in the eye. "We make no sound, got me? Anyone got an itchy throat? No? Yes? Then suck on a cough drop or press on your Adam's apple in a pinch. Stop a sneeze by pressing a finger to your upper lip, like this. Got me? Always whisper. Always. Don't bunch up, but stay in sight of the pack, and keep it moving."

His patrol headed out, filing through the forest, crouch-walking under the low branches. They had to cross a swelling stream. They hopped rocks to get across and a couple guys lost their footing and got dunked. Lett's boots held tight for now. They plowed onward. They approached the ridge as a wedge, spaced out at trunks, whispering their names out to know each other's position because it was still dim and foggy. Lett kept the newbies from bunching up. The ridge stood only about thirty feet high, but its crest got blurred in the haze. When patrolling ridges like this, Lett had learned to run his squad halfway up while sending a guy up top now and then to scout. If they stayed too low, the enemy could get on top of them and fire right down on their heads. They moved along, from bush to trunk and over fallen log, barely crunching in the underbrush.

The old anxiety pressed at the inside of Lett's chest, like hundreds of fingers prodding and probing at his ribs and under his skin, wanting to tear their way out. Something didn't feel right. He heard something.

"Hug trees!" he hissed. "Hug fucking trees!" He clambered through mud and slammed his body around the nearest trunk.

Nothing had come in. Not a sound. And no one had followed him. A few of the newbies let out nervous chuckles. A kid corporal shushed them. Lett hopped around on his haunches, saw guys whispering to each other, probably wondering if their sergeant had finally lost it. Lett glared back at them, his nose dripping like a tap. He wasn't going to tell them again. His chest rattled and worked out a screeching, burning cough that he suppressed with a wheeze.

He listened up. He needed to listen.

He heard it. The "whump-bangs" sounded, another and another. 88s. Incoming.

The men rushed for trunks and held on as the shells soared in. Time stopped and lasted forever as Lett squeezed his eyes shut, gritting teeth and yet screaming through the grit. The din and force and storm of it was like being inside a revving engine, a thresher. The dark day went darker and thunder boomed and lightning flared inside the woods.

Lett felt like someone was beating him with a rifle butt, then it was a machete, pummeling him into the bark. He was hit. Had to be. He held on. The earth rocked and the force of air rushed up under his uniform, puffing up the layers of wool and denim as the shelling kept pounding. Something struck his side. He went down, sideways. In flashes he saw dirt and underbrush erupting, men cowering, splinters and sparks, others running screaming, thick objects and jelly-like masses hurtling by. His tree trunk creaked, shrieked, shuddered. He dropped away from it and curled up, into the earth, and imagined himself digging ever deeper as the shelling pounded him and them, bringing on night, squishing him into the earth with the staccato rhythm of a jackhammer.

All went green, then black.

He woke. He had passed out. He couldn't feel his body, but he could feel the squishing crunch of soldiers slogging by, and something told him not to move. He was on his stomach, his head to the side in the mud or something slimy. He smelled grimy oily leather straps and gear, and vapors of grain alcohol. He knew these smells. It took all he had left to part one eye.

Germans soldiers were trudging past, but quiet as squirrels.

He shut his eye. He kept it shut a long time.

Sunlight beamed through the trees, sparkling, arcing. When Lett opened his eyes again, he didn't know where he was, or how long he had been there. Was this his first battle? Was he dead? Bodies and parts of bodies lay strewn among shards of trees and churned earth.

The mud had a dark red hue. A rifle stood straight up with its barrel in the ground, a gloved hand still grasping it connected to an arm, ripped off at the shoulder.

He bolted up, stiff and staggering, and he ran, hoping he was going the right way. A ridge was at his back, and he sure as hell was not climbing that. Keep moving, keep moving, stop and you're cornered. He came to a stream surging beyond its banks and didn't stop, just stomped right through, lunging for rocks to step along. A foot gave way and he plunged into the water, thigh deep, the water so cold he gasped. He reached the opposite bank, slipped and cracked his chin on a log. Kept going. He was calling out his name, his own name: "Wendell, Wendell," but in an urgent whisper, as if calling out the names of a whole patrol of Wendells.

He lurched onward but daylight kept flickering, like someone turning a switch on and off.

All went dark again.

The next thing Lett knew he lay outside a tent, on a pile of bedrolls. A few from his patrol sat around, some passed out, some staring dead into space, not blinking. This was the company aid station. He sat up. He remembered where he was, what had happened, and a deep, droning ache of despair gnawed at him, from deep inside his bones. He cried. Shaking his head. It was raining again. Where was that sunlight, so bright?

"You're going to have to get yourself washed off, soldier," a man said.

A stout little man stood before Lett wearing a pristine, impenetrable, double-breasted trenchcoat. Rain beaded on the shoulders.

Lett looked down at himself. His legs and feet were soaked through from the stream, but his upper body was still covered in blood and the slime of bodies ripped apart. His neck was thick with it, and it had trickled down under his collar. Intestines hung off his buttons, web belt, ammo pouches, congealing. He felt a sharp pain in his neck, shooting down to his hips. His lungs rattled and he tried to cough but it hurt too much.

"We can't have that all over men's bedrolls," the man said.

Lett couldn't tell the man's rank. He could have been anything from a sergeant to a colonel, but he was definitely rear-line. He was possibly supply troop, probably a quartermaster. He wore the same double-buckle boots as Lett. Combat Joes had been dying to get their hands on them for months, but word had it that all the rear-liners were trading high and low for them so they could look like real front-line types. The boots almost never made it to the front.

The rear-line man added a smile. A smile?

"Says you. What the fuck you know?" Lett said. He had shouted it.

Men's heads turned their way, and someone looked out the aid tent at them.

"Relax, soldier."

Lett shook his head again but the ache stopped him. It made him cry out in pain. Yet somehow he stood, groaning. The man stepped back. Lett lunged at him, dislodging the slime and entrails on his trenchcoat, hands, face.

The man squealed: "Orderly! Assistance here! This soldier's hurt awful."

"No!" Lett shouted, staggering backward. He reached to unsling his carbine but it wasn't there. "Fuck you," he muttered, pushing off the orderly that had come out to him, or was it a German? Who the hell knew anymore. "Who knows!" he shouted.

He tried to run, pick up his feet. "I'm going back out!"

He tried to stumble on but the pain seized his neck and his legs seemed to slide out from under him. He was shivering, and it wouldn't stop. He blacked out.

His eyes popped open. Men were speaking around him, holding him, but he couldn't understand them. He was on his back? On a litter? The heavy forest canopy above had given way to gray sky, and he imagined the leaden, shifting mass of clouds a dark sea, washing over him.

***

The curse had sold out to damnation. The sea had become an abyss of toil and torment and vengeance. By October 1944, Holger Frings had become a zombie war-sailor living only for the next torpedo run, for keeping his boat in one piece, for saving his fellow crew members from enemy bombers, mines, fast boats, destroyers.

He had written Christiane weekly for a time, pleading and then demanding that she come to her senses. She never wrote back. Scherenberg's boot-licking lawyers did write to him. They advised him to refrain from further communication. They would tell him when it was his time to know. Frings could only think of his little girls, the situation they were in. They didn't know better. He wondered if they even asked about him. He wondered if they called that brown bastard *Vati*.

On October 2, at 1600 hours, Frings' S-boat formation left the concrete pens at Ijmuiden line abreast, heading for a convoy reported in Quadrant 76. The afternoon promised high winds, rough seas, a hazy clear sky gaining clouds fast. They had seven boats, two flotillas patched together as one.

Hanssen's S-boat had finally become the lead boat. Flotilla chief Schirakow just had a heart attack, leaving *Obersteuermann* Baum as slave boat to Hanssen's now, the other six boats following lined up abreast. Hanssen pushed their rebuilt supercharged motors to the limit, cruising at thirty-five knots all ahead despite warnings of swelling waves to come, the bow riding so high that sailors had to climb uphill to reach the wheelhouse from midships and stern. The newer boats' heavier armor had made them unstable, pitching them from side to side in his wake.

Frings welcomed Hanssen's recklessness. This was a race with time, with weather, but it was also their time. They had earned this.

A few miles out from base, a haze had obscured the Dutch coast behind them. Before them, where their quadrant lay, a front of dark clouds loomed.

Frings quivered inside. His organs seemed to press together. He knew the old feeling. Something was not right. He could sense it.

But he didn't tremble. He snickered. Radioman Hahn stiffened at the sight of a possibly crazed helmsman and it only made Frings laugh out loud, the drool slinging in his beard. He pulled his unlit pipe, pocketed it, and reached for his black oilskin Southwester. Engine telegraph man Kammel held it out for him. Good man. Frings had been hard on the seaman but it was paying off. Kammel would make a great Number One someday.

"Planes!" the spotter shouted.

Frings looked out windows. The bombers were coming out of the North, a line of crows growing bigger, darker. Halifax bombers. No, they were Lancasters.

Spray slapped at the double-glass, the swells pounding at the hull. Frings planted his boots wider, his legs surging warm with strength.

"Sortie canceled! We head back!" Hanssen shouted in the voice tube to radioman Hahn.

Frings banged at the wheel. "*Verdammt noch mal!*"

Their bunker pens were only a couple miles behind them. Hanssen was ordering the flotilla to return. It was the safe bet, but it would be one ugly race to the pens. They could lose. The Tommy-bombers would lay on the full treatment no matter how much throttle they gave, no matter how much coastal flak they fired. The hopelessness pressed down on Frings, as if the very sky was dirt about to be shoveled on top of him. It would prove little better even if they made it into their battered pens. The din inside that concrete cave during a bombardment bored into the brain, the concussion rattling every fiber, bone, marrow. And boats not reaching the pens got shredded into charred heaps in the port, a hull here, a scrap of wheelhouse there, all smoldering. The port was a butcher's block. Men got hacked apart, or propelled right through railings and the body parts and entrails stuck to railings and concrete and planks as if glued. Survivors wandered through smoke and flames, crazed from it. One of his long-lost mates, Engel, his fingers scorched to bone yet clawing at Frings shoulders, half his face burned away, muttering, "Mother, mother," yet he wasn't calling for his mother—he thought Frings was his mother, and he buried his face in Frings' oilskins before Frings could stop him. It left the last of Engel's flesh right there on his leathers. A medic had come, led Engel away. Engel dropped dead before they got him on a litter.

How many times had it happened? It would keep happening. Christiane's Wonder Weapons would only prolong the madness. They could end up fighting with the Tommies and *Amis* against Commies. There was no end to it. It was the way men like Scherenberg wanted the world to work. The real men fight so one tin pretender can shine.

The bombers fired through the smoke, coming in low. Their boats fired back but had no stability for aiming on such a wild run. Frings saw how this would go down. One boat would burst, then another. Two might collide. They would run out of smoke.

But Hanssen hadn't yet commanded Frings to wheel around. They sped on, jostling, leaning into it, the bombs and guns lifting water in geysers and the salvos clinking at their sides, chopping away at their puny plastic armor. They heard a scream astern.

"We go on, forward," Hanssen shouted in the voice tube. "Stay course!"

"Good, good," Frings said to his wheel.

"Baum's boat stays with us. The rest keep going back. Maybe they make it."

"A good plan," Frings growled. He grinned at Hahn and Kammel but not even Kammel could force out a smile.

Hanssen ordered the other boats to return as Frings steered his onward, toward the stormy dark horizon. Baum's followed Frings at starboard quarter. Their two boats would play decoy. The rest of the flotilla turned around, speeding for the pens in zig-zag pattern, pumping out decoy smoke. Their two boats released no smoke, and showed the Tommies their bare asses.

The swarm of Lancasters pulled around, bringing darkness on top of the two boats. The planes dropped their loads, the individual missiles seeming to halt in the air a moment like cartoon bombs before plummeting down. The sea erupted around them. They kept going, Hanssen yelling for engines at maximum ahead, all they could give it.

Far behind them the other five boats blended into the horizon, heading toward the coast and the safety of their bunker pens. Maybe they could make it.

"Smoke!" Hanssen yelled in the voice tube. "Zig-zag!"

Frings worked the wheel, grunting, "Come at us, bastards." Their two boats discharged smoke, kept racing, zig-zagging.

The dark clouds seemed to lunge down at them. The bombers pulled up and away, slicing through the clouds as the weather front came at them and spread like a blanket yanked over them. They had more than clouds and storm in their favor. They ran with eight torpedoes total, and Baum's boat had new 4cm guns.

"Quadrant 76!" Hanssen yelled to the navigator poring over charts. "We go hunting."

1900 hours: The clouds hung so low above that dusk had lost out. Darkness had enveloped the two boats. They had entered their quadrant. The lay in wait in *Lauerstellung*, just like the old days—their two-boat *Rotte* ready to strike, bobbing along the swells, hiding behind a wall of fog. Right before a convoy came, when the wind was right, they could smell the peppery-rich odor of a coal steamer.

The mist thickened. The deck crew was wearing rain gear. Frings had pulled his southwester tight on his head. Hahn's radio crackled, fuzzed. Frings could see Baum' boat signaling, but the semaphores blurred and signal lamps fared little better. Such poor visibility was just what they wanted. Enemy planes and destroyers would have a tough time finding them before it was too late. Even with radar, a gap in detection existed between pinpointing an area and the exact location. This was also the horror of it. Escort ships hunting them down at close range sometimes ended right on top of them.

They scanned the horizon for bow shapes, for one juicy convoy goose. The wind was not right though. They had smelled nothing telltale in the air. Now rain surged down as sheets and rolled down their decks, windows and floppy southwesters.

In the wheelhouse, Frings felt a twinge in his fingers, a slight vibration of the wheel.

"Flares!"

Gun bursts pierced through the wet blur, the hits clattered against their boats like gravel. MTBs. British motor torpedo boats charged at them two by two. Hanssen shouted "All maximum speed" as the MTBs passed with guns swinging around, Hanssen's and Baum's boats firing back. Hanssen called for more smoke and shock bombs— floating charges that burst in their attacker's path. They sped away.

A massive bow appeared, like an island erupting from ocean—a light destroyer. Baum's boat veered starboard and the wall of steel passed between their two boats. To avoid keeling, Frings steered into its tsunami wake and they crashed into it, the sea washing over them like poured wet concrete. Sailors might have gone over. He had no choice.

They sped on firing at the massive stern and the ship's smaller guns fired back, its big barrels too close for a good shot.

The shock bombs had exploded half a mile off starboard but burst only sea water and their effect was lost in the chaos.

The MTBs had vanished. Where was Baum? They couldn't see him. Hanssen had Frings wheel back around, the smoke canisters still pumping as more flares and search lights lit up the low clouds, creating a cave of flashing whites and reds and yellows.

Off portside they spotted an MTB burning, sinking fast, black smoke piling out the back as sailors scrambled along the deck.

They sped on, Frings still wheeling around, searching out Baum.

An object came at their starboard midship. The crash lifted them off their feet in the wheelhouse as they listed hard, Hahn and Kammel slamming into each other, wires snapping and charts flying. Frings kept one hand on a wheel handle and pulled himself back up. A hatch hung open and black smoke rolled in, burning in their lungs. Sailors coughed, shouted.

Frings saw Baum's boat starboard, burning midships, just meters from them.

They had collided. Frings steadied his wheel and heard Baum yelling from his open bridge. His engines had to be dead.

Where was Hanssen? *"Herr Oberleutnant!?"* Frings shouted into the voice tube.

Sailors flung out lines. They would tow Baum's boat. Frings worked the wheel for it.

Salvos spewed water, rattled their armor and ricocheted off railings, the bridge. MTBs came at them again. They held on, firing back. Frings' head swirled from the flashes of guns, the rain like rocks, swells flickering, shouts and cries, MTBs coming back around firing, men in the water, arms flailing.

The wheelhouse double glass went dark with a chunky red liquid. Blood.

Frings screamed, he didn't know what. Hahn had crumpled into a ball, shrieking, howling. Kammel stood stiff, bloodied. Frings ran out the hatch and bridge wing onto the rocking deck, stomping across the planks and grabbing at railings. He saw seamen only as shapes in the smoke and flames and bursts coming at them, the water flogging them. Baum's boat had sunk lower, the bow underwater now. His men jumped off, some trying to leap across, others hanging on a rescue ladder Frings' men had thrust out for them.

The MTBs passed again, this time slower, using searchlights to pick out targets. Single shots clanked at metal. The midships gun was unmanned. Frings scrambled over and worked the wheel to lay the barrel on an MTB, staggering with the rising swells. He fired screaming.

He got off a few bursts but the gun kicked up into the sky. The ammo ran out. A jolt seized him and pulled him backward, his feet swinging out from under him.

***

Wendell Lett moved from a battalion aid station to a field hospital, then to a rear-line Army hospital in Western Belgium. He got white sheets. The whole place was white. He saw white in a new way, as a new color. It didn't uplift a guy. Take white far enough and it turned to black. Men around him were muttering and whimpering, snoring through raw inflammations, exuding strange noises from unnatural holes and crevices in their bodies. Under these conditions, Lett could only welcome the strong smells of antiseptic. He never thought he'd see any manner of cleanliness again. They had a few Army nurses, beautiful things all of them despite their blood-soiled OD fatigues. One of them shaved his beard with the touch of a butterfly. Natural light streamed in from the high windows. The place had been a church, it turned out. The ambience only made everything seem all the more unreal.

A gaunt young doctor had given him the lowdown: He had whiplash, dysentery, pneumonia, various infections and boils, lice, bits of shrapnel and wood slivers embedded in him, and early signs of trench foot, and that was just the physical part. He suffered from a clear case of battle fatigue, what doctors used to call shell shock. "All out of change," they called it up on the line. His treatments included a neck collar, assisted movement, infusions, pills, copious liquids, more pills, and stern words from a mousy chaplain about the horrors and temptations of battle fatigue.

He tried to bolt the joint after a couple days and make it back to his unit but the orderlies followed him. After that he gave in to the rigmarole, only so he could get to the line sooner. They were going to return him anyway, so why not get it over with? His horror was fixed, death predestined. Anything else was fooling. His limbo had let him do some thinking. He realized that his existence, and those of all true dogfaces, had become something out of an Edgar Allen Poe horror, or a strange terror tale from the writer H.P. Lovecraft. They were worms. They were ants. They had no eyes, no arms for grasping free. They would be crushed. There was no way out of it, and the universe cared not one wit. Gods were a cruel joke. Nightmare was the reality, not the aberration.

They kept him off the line for a little over two weeks. After his release he was supposed to rotate through a repple depple. He skipped it and hitched a ride back with a combat engineer unit doing their magic to punch holes in the dragon's teeth of the Siegfried Line, the Germans' concrete obstacle stumps used to stop tanks. They were really going to need those tanks.

Lett and Tom Godfrey hugged and didn't give a shit who saw it. They held each other by the shoulders to get a good look at one another. Lett couldn't stop staring at the burn scar on Tom Godfrey's upper lip. Godfrey's new mustache couldn't fully hide it.

"It's not bad. Hey, you still have your lip," Lett said.

"The old silver lining," Godfrey said. "I've never seen you without the beard. You're just a laddie. Look like your own son."

It was raining, the middle of October, and the sun was already going down in the afternoon. Lett had returned to a new surreality, ad hoc as it was—his battalion had been pulled off the line. The Army had no choice. Guys were breaking well before those 200 days straight if they weren't dead already. Patrol after patrol, assault after assault had been beaten back in the Hürtgen and tree bursts were finishing off the rest. Casualties were higher than ever. Crackup cases had skyrocketed. Some doggies had up and walked off, never to be seen again.

They billeted in a forest area near the German border south of the Hürtgen, inside a Belgian forest region called the Ardennes. The post was sodden and remote, among a few stone farmhouses and huts— not what the guys wanted, but probably better for their heads than an extended warm bender in a wild town. By staying put, they found ways to keep the water out. And Lett had a new skin: He had gotten new underwear, shirt, trousers, battle jacket, most any other gear he wanted. Some of his old gear he kept as good luck, including his trench knife.

In his new windcheater, belted overcoat and double-buckle boots, Godfrey might have been another rear-line swell. They chuckled at that, shaking their heads. To get out of the rain they sat under a half tent on a bench cut out of a log some wiseacre had painted with the words "Central Park East."

Godfrey said the burn injuries were second degree, most superficial except for the scar.

"I never was able to find out if you made it," Lett said. "Hoped maybe you got the million-dollar wound."

"Never been that lucky. Went AWOL from my hospital once I heard they were sending me back up on the line. Came straight back here. Didn't want to end up in some other unit. What are they going to do—send me to the front?"

They laughed about it.

"Thanks for pulling me out," Godfrey said.

"You woulda done it for me," Lett said.

"I heard what you guys have been through since. It's no picnic."

Lett nodded. "See what happens when you're not around?"

Godfrey had a musette bag with him. He pulled out a bottle of gin and two ceramic mugs, painted delicately with farm scenes but sturdy. He poured, they sipped, licking the heat off their lips.

"I got you limited duty. Company courier. Don't know how long it will last though. Word was we'd stay off the line for at least a month. But who really knows? Only a general."

Lett knew how limited duty worked. It had become routine to put a cracked dogface behind the lines a while, see how things went. "I'm no good hanging around the rear," he said.

"It's not like that. Some charity case. This is only till they send us back out. One of the others can play platoon sergeant meanwhile. Let them be my gopher. Besides, we'll need all the guys with some experience we can get."

"Yeah. Sure."

"You'll get some fresh air. Sort things out. Be on your own from here to battalion, all the way back to division some days. Maps and special mail, mostly. Do the occasional interrogation or translation for me should our patrols pick anything up—that's valid right there. You're in reports for knowing German."

"I said, sure. Why convince me? You're the looie."

"It's not for me."

"Thanks, Tom. That what you want to hear?"

"I already heard it."

Lett lifted the mug. His hand shook.

Godfrey looked away, till Lett got it to his lips. They toasted, and Lett noticed Godfrey's hand shaking too.

***

Holger Frings ended up in a field hospital in a former schoolhouse farther north up the Dutch coast. For a time, days maybe, he had been left to float in a warm sea of morphine. In such a state the hospital worked on him in a macabre way, with all its layers of unreal white mixed with a smell of gangrene, of burnt flesh from patients worse off around him. He remembered: He only suffered from smoke inhalation and a severe concussion, his symptoms ranging from a burning, wrenching cough and retching to nausea and confusion. The skin of his face felt tender, his eyebrows and nostril hairs had singed and his beard shrunken from heat. His saliva had tasted burnt for days. He was more shocked to find out that he had lice, like some sorry foot soldier.

The morphine gave way. Then a man was talking to him, a Navy ensign with the silver piping of Administration, squinting, a quivering chin—the type who probably used a magnifying glass to find the lint on his tunic. Hanssen was dead, the ensign told him. All on the open bridge had died, which explained the blood Frings had seen running down the wheelhouse windows. Frings demanded details. Shrapnel had ripped Hanssen apart from shoulders up. Another flotilla on return march had found them just as the weather turned so bad the British MTBs pulled out and the light destroyer didn't bother coming back to finish them off, this after Kammel had hurtled them to safety—his throttle-up must have sent Frings falling on his back. Kammel had lost a hand and an eye from a burst that shattered the wheelhouse window; they had to amputate his hand right out on deck. Both Hanssen's and Baum's boats had to be left to the sea. Baum went down with his. More sailors had been lost than survived.

The ensign had pulled up a chair. He kept his attaché case upright on his knees, like a shield. Frings had sat upright on his bed, lining up his angle of attack.

"You look like you have a question," the ensign said.

"I have one for starters. I don't understand why all the morphine."

The ensign looked around, as if for a nurse, an orderly. "I'm not a doctor, mind."

"My injuries aren't that bad. I just want to get back out there. So what's this all about?"

The ensign cleared his throat. "We would like to know why your boats did not return to the pens with the rest of the flotilla. What were your last instructions, as you understood them?"

Frings didn't answer, at first. What was this? They were building some kind of case against them? A heat seethed in his inflamed lungs, sinuses. He wheezed and glared at the ensign, who seemed to shrink behind his attaché.

Frings said: "*Oberleutnant zur See* Hanssen wanted it. *Obersteuermann* Baum did. And I think they were right. It gave us something like an opportunity. Odds. The Beefs thought we were all heading in. We thought we could decoy. It's called sacrifice."

The ensign paused a moment, as if referring to notes in his head. "We understand you left the wheel. Why?"

Frings pushed off his blankets and swung out his legs, brushing the ensign's knees.

"Where is Kammel?" Frings shouted. "I want to see him. He'll tell you."

"That's not possible. He's been moved to Germany for convalescence." With that, the ensign added a sick little smile. The man had gotten in Frings' head, he appeared to believe, and that was all he had probably ever wanted. This binder commando had a cruel streak.

"What about the rest of my flotilla?" Frings said.

The ensign shook his head. "More bombers came. They caught our boats right before they could reach the pens. Only two made it inside. The rest scrambled away but were sunk." The ensign pushed up his glasses. "The total able survivors? Well, they could barely man one boat," he added.

Frings thought he saw the hint of a smile.

He lunged at the ensign, grabbed him by the collars, pinning him to his chair. The attaché tumbled away. "What about all that intelligence that's supposed to alert us to all these goddamn planes, eh? You can wipe my ass with it. What about the radar owed us going back years, and for so many dead? Huh? Where's that leave us?"

It took three orderlies to pull Frings off the ensign. The ensign hurried out, gasping.

He never returned. No one did.

And Frings came to understand why they had first given him the morphine.

After two weeks in the field hospital, Frings was ordered to a billet nearby, a hotel on the coast just outside Den Helder. He got a room of his own, top floor, low gable ceiling, one tiny dormer window, a cross on the otherwise blank walls, what had probably been servants' quarters. It was a cell, more or less. He had been told to bring whatever things he had. He would have preferred the brig or a penal unit to this, even a training flotilla. At least there he would know the score. They had their sharp hook to hang him on. Their two boats had not radioed in to report the approaching planes nor their plan to turn around, the ensign was clear on that. Frings didn't know if it was true. Radios cut out all the time. It didn't matter. It was a formality. Maybe they would try and pin it on him, or maybe on dead Hanssen. Frings wouldn't put it past them. Not when the likes of Scherenberg were running the land. They always needed a scapegoat.

In the hotel's dank and narrow cellar bar he huddled with a Number One from the other flotilla, *Obermaat* Schenkel. Schenkel had been there that day. Their own boats had already radioed in that bombers were heading for them and their pens, Schenkel told Frings, so no one needed an alert from Frings' boat or any other. Schenkel set down his beer mug. He stubbed out his cigarette. "The worst thing is: There was never even a convoy."

"What?"

"The intelligence was shit all around. There was no reason to venture into Quadrant 76, period. For all we know, the Beefs had been luring us all into a clever trap. Got me? The bastards got so much control, they can do anything they want now. It was like they're reading our goddamn minds—or at least our secret codes."

***

Wendell Lett liked the illusion of freedom a motorcycle gave him. At division motor pool he had chosen a 500cc Indian Scout, so worn its OD green silvered at the edges, the hefty leather side bags well rubbed with mud and grime. He could have had a jeep and probably should have for any large packages. A bike offered extra mobility. If the call came down he could get back to Godfrey and the platoon that much sooner. And something else had entered his noodle. He had heard guys talking in the hospital about all the desertions—the Army was losing Joes by the thousands every day. They would just up and disappear but had nowhere to go after a few weeks at best, so most came back and got a second chance unless they were head cases. Sure, others found a way to vanish. Paris was full of them. But what then? Lett told himself he would never choose that. He'd had his chance. Back in the states he could have claimed CO—conscientious objector status—on account of his Mennonite upbringing. It was too late. This was all he knew. The only way he would desert, he told himself, was if they did not send him back to combat. Two weeks in that hospital had shown him that he'd lost any connection to a normal world.

The battalion was spread out for this close to the line. The company command post was a couple miles behind the line. Division was at least fifteen miles back, at the base of a hill that had a grand villa on top. Lett had only been down below, where farmhouses and barns endured like serfs below the great lord up in the castle, now turned into US Army depots and service and supply posts. He stopped for chow there. Locals often lined up across the lane from where they dumped leftovers, women and children mostly. After mess Lett, like the other lapsed dogfaces, always crossed the lane and set down his mess tray, then turned away and crossed back over and shared a chat with some of the other guys, to give the poor people some privacy while they scooped into their pots and bowls. Sometimes Lett went back two or three times for chow and left out more for them. He'd keep doing it till the mess sergeant would wink at him and cut him off like a seasoned barkeep.

Riding the narrow, snaking country roads gave Lett room to breathe again. Rumbling along when the morning fog burned off was best. He didn't need the sun to come out. Just to feel the light, to see it sparkle in the dew of the hill grass when he'd come roaring out of a turn and a wood. The mornings were getting colder, so he traded a Joe for thick leather German motorcycle gloves, and he pulled his helmet beanie down tight under the straps of his goggles. He allowed himself to appreciate the countryside. It was beautiful, like something out of Grimm's tales. He told himself not to get too used to it. Reminders were everywhere. He sometimes passed forest battlefields that graves registration hadn't found yet and could make out the distinct smells of American and German—the two enemies smelled differently when decomposing owing to the different fabrics they wore, the various wools and denims breaking down along with flesh, muscle, organs. He himself would reek a certain way, and he took some solace in that.

His billet was a standard Army wall tent with stove. He shared his canvas with five other diehards from across the company—the doggies had taken their own tent, ignoring billet assignments. Lett would try to sleep but he twitched and gasped as if choking, as if trying to scream. Combat plundered his dreams. Anxiety robbed reality. To get over the rough humps, he would hole up with Tom Godfrey in his tent and listen to music. Tom had scored a record player and records—musicals mostly—from a captain who had showed up at the front with a trunk. All that was missing was the valet and personal porter. That fat cat found a way to get transferred out of the company within weeks, yet he could tell all back home that he'd been on the line.

"That's the way a lot of them are," Godfrey said. "We should be happy to see them go. It's when they want to stay that we start praying."

When Lett had time, he would fan out and drive more skinny roads and discover the valleys, ravines, junctions, towns and villages farther off the straight line from company. Taking it slow. The ritual found him within a few days of starting courier duty. He kept coming back to one village—Stromville. It stood on its own like others but wasn't crammed into the rugged land like many were, crowded around swelling secondary rivers or their backs up against some rocky hill. Stromville had its own valley and occupied one end of it. It was no bigger than a few football fields squared together but the open yet secluded space felt like a sanctuary, ringed as it was with the ridge and trees and Stromville's quaint skyline. Stromville had the requisite village steeple and the gables and old stone buildings like all. But Stromville had a special obscurity. It had insignificance. It had no junction to fight over. The place didn't seem to want to be anything it wasn't. Walking through the brief main street, taking in the few sights, Lett saw no references to this or that bishop seating here in the Middle Ages, or some plaque pointing to the birthplace of a certain poet or national dish invented here. The population? Nor more than a few hundred, if you counted the outlying farms. He visited the place four times in his first week, and each time heard no thumps of far-off battles or shelling, no clanking of armor columns, hell, he didn't even hear planes overhead.

Without the few cars, the place might as well have been three hundred years ago. He saw no other GIs here, no Off Limits signs left behind by a battalion XO or his rule-bound German equivalent. The people left Lett alone, too. No one wanting to hustle him. The place didn't smell like war either. The worst odor was when the cobblestones got damp.

Lett always did the same thing. He would park his bike inside the half open rear courtyard of a nondescript, two-story red-brick house on the main street. He would stroll the town. Each time he ended up on a bench, or overlooking the valley, or leaning on a lamppost. And he would start trembling, uncontrollably, as if in an earthquake, as if a hundred hands were shaking him from all sides. And he would cry.

On his second week, he found himself on the bench near the small main square, under trees. It must have been about noon. It was colder now, approaching the end of October. He had kept his motorcycle gloves on. He shivered. He felt his fellow dead Joes around him, but he couldn't see them. He tried to shake them off. He squeezed his eyes shut but it only made him see them. His foxhole buddies sat on the bench with him, others at his feet. They offered him smokes and hooch, played cards and shared mail from home. They joked about Lett. What a sad sack. How could such a nice bub let them go and die?

Lett cried again. His head lowered, between his knees. Once he was finished, he stretched his legs, letting his boots rest on their heels, and sighed. He couldn't wipe his tears with the gloves on, so he'd just let them dry. He closed his eyes, listening to nothing at all. The silence awed him, but he didn't know if it was from the beauty or frailty of it.

Someone sat next to him. A woman. He hadn't heard her coming? He sat up. Gave her the top-to-bottom. She wore shiny loafers with soft soles.

"You're good at that," he said.

A corner of her mouth fought a smile. Her hair was neither blond nor brown but could be either in the light, parted to one side in a way that reminded him of Veronica Lake. She could only be a couple years older than he. Her eyes were blue with sparkles of mischief, her skin light and face a little lean, Lett thought, until her smile began to lengthen, lifting her cheekbones and eyebrows, which seemed to spread her eyes farther apart even as it widened them. Wonderful.

"I mean it," he said, turning to her and taking in her smart blazer over a dress with buttons that ran from her collar down. What was she? She could be anything from schoolteacher to town hall secretary to shopkeeper, but probably not a farmer girl. She was the village girl with smarts, he decided. "Do you speak English?"

"A little," she said, pronouncing it like "leetle."

"I said, you are good—sneaking up on me like that, I mean. We could use you in my outfit."

"Outfeet?" She looked down at her blazer.

"Oh, no, not clothes. Like a unit. A platoon."

"Ah. I know it," she said, smoothing out her skirt, her smile fading. Was she scared of front-line GIs?

"I'm harmless," he said.

"I know," she said.

She pulled a hanky, and wiped at his eyes.

He'd forgotten about the tears. Tough luck.

She pressed a finger to the divisional patch on his arm. "Your outfeet, it stays near here, yes?"

"That's right. We're getting the royal rest treatment. Damp forest, cold chow, latrine tent, the whole works."

"You have seen much fighting."

"How can you tell? You know what? Never mind."

They stared a moment, she with her hanky clenched in her hand, he with those German motorcycle gloves hanging off his knees like two rabbit skins. He pulled them off.

"You are parked in my court," she said, leaving off the "t" in the French way. Like this it sounded like the word "heart"—*cur*—to Lett's untrained ears. "Once again, you are," she added.

Lett's face flushed, and it surely showed on his cold cheeks. "Well. It didn't seem to be bugging anyone, so I just . . . kept doing it. I'm not hiding anything."

"I know."

Lett sat up, feeling an actual smile push through his dogface mask. "Oh, you do, huh? You've been following me, have you?"

"It's true. I watch you. Someone must keep an eye on the invaders."

"I'm not invading anything."

"I know that too. But I have not informed the authorities proper. So you are safe."

They laughed.

"You know what? I have an idea. I got a couple hours to kill, and a bottle of Riesling in my cargo bag."

She cocked her head at him.

"Understand? Wine. It's *boche* stuff, sure, but it would probably go good with bread."

"I understand."

She walked him to a picnic space just inside a wood, along a creek. She had stopped on the way in a shop for bread, half a short baguette and a couple inches of hard salami, telling him to wait outside. So he had waited. He could get used to taking orders from a CO like this. The picnic space had a little table—blocks of pocked stone and a narrow old door atop it, wood benches. They sat across from each other, their knees touching often. She had slung her satchel-sized purse crossways, in the military way. From it she pulled a large and sturdy knife and used it to cut thick slices of the salami. Godfrey would be proud of him. He had managed a meal with a local girl all on his own. They ate staring at each other, she tearing off pieces of meat and bread and he making a little sandwich that made her chuckle. He drank straight from the bottle and so did she, which surprised him. She had a little roughness in her background. For a moment he imagined her doing the same with some German NCO the previous year, then lost the thought. Who cared? That poor bastard was a goner too.

"I hope you didn't use too many ration cards for this, or whatever you have?" he said.

"I did not," she said. "We have none left."

For a few minutes, maybe more, he didn't think of the war. He wasn't in a war. Though it didn't remind him of the back-home stateside world either. That was still lost to him. This was a new place.

"A special occasion," she said, chewing. They finished off the short loaf and few slices of salami, devouring it and speeding up to do so as if needing to catch a bus. They each took longer slugs off the bottle without taking their eyes off each other. His fingertips had found her upper thigh. She kept her hands on the table, as if hoping to fool imaginary fellow diners. He leaned across the table, and his face loomed over hers. He felt ten feet tall. He saw hesitation from her—a flicker of the eyes, looking away. When she looked back again, her mouth parted. He kissed her. She wrapped arms around him. He pulled back to get a look at her, held her face a moment in his calloused, bony, prematurely aged fingers.

They rose and met at the end of the table and kissed deeper. They tore away clothing, panting, looking for a spot. She led him to the base of a tree. Lett kept her standing.

He entered her with one arm propped against the tree, his other arm around her to protect her from the bark. She pulled him closer, her fingers searching inside his field jacket, his shirt.

The surge from him to her made him gasp, groan, hoot with relief. She laughed, and buried her head in his chest.

They caught their breath, then put themselves back in order like two teenagers caught pawing each other at a dance. They stood back at the table. Each smiled, now more nervous than before.

"You may smoke if you want," she said.

"I don't smoke anymore," he said. "I will if you want," he added.

Something about that made her laugh, a hand over her mouth.

"My name is Heloise. Heloise Vérive," she said. Her hands clasped behind her back and she swung her hips, as if embarrassed. "I never have done such a thing as this," she said.

"Me neither. And I never thought I would, either."

***

On the morning of November 10, 1944, Holger Frings was ordered to report to the *FdS*, the *Führer der Schnellboote*. He wore his Navy undress blues, the double rows of gold buttons polished, his S-boat War Badge gleaming. The S-boat flotillas' headquarters was just up the road from his billet in Den Helder. They didn't tell him how to get there, so he walked. His head was clear. He had quit drinking until his limbo was over, needing to stay alert for whatever they had in store for him. His resolve had been sorely tested the previous day, when he got word that Number One Schenkel had gone missing at sea. Instead of mourning in the hotel bar, he had written to Christiane again. He knew he would get no response.

Their Commander-in-Chief occupied a brown stone box of a villa. It looked like a provincial girl's school with its tall mansard roof and ornate black iron fence tipped in gold. It had an excellent officers mess next door, Hanssen had once told Frings. Now utility vehicles and motorcycles raced in and out the front drive. A supply truck had pulled up to a side entrance. Men loaded all manner of crates and papers onto the truck, another truck waited, and a third pulled up while Frings stood before the front steps. The *FdS* was pulling out. The great retreat was pressing onward. On land, the Allies had rushed into Holland and pushed farther east, into the Hürtgen Forest, aiming for the Northern Rhine. Cologne lay in their sights now. Frings watched pale-faced officers and adjutants rush by and had to laugh at their eyes wide in shock. You fine fellows want to know what shock is really like? He wanted to shout it at them.

A well-groomed aide with suede gloves and an Iron Cross in manservice met Frings, and Frings wondered if he was going to face the Commander-In-Chief himself. Suede aide ushered Frings into a second-floor office. Crates stood open, half-filled or ready to be carted off. Files and charts had stacked up on a billiards table. A *Korvettenkapitän* strode in carrying bottles cradled in his arms like two puppies. Frings saluted with the regular military salute, hand to brim, though all military had been ordered to use the Hitler Salute exclusively after

July's assassination attempt. The Lieutenant Commander set his puppies on his desk, one by one. They were bottles of Scottish whiskey, the labels water damaged, booty from a sinking no doubt.

"At ease," the Lieutenant Commander said. He removed his peaked cap, sat at his desk, saw the file dead center in front of him, and smiled at Frings. Frings thought the man looked familiar now, and it wasn't just the high forehead and aquiline nose all these career-path officer types seemed to have.

"You're Lieutenant Hanssen's brother," Frings said.

"I am. Reinhard Hanssen."

Hanssen had talked a lot about his brother. Reinhard was the older one. He was the reason Frings' boat captain had chosen the Navy.

Their smiles faded, and they bowed their heads.

"He turned into such a damn good *Kommandant*," Frings said.

"He said the same of you. Said, he wouldn't have made it so far without his Number One."

Frings nodded. It was more like a bow.

The elder Hanssen closed the file, set it aside. "So. What are we going to do with you? There may still be punishment. The *FdS* only has so much control over cases like this. They could use anything they want against you. Say you have a habit of abandoning your combat post, whether it's the flotilla or the helm. They always have choices, you see."

"*They* could say I harass a certain *Gauleiter* and his new girlfriend, who happens to be my wife," Frings said. If *they* were in control of this, surely his file contained family information.

Hanssen pursed his lips. He drummed his fingertips on the table. "I may be able to get you back out on a boat eventually, but by then? I wonder if you really want that."

"I just want at the enemy," Frings said.

Hanssen nodded. He reached over to an inbox and held up a page. It was a teletype.

"You speak English, yes?" Hanssen said.

"I do, sir," Frings said.

"How much? Some measure of fluency, would you say?"

"Close enough. American and British ports, English-speaking shipmates. Did so for years."

"Ah, yes, a former merchant mariner. That should do it. Do you have anything against being deployed on land?"

The question should have slapped Frings hard on the jaw. Burned in his ears. Fight on land? Two years, even six months ago, he would have spoken his mind. Remembered his father.

"None at all, sir," he said.

"Fine, then. This should take care of your situation. It seems they're looking for a special sort of volunteer. They'll take one look at you and know just what to do, I'm sure."

Hanssen asked Frings to sit, and handed him the page. The teleprinter had received a general order request signed by the Wehrmacht General Staff:

VERY SECRET: *Officers and men who speak English are wanted for a special mission. . . . The Führer has ordered the formation of a special unit for use on the Western Front in special operations and reconnaissance . . .*

The communiqué went on at length. They sought men with American dialect. When Frings finished reading, he saw Hanssen shaking his head at the mess around him. The Lieutenant Commander pushed one of the Scotch bottles to Frings' edge of the desk. "Please do take one of these before you go, *Obermaat*. A memento."

Frings was ordered to a place called Grafenwöhr, in Northern Bavaria. He meant to travel in his Navy undress but the supply master made him wear the Navy's gray-green field uniform that left him looking like any other land rat if one didn't look closely and see that his war eagle and insignia were gold, the buttons bore little anchors, and his left pocket his S-boat War Badge.

He left Den Helder the next morning. He was supposed to switch trains at a station outside Cologne and report to a transfer post the next day. He hitched a ride into the city instead.

The Cologne he knew had been destroyed by '44. He had been back before. The last time the previous spring. He had gone to his old town street in St. Martin's Quarter where he grew up, when working people were crammed into the quaint but dilapidated blocks down by the river just as they had been since the Middle Ages. In the 1930s, the Nazis had tried to restore the area into an "island of tradition" that mimicked their make-believe ideal of medieval glory. Those ideals of theirs had gone too far, of course, as ideals did, bringing on the Allied bombings that had returned his old neighborhood to some primeval outpost after the flood. Old St. Martin's Church was gone. The ambitious Rheinau Harbor peninsular running parallel to the bank had been bombed into oblivion, left a junkyard and a fire hazard. Only the main cathedral and its high spires stood, along with one bridge—Hindenburg Bridge— now constantly loaded down with trains of refugees and ragtag retreating forces. He had trudged along the rubble-strewn lanes near old town like one would on an obligatory cemetery visit, and was amazed to find people still living among the ruins. He had seen little girls having a tea party with a salvaged table. A sentry passed and stopped to admire them, and patted one of the girls on the head. The sentry was an older man, in a civilian overcoat but an army-style field cap, on one sleeve a black armband with red piping and white letters for the *Volkssturm*, the Nazis' new last-ditch home guard. He had a vintage Mauser from the previous war and a whistle, of all things, looking without the rifle like an aging football manager. That was probably the moment Frings had known, deep down, that the war was lost for Germany. He had never told Christiane this. By then she was already calling such doubters weaklings, cowards. Among the rubble he had wanted to shout at the little girls and the old sentry and anyone else he could grab by the collars and scream at to get out, flee now, find a different city. Cologne was fucked and would have to start all over. He had wanted to scare those little girls. Maybe it would save them. But he had only staggered onward, head down, his damp cigarette hanging from his mouth.

He would not revisit the ruins of St. Martin's Quarter this round. He had been drinking too much of Hanssen's scotch, already felt a lump of grief in his gut like a stone dumpling, and didn't have much time. He found a cluster of watercraft along the river at the south end of the bombed-out *Rheinauhafen* peninsula, tugs and watch boats mostly. He saw no one aboard from the old days, and it left him breathing easier. He'd rather not talk about his father, or himself, or have to admit he was transferring to the land. He spoke with a kid in a leather cap like the ones the onetime street-fighting Socialists and more recently the defiant young Edelweiss Pirates probably wore, his longer hair wanting to spring out from under the brim. He manned a skiff and probably ran black market goods. Frings' dad had probably kept an eye on the likes of him. It didn't take Frings long to talk the kid into running him downriver. Seeing Frings' leather peacoat, gold Navy insignia and S-boat War Badge on his tunic would have proved enough, but hearing Frings' Kölsch dialect had cinched the deal. Frings added five marks into the bargain anyhow.

"Why can't yoush take da train?" the kid asked when they were halfway there, keeping close to the bank, the kid knowing his way like Frings remembered.

"I'm a sailor, ain't I?" Frings said. "Me, I don't like da trains, even if there was one runnin'. They get bombed, see."

"Yeah, sure do," the kid said, nodding, steering them along.

Frings pulled his peacoat tight around him against the river cold. Supply had issued him a new holster for his service Walther p38 semi-automatic. He had never used his sidearm in any S-boat sortie, and rarely wore it. It was good to have now, though he doubted he would use it.

There were easier ways.

Königswinter lay just ahead, a modest pier with a ferry landing. Trees lined the bank before it. The kid dropped him off onto the sand there. Frings marched inland through a wood and into this village where tourists came to see the Drachenfels castle ruin. He hit a pub.

One healthy pour of a fair but strong Rhine wine and a little banter with locals told him where former *Gauleiter* Scherenberg lived—requisitioned not some ten years ago and the most posh villa on the hill, he was told, which meant it was stolen.

Frings could see the place well before he reached it, recognizing it from his days on the river: a dense cluster of steep gray-roofed spires and phony towers in an emulation of a castle, all crammed together as if for some fancy cake. Fitting, that, Frings thought and laughed. He was glad for the scotch in him, because his heart was beating now but not like when on an S-boat run. His heart twanged, as if fingers plucked at it. He knew why. This wasn't about Christiane anymore. The girls might see him like this. They might even see him kill a guy. If they had to see it, he only hoped he could share a few soft words with them before he did it.

He had thought about it many times. In the latest scenario, he would be able to watch the girls a while through a window, painting, reading or playing chess maybe, while Christiane brushed her hair in the mirror. Finding them safe and secluded, he'd hunt down the brown bastard in another part of his stolen castle. Maybe it could be on a top floor. Maybe Frings could make him join the Luftwaffe, take a little flight off one of his fancy turrets.

A calmness came over him as he strode up the little lane, sticking to the side of the road. A drizzle came down, put the river fuzz on him and he liked that, he knew it. He unbuttoned his peacoat, unclasped his holster, and unlatched the side safety on his loaded Walther. He slowed, assessing the target.

A wrought-iron fence stood about his height. A gate waited down the way. He kept behind a column, and looked through the bars. He saw no sign of a guard, so he climbed the fence. He kept to the perimeter, using the fence and bushes, keeping clear of any open windows.

The lump in his gut had turned to pure muscle that radiated through him, fed by adrenalin. He was meant to be here, he knew. He had so wanted this. Hanssen would want this for him. The windows were blocked with closed curtains, even on upper stories. He moved to the wall, keeping close to the cold red sandstone, inching along, looking for a way to peak in. Around back he found a patio window, saw a gap in the curtain. Crouching, he moved across the patio until he reached the gap. He looked in.

He saw white shapes, silhouettes. All was draped with sheets. What looked like a grand piano, a double chaise longue, a standing globe taller than his daughters, and in this one room more furniture total than they could probably carry on their S-boat deck.

He heard something, the crunch of feet. He backed away on his toes to the base of the patio steps, hugging a column for cover. He pulled his Walther, keeping it between his legs, both hands clenched around it for steadiness.

Something flashed in a corner of his eyes. A barrel?

He swung around aiming.

"Don't shoot!" yelped a man. He wore work denims and might be slow judging from his misshapen, childlike face. He carried a rake, spiked with autumn leaves. A gardener?

Frings sighed, holstered his sidearm, and tried a smile.

The gardener's mouth hung open. His eyes rolled around, taking in Frings' odd livery.

"It's Navy. I apologize for scaring you. I thought I heard something back here. I guess I've been at the front too much."

"Uh, huh," said the gardener.

"I'm a relative, you see," Frings said.

"Uh, huh," gardener repeated, and Frings wondered if he had exhausted the man's vocabulary. "Me too," gardener added.

"Ah," Frings said, wondering if this man was a Scherenberg brother or son or had even belonged to the family who had truly built this place.

"I'm surprised not to find them at the house," Frings said. "They wrote to me about coming here."

The gardener took a big swallow, nodded, and said: "Sir, I'm sorry you didn't receive word. They have moved to Prussia. They believe it's safer there, for the time being."

This gardener might as well have run him through with his rake. The booze rushed to Frings' head. He took a step back, almost stumbled. "Prussia. You mean Brandenburg," he muttered.

"Yes. East of Berlin even. There's an estate... Are you all right, sir? Need to sit down?"

"No, no." Frings' feet seemed to float. The villa whirled around his head.

He vomited on the steps. The splash forced the gardener to jump back.

"Oh, dear. I can call someone. Should I call someone?"

"No... No..."

Frings heaved till it was only strings of saliva and bile. The gardener had placed a hand on his shoulder, patting him as if burping a baby. The last of it came up tasting like that burnt saliva, which made Frings want to throw up again. The gardener didn't seem to mind any of it.

Frings stood, finally. The gardener handed him a rag, and he wiped at his mouth. "Thank you. Did they say when they would be back?"

"They did not say, but it may well be some time. I expect not until the war is won."

Frings almost wanted to laugh. Here on these grounds, it might as well have been 1914. Or maybe Christiane had assured him those Wonder Weapons were coming.

"Very well. Thanks again," Frings said, and made his way out. He didn't wait for the gardener to open the gate. He climbed back over the fence and headed back down the lane, stopping to brush his boots against high grass, to wipe off the vomit.

White sheets, he thought. Talk about weaklings, cowards. White sheets were for hospitals. White sheets were nothing more than surrender flags, he told himself as he stomped around the village looking for a rail station—if that too hadn't been bombed already.

***

In November 1944, everyone from new privates on the line to war correspondents back at division was talking about a German surrender coming and the war ending soon. The krauts were licked, they said. Wendell Lett was hardly fooled. The Germans would not just give up. It was true American troops had taken their first German border city, Aachen, but only after gory and grinding street battles. Rear-line officers, thus inspired, had started taking longer leaves to Brussels and Paris, but meanwhile the slaughter soldiered on among the killing trees inside Hürtgen Forest. And Allied troops would still have to enter Germany proper. Defeating them could take years. They would need Lett for whatever it took.

Somehow, the Army had kept Lett's battalion from the immediate front line. Though it was always near. They were still near the border. Lett coped with it. He knew the dates, time, days of the week again. He needed them to spend as much time with Heloise in Stromville as he dared—whole days, afternoons, a couple hours, whatever it took. Sometimes he returned to his billet well after dark, which the green sentries never got used to.

He and Heloise shared her second-floor room overlooking the main street. They often just lay on the made bed. It was safer there. Breaking down in front of her had only been the start of his episodes. Everyday sounds—a zipper even—made him jump, scramble under the bed, hug a tree. She let him fall asleep on the bed, but knew he muttered horrific things in his sleep by the way he woke up gasping, sweating, whimpering. She didn't dwell on his fits of terror. She was just there for him. She had stroked his forehead, wiped away cold sweat, helped him breathe right again.

He had forgotten what it was like, just talking with a girl. Pledging such sweet things to her one moment, then joshing with her the next moment. Suddenly all that he had given up for dead had landed, softly, as if from a parachute, right down in front of him. It was like some kind of rapture, like a guy finding religion—that bliss he'd always heard the nuns talking about, that he had snickered at. The only problem was, this realization made him tremble all the more. It only made the prospect of going back up on the line look even worse. This was worse than dying. Now, he stood to lose the only good thing he'd ever had.

They lay on her bed in silence, staring at the ceiling. The afternoon was darkening outside, from more clouds moving in, the shadows creating dim shifting shapes above them. Lett had his shirt off. Heloise felt at the thin purple-red welts he had from shrapnel, on his shoulders and back.

"I was married," she told him.

"Was?" he said.

"Paul. He was in the *Résistance*. In the *AS*, the Secret Army. Two years ago, they send him on a *stupide* mission with no hope. He was shot in the back by the German military police."

"I'm sorry," Lett said. He told her about his not-so ideal upbringing, how it had left him without those deep roots the other Joes felt so strongly. Heloise understood the loneliness. She had gotten used to loss, she told him. Her mother Amelie had died of a cancer when she was twelve. Her father, Jean, had opened a stationers shop after the last war. It never did well. Now this new war threatened to wreck it for good, so Jean had settled for waiting out the battles with drink and sleep. Some called him a *dipsomane*. And who could blame him? The father didn't mind having Lett around. Jean often kept watch at the entrance to the courtyard when Lett and Heloise came and went. When they had to go out on the street, Lett let her take the lead. This was her town. She knew the ropes. She was twenty-six, four years older than he. She didn't let him hold her hand on the street. She said they had to keep things secret, just in case the Germans came back—they didn't want anyone finger pointing. She had already secluded herself. Many suspected she helped out with the Resistance and didn't want anything to do with her. What if the Germans found out? They could shoot the whole village, not just those who kept their mouths shut.

"I don't know why it is," she said, "but I feel I can tell you: I had, euh, *la fausse couche*. I lose our baby. Is this how one says it?"

"Yes. A miscarriage."

"Ah. It was the baby from my Paul. *Le Docteur*, Doctor Servais, he says it is the stress."

"I'm so sorry. But I like that you feel you can tell me."

"Yes, but do you know what I think? I fear I did not have enough hope for this baby. In my heart. It is the war. It is the fear to bring a child into this bad world. That is their big crime, the men who make war. They make us mothers think: Why make one's child suffer this life?"

"I can't say I disagree there. Not from where I'm standing."

She said nothing. She turned her face away, staring off. Lett didn't like that stare on her. He knew it too well.

"The Germans, they won't come back," he told her.

"Oh, they can," she said. "You have not seen the *boche* with his back against a wall."

"Fighting the Resistance, you mean."

"Yes. Paul told me horrible stories. Sometimes he just stared into the air. He trembled like you. He had so many nightmares. I went on some missions, to help them, but he stopped me from doing it."

"I wouldn't have let you either," Lett said.

"I will not let you," Heloise said.

"Let me what?"

"Go. Let you go."

"I will come back. After, I will," he told her.

"And when is this 'after'?"

"I can't say. There is no plan for giving us a real rest. There's always a plan for sending us back out. I do know that. But we never hear anything, not until we hear it."

Lett hadn't meant to say it like this. It just came out.

"You can stay here forever," Heloise said.

It sounded fanciful with her accent, but she meant what she was saying. Lett knew her well enough by now. She always knew the score before she spoke.

He turned to her, propping himself on an elbow. "Don't get me wrong, *chérie*. I do want to stay, for good. I'll come back when I'm done, when I've done my job."

He had expected a tirade, the silent treatment, a huff, something. Heloise only nodded. She snuggled up to him. They closed their eyes a while. When Lett woke again, he found her staring at him with larger, unblinking eyes. She said:

"Do you know, I still help the *Résistance*? I keep fake identifications and other materials for them. We help escape American and British pilots. So now I help you."

"What? No. I can't."

She punched at the headboard.

That same afternoon Heloise's father crept up the stairs, knocked, and whispered to Heloise through the cracked door. She returned to the bed pale and shaken.

Lett sat up on the bed, listening.

"There. Do you hear?" she said.

"Yep." The curtains were closed, leaving a crack. They went over and peered out. They saw an American jeep slide to a halt below. The jeep had white trim and the occupants white horizontal stripes on their helmets. "They're MPs. Military Police," Lett said.

Two of the three MPs pulled batons and rushed into the inn on the opposite side of the street. Another jeep and a staff car rolled up, unloading war correspondents and officers in dress too crisp for the front.

The MPs hauled out a GI scruffy from the frontline. The MPs played it up for the correspondents who snapped photos, shaking the poor Joe to make it look like he was resisting.

"What happens when a man goes AWOL. Those officers you see? Staff-level creatures, rare as a good latrine where I come from," Lett said.

"Your commissars, yes? To make the strong warning for others."

"We don't call them that, but, yeah. Desertions are getting worse. So you see? This is what happens," Lett said, his hands shaking so much that Heloise had to close the drapes right. "They could take me away from you," he muttered. "And they would, too." He fought tears. They came on just like that, a flicker of heat. "I'm not fooling you. It's almost as if I was meant to go through all I did, just so I could find you."

"You only fool your own self." Heloise turned away from him. "One day, you will see how they use you, all these self-important commanders," she said to the wall. "You will see."

November passed into December. Back at the billet, Lett hadn't told Godfrey where he went all the time and Godfrey did not want to know. Often Lett just dropped off his delivery and headed right back to Stromville, even if it was for an hour before dark.

"Sometimes I wonder if you'll come back," Godfrey told Lett finally. "It sounds like you got a better reason than most, by the looks of you. Or should I say, 'she'?"

"You shouldn't. What you don't know can't hurt a guy. I don't want to put you in a spot."

"Touché."

Back at division, Lett's offers of captured Lugers and German medals got the rear-liners drooling so much they unloaded their bottles of Johnnie Walker and vintage champagne on Lett like they were used bandages. Godfrey was acquiring quite the taste for vintage champagne. It went well with his records. He even thought about putting together a little revue for the boys.

One evening when Lett returned, Godfrey wasn't looking like a man fixing to put on a show. He had bags under his murky eyes. Lett could smell the drink on him, a mix of sweet champagne and mossy scotch. Lett sat with him in the command tent. Lett wasn't dumb. He had been delivering more maps, which was never a good sign.

"They got us sending out more patrols," Godfrey said. "Evidently the line's a little thin in front of us. The Germans seem thin too, but you never know. We're moving some positions further up, nice and dug in, and the OPs will creep farther forward. Don't worry. I see that look. We're officially still at rest. The whole damn front is."

"Any steak dinners yet?" Lett said. When mess ran steak to a unit at rest, it meant they were going back out sooner than later.

"Apparently there is word of real pork chops coming. Look. I'll be sure to let you know when it's the real thing. The problem is, who's gonna let me know? You don't know those brass the way I've seen them. The way they justify their moves in a briefing, all puffed up like they get. It's worse than the shelling, a horrifying sight."

"So you tell me. It's because you can't do anything about it."

"That's right, Wen. And I'm telling you, I hope you never have to see it."

December 10, 1944. In their upstairs room in Stromville, Lett made love to Heloise. The windows and room trembled from a constant roar outside. US Army troop trucks rumbled along the main street below, the bulky tires mashing the freezing mud. Lett and his Heloise did their best to ignore the blare, and the bedside clock, and the calendar on the wall, but the traffic roared on, a grinding drone.

Wrapped in the same blanket, Lett and Heloise went to the window, parted the curtains and wiped the glass to watch the trucks pass, crammed with new troops.

Heloise's face hardened as she watched. It reminded Lett of a ballet dancer's, poised on her toes. "You see? There they are. More cannon fodder," she said, in French. She had taken to saying more things—the important things—in French.

Lett still didn't know much French but he looked at Heloise with that open face of his that wanted to understand. "You don't have to translate," he said. "'Replacements' is the official title. They're even younger than me."

"Yes, and what do they replace, eh?"

Lett didn't answer her. That morning, he had learned, a load of pork chops had been delivered to the division mess depot.

The column passed on through, revealing the frosted storefronts below—their quaint and wintry Belgian village had returned.

Heloise hadn't lost the hard face. "Something is missing in those trucks," she said.

Lett pulled the curtains together. "Is that right?"

"Oh, yes. There are no generals. No grand officers. The big leaders."

"Brass," Lett said.

She had learned the word. She nodded. "Yes, and where are they? Where? In comfort. It is the same everywhere, in every land. Streets and schools will have the big names of those brass officers one day. But you? What happens to Wendell?"

Lett showed her a smile. She didn't have to tell him. Godfrey didn't. Hadn't he just spent the last six months seeing what happens?

He pointed at the clock, just striking four. "What happens is, I gotta get back to post." He unwound the blanket from his shoulders and wrapped it around hers. He pulled on his long underwear, wool shirt and sweater, his fatigues and boots, web belt and courier bags. He shouldered his M1 carbine, and hung his helmet on his gear.

The day before, Godfrey had warned him to start carrying combat gear, just in case.

Heloise watched him dress. She yanked the blanket off herself and pulled on her red robe of Asian dragons and gold swirls that set off her fair skin and wide blue eyes, far and away the rarest piece of art in the village, Lett thought.

They held each other. Heloise touched the coil of hair on his forehead, pushing it back to show his face. "Cannon fodder," she repeated in French.

"I'm hearing you, doll, but I still can't know what you're saying."

"It is time. This is what I say to you. It is now."

Heloise took Lett by the hand. She led him to a dresser in the corner, knelt down to pull open the lowest drawer, and lifted out the drawer's false bottom.

Lett saw passports, ID papers, and forging supplies—glass vessels and papers, pens and brushes of all shapes and sizes. He saw documents in French and Dutch and German, but also US Army leave passes, trip tickets, and GI ID cards, some of them blank.

"Many of your GIs desert. Some are criminal. They steal trucks, they sell gasoline. But not you. You have the best reason. This can help you, until the Americans leave here."

He looked away. "I can't know about it. It's *marché noir.*"

Heloise shut the drawer. "What do you know about the black market? Against the Nazis, our forgers keep the *Résistance* going. The Secret Army fights with more pens than guns."

"You don't want me to fight any more. I understand that. But wasn't that fighting what you were doing—'V for Victory' and all that?"

"It was not for *victoire*—it was for our survival. Victory, that is a club for rich men and powerful men and they do not let in you." She added a huff.

"I am talking survival. That's all I'm doing. You gotta understand." Lett pulled Heloise to him, holding her tight. "It's almost over. I promise," he said. "And then I'm back."

"I don't want promises." Heloise pushed off him. "I lost a man once."

Lett moved to speak—

"Paul believed their words of victory, their promises," she said. "And look at him now. And you? You do not even believe."

Lett sighed. He stared down, at the worn bouclé carpet doing its best to adorn the worn plank floor. "There's not a lot of Joes believing in much. It's not how a guy makes it on through." On through to what, he did not specify.

Heloise had stood back, her hands on her hips. She nodded at the drawer. "This is here for you. I am. When you are ready. No more talk. You understand? You take a new name. It will be my name."

Lett drove his mud-caked courier bike back into the forest. For the increased patrols, the medics had set up an aid station near the company CP. Lett had to walk by it to get to Godfrey. Crying was coming from somewhere inside the tent. Near the entrance, GIs sat with bare feet blackened from trench foot. Lett kept his head down and almost stumbled over three corpses covered in frosted blankets. At least the growing cold was good for muting the smell, he thought.

Replacement GIs kept their heads down as Lett passed them. They had arrived from those troop trucks he had seen pass through Stromville, in their crisp field jackets and shiny helmets. He looked back over his shoulder at them shivering and gaping at the ancient stone farmhouses and huts and mass-produced American tents, the piles of trash. Wait till they see the foxholes and OPs farther forward, Lett thought. The veteran GIs, bearded and bundled up with threadbare scarves and rags, were building a fire in an empty drum despite the regs. It must have looked like a hobo camp to the new kids. Hoovervilles abroad.

In the command tent, a Broadway musical played on a record player. Maps, files, a typewriter, the field telephone, and a mess of bottles stood and lay around. It was a hobo tent with appliances. Godfrey smiled to the music, sitting behind a fold-up desk. The CP was designated for their newest captain, but no one had seen the man for days after ordering Godfrey and the other platoon lieutenants to "man the fort." Godfrey did so by deploying his record player. Lett stood before him.

"This one? It's 'Top Hat.' That's easy," Lett said.

Godfrey, nodding, lifted the needle arm and record with fingertips, sliding it back into its sleeve. "Irving Berlin. Well done. Sit, sit."

Lett sat. Godfrey pointed to the newspapers on the desk. The headlines read: "Krauts Kaput, Hightail it Home" and "Surrender Before Xmas?".

"You believe any of this? Actually, don't answer that." Godfrey sighed. "We really don't know what the Germans are doing over there.

Division sure doesn't. Even with the replacements? We're far below strength. Ever since . . ." He let his words trail off.

Lett set a bottle of champagne on the desk. "Prestige cuvée, they call it. Cost me my nice kraut gloves."

"Thanks," Godfrey said, but his eyes didn't light up like usual. He opened the champagne and it popped, making them start. They traded drinks from the bottle, foam and all.

Godfrey smiled. "Well? Did you see her again?"

Lett nodded, and a smile broke out. Godfrey grinned.

"Good. That's good. Better news to me than those headlines."

Back in his wall tent, Lett fired up the stove and gave sleep a shot. He must have slept fifteen minutes before his dead buddies visited him. They sat around a fire, roasting something on a spit. Shells were shrieking in on them but no one was ducking. On the spit, revolving and smoking, its skin blackening, was a creature the size of a dog but unknowable. The shells pounded down. Lett pleaded with all to take cover, with Sheridan, Tower, Mancuso, Bartley and all the rest. They only laughed at him.

Lett woke whimpering and sat in the darkness, expecting to get the business from the others in the tent. Nothing doing. The rest were snoring, or whimpering too in their sleep. From his breast pocket, Lett pulled out his photo of Heloise, a younger Heloise with fuller cheeks and brighter eyes. He didn't need to turn on the lantern. He had her face memorized. He cradled her in his hands, and winced at the thought that her dead fiancé who'd fought for the Resistance had probably once done the same, with the identical photo.

***

Lieutenant Colonel Lucien "Archie" Archibald of S-2 (intelligence) assumed his latest divisional post after a delightful leave in Paris. It was December 10. His new war room was once an ornate throne hall, in a lavish 18th-century villa that topped a hill just west of

Belgium's Ardennes Forest. Aides carried in maps and file cabinets as local workers removed wondrous paintings, antique books, and all that Archie deemed superfluous decoration. The aides and workers did their best to avoid Archie's squinting stare; Archie squinted always, it seemed to many he met, making his large yet compact face resemble the grotesque visage of a stage mask.

"Selfer? Selfer?" Archie said.

"Coming, sir." Captain Charlie Selfer sauntered in around the room's frantic redesign, calm as ever, files neat under his arm. His smooth good looks with a hint of dimples suggested he was a singer or actor attached to the USO rather than Archie's steady right hand. Selfer had even perfected the mid-Atlantic accent popular with entertainment types.

Archie stood behind his expansive metal desk. Selfer passed him a folder that read, "Strictly Confidential." Archie, smirking, flipped it open.

It was empty. Archie closed it, opened it, his smirk gone. He clapped his hands in machine-gun rhythm.

"That means out, everyone," Selfer said to the aides and befuddled workers. "Five minutes. Thank you."

The aides and workers filed out mumbling as Archie stared at Selfer for an answer.

"Well? Where are they?" Archie said.

"It's quite simple. The enemy intercept reports are unavailable, sir," Selfer said.

"Unavailable? How can that be? They're top secret. Inside information. No one even knows we have them."

"Unavailable only in the sense that there's no data. Possibly from here on out. It seems the Germans—the krauts, I mean, have stopped using their special ciphers," Selfer said. Archie insisted Selfer say "krauts" like the front-line boys. It played well.

"Ciphers that our code breakers were intercepting. The damn krauts can't stop now."

"It's unfortunate, but true. Once they retreated over their borders, the krauts can now use their normal telephone lines, and any old code they well wish."

Archie squinted at his empty outbox. "Well, did it go out? Tell me. It go already?"

Selfer nodded. He knew where this is leading but he would let Archie tell him, as always:

"In Archie's latest issue, Archie maintains that the krauts are done for," Archie said. "And it was those top secret intercepts we had our hands on that told us just that."

Selfer nodded again. This was the game they played, like a grumpy old radio duo, especially when it came to something as vital as "Archie's Account." Nicknamed "AA," Archie's self-styled independent field reports gave away no top secrets. Rather, as his promo copy described: Archie "makes his bold predictions and shares his wise hunches. Yes, friends, Archie's got the wits and tells it like it is." It had become the one bulletin every freethinking staffer on every keen rear-line staff had to have, like that novel everyone bought because the ads in Colliers told them to. Few noticed that Archie's previous division had been decimated in the Hürtgen Forest. The bulletins never had as much pull as they did now, with the final push into Germany coming in the new year.

"Yes, sir, they told us a great deal," Selfer began, "but—"

"Don't! Do not appease me," Archie growled. "We were coming up roses. This is my horse I rode in on, and yours too. We had an inside guy. My guy."

Archie had never told Selfer who was passing him the top secret reports of enemy intercepts. Was it a similarly rich cousin on Supreme HQ staff? An old friend of the family in the War Department? Selfer didn't care. All Selfer knew was, the reports made his patron Archie look like a soothsaying genius and a maverick to boot. Selfer suspected brass much higher than them were using the broken-code secrets to appear all-knowing, so why not they too? The market in military success was just as dog-eat-dog as any other.

In any case, Selfer had come up with a new ploy. All he had to do was convince Archie of it. "Indubitably," Selfer began. "We had a swell run going. Yet, who says it's over?" He opened his body to the room, to show Archie their large maps of the Belgium-Germany border that displayed thick and overwhelming Allied green arrows compared to a jumble of shapes in enemy red in retreat, just inside Germany. "We're a juggernaut, as you see."

"Which, of course, was the very point of 'Archie's Account' number thirteen." Archie nodded, with chin high—he got the drill now. "Right, yes. So what we do is, we just find a way to confirm it. We go and we reaffirm AA thirteen."

"Indeed. We don't need egghead data for that."

"Indeed! I'm back at the front now," Archie said. "I've got men here, a whole new division of them. They can serve as my eyes. Fine, fine! A sound investment, I say. So we will use these men, and we will only need a good few."

***

The next morning, December 11, Wendell Lett found Godfrey in a corner of the command tent with his back to Lett, standing over maps and files. Godfrey wouldn't turn around. Lett felt that ache low in his gut. Something had come down from a great height, he knew it.

"You called for me. What is it?" Lett said. "Please. Sir. Tom."

Godfrey turned showing a long face that made his scar shine in the light. "S-2 has a new colonel who's one verifiable bear of a cat, apparently. Archibald. His deputy called, a Captain Selfer."

"Okay, just tell me what they need, I'll run it out to them—"

"No. They want you. You is what they want. This Selfer, he asked for you by name."

"Me?" Lett felt heavier than his hulking army motorcycle, and he didn't have a kickstand.

Godfrey spoke with a snarl, as if he was dressing down Lett. "Well, it's all on paper about you, isn't it? For anyone looking. You got your Combat Infantryman Badge and then some. Proved yourself. Survived. And your name is on our interrogations, and you're down as translator, so they know your German's been tested."

Lett's pulse raced. "My German's a crock."

"Maybe so, but it was good enough for after-action reports."

"What else? Tell me."

"He asked all about you, but in the way those lawyers do in the pictures, you know, when they already know the answer? He knew you're an orphan even. Oh, he was a smoothie, let me tell you."

"I need a leave," Lett blurted. Just like in combat, instincts had kicked in—the leave request had shot out his mouth before he thought it. He needed to see Heloise first.

"You know I will. When I can. Meantime, no one gets one till division says. I'm sorry, Wen. You go now."

Lett drove west along winding roads and up hills to the rear-line villa with its wondrous view, what locals called a chateau. Division HQ. The whole corps staff was there now. Lett had never been above. It was no depot up there. Trimmed hedges ringed a courtyard of staff sedans freshly washed and jeeps parked neatly. Tightlipped adjutants put him in a chamber that was like a courtroom, with wood paneling and antique portraits of grim old faces glaring.

Other front-line GIs had wandered in, eight of them total, none from his outfit and eyeing each other like low-grade gladiators thrown together before the bloodsport. Lett wondered if they were all orphans like him. He had always felt expendable as such. Surviving as a footslogger was the only thing more so.

A captain in a pressed tunic worked the room like a politician mingling with donors, shaking hands, smiling, offering cigarettes. Few of the dogfaces around Lett had saluted, and the captain didn't seem to mind. He had the aristo's cheekbones and jaw, not quite movie idol material but in the running. Lett planted himself away in a corner, next to a gold-adorned planter that looked like an oversized chalice. The captain made his way over to Lett, a slim French cigarette hanging from between his manicured nails. Captain smoothie.

"Care for a smoke, soldier?" the captain said.

"No, thanks," Lett said.

"Charlie Selfer," the captain said.

Lett didn't give his name. They already knew it.

"So, you speak German?" Selfer said.

"Not really, sir," Lett said. "It's like I tell everybody. Nuns in Ohio don't speak like the Germans here. Prisoners we nab think my Deutsch sounds oddball, and I barely follow what they're saying."

"You sell yourself short, I'd say. Your name is Wendell Lett. From Ohio. Hometown?"

"It depends, sir. I didn't have parents."

"Thus the nuns," Selfer said. "What sort of nuns again?"

"Mennonite."

"Do tell."

"Some get them mixed up with Amish, Quakers even," Lett said. His implication was clear: The old sects like these raised noncombatants, conscientious objectors.

"Ah. They raised you, but you didn't take the faith."

Lett shrugged. "It didn't work out that way."

"You didn't stick around. You wanted something bigger."

"I had a foster home for most of high school. I liked being in a regular school. But I still felt like a boarder."

"I think I follow. What was it like, on the front?"

Did this swell really want to know? "Up on the line, you mean. Tough. Just us dogfaces. I never saw an officer higher than lieutenant."

"I see." Selfer looked toward the others, and placed an index finger on his chin as if working out an exceptionally complex math question. He turned back to Lett smirking, as if ready to share gossip. "I'm not just any officer. I'm S-2, as if you couldn't tell. I'm Archie's aide—Archie Archibald, I mean. You'll get to meet the man.

Then you can say you did. Archie really knows his intelligence. He rode cavalry in the Great War."

"In trenches, sir?"

"Droll, aren't we?" Selfer smiled, a show of bright teeth. "Archie's run oil fields, railroads, even owned thoroughbreds. Why, he's the horseback hero. Yes, people are saying he's right off the old Archibald family block. Heard of them?"

Lett shook his head.

"Well, you will."

Captain Selfer clapped like a stage director for them to take their seats. Lett sat on the end of a row of fold-up chairs along with the other GIs. An easel map of the German borderlands stood on a dais. Out strode Lieutenant Colonel "Archie" Archibald, and as he spoke he strutted around the propped-up map like it was a goat he was about to throat-cut.

He announced the mission in broad strokes, and Selfer joined in to add details.

Lett couldn't believe what he was hearing: The nine of them were going on a secret recon operation. They were going behind the enemy line and over the German border disguised as German soldiers. The goal: gain new intelligence on German troop movements, tactics, equipment and general constitution. They would be the eyes and ears of military intelligence.

Lett would do anything. He would take the next ten night patrols out. He would take a field commission as platoon leader. Anything but this. He could only imagine what Heloise would say.

Archie had come around to the front edge of the dais. "Very well, men. You head out PDQ and pronto."

A silence had fallen where Archie had probably expected applause, cheers. He looked around, squinting.

"Questions are welcome," Selfer added. "It's your right, considering."

Lett sat up, raised a hand. Selfer nodded to him. "What if we're caught, sir?" Lett said.

Archie and Selfer exchanged glances. They had to know what Lett meant: Going on a mission in German uniforms made them spies, not Joes. Spies got shot on sight. POWs, not as much. The Geneva Convention could only save them if they played by the rules of war— and came out luckier than a straight.

"That's a heck of a question," Archie barked. "Let's not be defeatist now."

"All I mean is, have you done it like this before?" Lett said.

"Oh, so it's 'precedent' he wants? The barracks lawyer," Archie said.

Selfer gave Archie a stern look, despite his lower rank. Archie added:

"All right, all right. Men, what I'm to tell you is confidential: In October, in Aachen, crack Army Rangers—directed by OSS—did pull off something like this and well done too."

"That's different, sirs," said a gruff voice. It came from one of the scruffier GIs, an older sergeant named Weber with a pockmarked face and dark bags under his eyes. "Those there are real commandos. We're only grunts. And we got some puppies here." Weber glared down the line of chairs. Some of the GIs had to be pretty new footsloggers, Lett saw. They didn't have the stare, for one thing. Put them in neckerchiefs and they had themselves a boy scout troop.

"You know the great Teddy Roosevelt, don't you?" Archie said. "He did more with far less. That's war. You ride into it with the mounts you mounted."

The GIs spoke up at once. Four hands had gone up along the row.

"No more, men," Archie said. "That's it. It's heave-ho time!"

Selfer clapped twice. "You heard the colonel. You'll be three teams of three—X, Y and Z team. Now, file on up here and exchange your ID tags."

A bulletin board stood on the dais. Nine GI dog tags hung from pins in the cork, tags they were to use in place of their own. Lett and Weber were the last to exchange theirs, sharing the same wary look.

Back in the forest, near the front line, stood a secluded farmhouse and barn requisitioned by S-2. Lett and the other eight GIs rode in a truck there and were left to wait in the muddy courtyard. Lett had been put into Z team with Weber and the one GI of the eight who looked the least dogfaced: eighteen-year-old Auggie, fresh off the boat from an Infantry Replacement Training Center. The three stretched out on an old farm cart. Weber and Auggie chain-smoked. Lett and Weber traded unit stories. Weber's company had seen the same blood-drenched casualty rate as Lett's, no surprise there.

The sun had only just gone down, but here it was nearly dark. Lett peered around the perimeter, inspecting the shadows. He counted only one sentry out there between the trees, maybe two. The idea nagged at him: What if he did just walk away? In Northwest Europe tens of thousands of them had done it, from all along the line, enough to fill a few full-up regiments. Paris alone was said to harbor thousands of them. So wouldn't a rural vanishing act be a sure bet? Only he and Tom Godfrey knew about Heloise, and Tom didn't even know her name let alone what town.

The six GIs of X and Y teams sat around a well fountain, laughing and joking, seeing no reason why they shouldn't shoot the shit before getting themselves killed. Auggie watched with a smile, as if wanting to join them, but soon his pug-nosed and freckled face lost its wonder look. "Some of those GIs in the other teams say we got a real fightin' chance," he said, as if to convince himself.

"Chance? A fuggin' chance?" Weber said. "On account of what? That we don't even got no proper kraut papers to show a sentry even?"

"We could come back heroes," Auggie said.

"Heroes? Oh, do indulge me," Weber said. "Who you want to play you? Gary Cooper's too old, but maybe Errol Flynn is free? Sure, we never had it so good—"

"Shut up. Both of you," Lett said. "I'm trying to think."

Perhaps worst of all, they weren't getting any German papers—there was no time to work some up, Archie had said. Didn't that make them spies all the more? They had to remain GIs first, if caught. But how?

Weber said: "Wrap your noodle around it all you want, Lett, it still don't hold up."

Soon after dark, S-2 sentries opened the barn for the three teams. Inside they found a long plank table of German uniforms and equipment, along with a War Department handbook on German forces. Weber stood back, eyeballing the enemy materiel as if it was booby-trapped. Lett stepped so far back his heels bumped up against the barn siding. The calm of shock was giving way to reality.

At the table, Auggie and the GIs of X and Y teams fought over the enemy swag as if it were souvenirs they could ship home APO. The more Lett watched them, he decided only he and Weber had been up on the line very long. The rest were only grimy on the outside.

Weber moved over to Lett, watching the GIs rave and haggle. "Just wait. They'll look so much better with blood on em," he whispered.

"If we only had more time," Lett whispered. "Figure this out right."

"Meanwhile? No time, like that goddamn Selfer says."

"S-2, they just want the low-down, what the Germans are up to," Lett said. "Am I right? It sounds simple enough."

"Says you."

"Well, wouldn't you like to know, what they're up to?"

"Sure. But facts are like pork bellies to brass wonders like those two and just as cheap. You said it. What if we get caught? What then?"

"We won't."

"Come off it, Lett. Just look at those ersatz GI dog tags they gives us—tags of Joes what don't exist, or at least not anymore?"

Lett felt a cold pinch in his stomach. Weber was right, of course. "They're hanging us out. That's what you mean," Lett muttered.

"I mean. This way they can claim we don't exist, anything goes snafu. Good and erased, like. See?"

An engine sputtered outside, and another, another. The barn door swung open. Archie and Selfer stood before three contraband German jeeps—two Kübelwagens and a Schwimmwagen.

Archie held out his arms as if he'd just rolled in a humongous birthday cake with a victory girl inside. "Here you are! See now? All a man needs is a good horse," Archie said.

"Take your pick, men," Selfer added. "And do get some sleep. You have a few hours."

***

The masters of the machine had grown more delusional and desperate than Holger Frings thought possible. His first thought had been, they had tricked him and sent him to a concentration camp. The sprawling garrison and training complex of Grafenwöhr filled the Bavarian forest. The SS camp guards were Ukrainians with steel balls for eyes and didn't understand German or English, so how could they really know the secrets going on here, no matter how ridiculous?

The couple thousand volunteers and recruits housed at Grafenwöhr came from all branches and many ranks, all housed together. They had to give up their insignia and identification. All letters were censored. When a couple men hinted in letters that they were on a secret mission, they soon disappeared and it was whispered the Ukrainian SS guards had put them against a wall. From then on, all outside contact was forbidden. Frings kept his head down but his eyes open, like many others. No one trusted anyone else, he saw.

This place was supposed to turn them into American GIs. They had sessions practicing *Ami* conversation, with slang such as chow, booze and moola, shit and fuck, dogface and foxhole, FUBAR, AWOL. Jeep. Joes. They learned American insignia and commands. They learned how GIs opened packs of cigarettes: Slap the pack, then flip out a smoke. They smoked like *Amis*, with the cigarette between index and middle fingers. They opened GI ration cans, and ate using their forks with the right hand. Instructors forced them to slouch, lean against walls, shove their hands deep in their pockets like traffickers and vagabonds. Frings had shaved his beard. Grow it back, they had said—you'll look more like a dogface that way. They watched Hollywood war films, sappy propaganda but effective. A ten-year old musical, *Top Hat*, Frings had seen in a New Jersey port town in 1935. He could only shake his head at that, and when they had gum chewing practice he could only laugh. American vehicles appeared on the grounds, including jeeps and light trucks and a few Sherman tanks, but the jeeps seemed to be the only buckets the mechanics could keep running. They received rushed training shooting American weapons and were urged to "shoot from the hip," as if Americans truly fired like cowboys. They were issued olive, green and tan American gear, most all of it ragbag or worn. They marched around in American field jackets, mishearing commands and colliding into each other as gray-haired German-Americans cursed them with shit and fuck and words they would never know before they were dead.

Frings only laughed harder. And the Ukrainian SS-pretenders did the same, pointing at them from up in the guard towers.

Grafenwöhr had many sailors because so many had been exposed to real English. Many had been merchant mariners like Frings. Few would have lasted on an S-boat. Out of all the soldiers from all branches, only about twenty turned out fluent in English and knew the slang. Frings barely made the next cut of about thirty to forty who spoke well enough, but with little slang and an audible accent. The remaining pack were hopeless, wishful thinkers, innocents or blind patriots and Führer-worshippers mostly. To test them, some did simulated time in a POW camp full of Americans. They came back looking like they'd spent a year in Eastern Front trenches. A few had broken bones, bruises.

Frings ended up in a select group the officers had christened commandos: They were the new Stielau Unit, the spearhead force of what was now called *Panzerbrigade 150*.

On December 11, after a month in Grafenwöhr, Frings ended up back near Cologne. His new commando unit bivouacked in a forest after debarking from a train painted with the words "Christmas Trees for the Western Front." The train carried some of the captured American vehicles, mostly jeeps. Their forest bivouac lay southwest of Cologne, close to a village called Schmidtheim. The Belgian border awaited, just down the road. The surrounding woodlands hid hills, ravines and mud, the opposite of the open sea though visibility could be as bad with the fog they had. Frings and some of the commandos had a barn to hole up in. Like all, he covered his GI uniform and gear with a German overcoat so that any troops witnessing them would not panic or worse. Yet whenever he went outside, he felt the eyes watching him from inside the forest—there the regular soldiers crowded out the greenery with their pale-gray faces, gathered around their camouflaged armor in untold clusters. There must have been thousands of them in there, waiting, surely a whole panzer division.

Frings had learned of the mission. They would travel in teams, four to an American jeep. The better English speaker often had the identity of an American officer and would do the talking. Each jeep team ran its own sortie. Frings' jeep team was to disrupt communications by cutting telephone wires and knocking out any radio stations and information posts they could find. Along the way, all commandos were to mix up signs and move minefield markers, pass on false orders, and cause confusion, panic and traffic congestion whenever possible.

His masters had given him the American name of Clarence Arthur. They made him a US Army sergeant. He wore an olive-colored US Army overcoat, thick enough but too short for the land. He wore this over a GI field jacket. The *Amis'* brown boots with the leather rough side-out and rubber soles made him want to sneer and admit awe at the same time. These were fit for a lumberjack or a carpenter, and yet those soft soles would be perfect on an S-boat—or for sneaking up on someone for the kill. His trousers were British but close enough, they said. They had run out of American pants.

Under the American field jacket he wore his tighter fitting gray-green German Navy tunic complete with S-boat War Badge, the collar well hidden with the help of a wool US Army scarf. Their team leaders had told them that wearing German uniforms under their American garb was to protect them. It might, if they were lucky, comply with the Geneva Convention and save them from being viewed as outright spies—if they had to fight, they would simply shed their disguise enemy uniform. Frings knew the score. Shedding a US Army field jacket before shooting was ludicrous, like an S-boat signaling the enemy destroyer before firing torpedoes. A commando was a spy, and spies were shot.

Dogface, meet Number One. The forces of fanaticism, idiocy and glory-seeking had released him from his S-boat damnation, and he had volunteered for the madness. So be it. If he was allowed to write to Christiane, he would have assured her: "I am your Wonder Weapon."

***

In Stromville, Heloise Vérive stood in her family kitchen over a cutting board of meager weeds and turnips, waiting for a pot of water to boil on the stove. She gazed out the window at their courtyard blurred in the late morning fog, and tried to imagine her Wendell's return.

Her stomach shuddered and roiled inside. She convulsed and lunged to vomit, into a basin. She wiped her mouth with a towel, eyes wide with shock.

She vomited again, heaving till nothing came out but strings of saliva.

She hovered over the mess, confused, the sour waft easily overpowering the bitter scent of the vegetables—her retching had only brought up more weeds and turnips. It was all they had to eat today.

She needed fresh air. She got outside. Every day, when she had a few minutes, she stood beneath one of the two lampposts on the main street, near the highest point in town. The spot let her keep watch on the road that stretched out of Stromville, waiting for her Wendell to return. They had joked that this made her Lili Marleen, as in the famous song, but from here she could see, and be seen from, the broad valley and forests beyond. That was on a clear day. Today wasn't so clear. It had been two days since Wendell had last come. It was colder now. Snow fell in wisps, yet she didn't cover her head. She was steaming from a heat inside her. She allowed herself to think it—could it be a baby from Wendell inside her?

All the more reason to keep her Wendell alive. The poor man was about ready to come apart in a way that no amount of thread could mend. She had to do something.

That afternoon she made her way east into the forest near the American front lines, among all their vehicles and depots and tents, smelling the sweetness of their Virginia tobacco and the linger of cognac and vermouth, then the stench of outdoor latrines and unwashed men. Bearded GIs—whom Wendell called "dogfaces"—rose from tents and stone huts to whistle while others stared slack-faced, simply saddened, she feared, by the beauty of a girl. "It ain't right," one grumbled as she passed.

She came to another sentry. The American straightened but sighed as he did so. She carried a basket hanging off her arm. She pulled back the basket's flowery cover. The deep plate inside still held a few pieces of glistening *pain perdu* she had made using bread about to go stale, milk and eggs and butter and sugar and vanilla hoarded top-secretly and probably the last in town. Americans knew it as "French toast." The others sentries had taken thick slices, but not all.

"I look for your courier, Joe," Heloise said in English. She described Wendell but didn't name him and waited while the sentry asked around, licking the powdered sugar from his lips. He had another Joe shuttle her to a command tent. There she met a Lieutenant Godfrey—Tom Godfrey, the only American Lett had mentioned by name that was not dead. Godfrey smiled for her, but it didn't do his recent scar any favors. Such a genial man, she thought, though now he would have to keep his mustache no matter the fashion.

She stood before Godfrey's desk, alone with him. She set down her basket, now empty.

"How did you make it this far?" Godfrey said in excellent French.

"Real butter," Heloise said.

Godfrey laughed.

"I am looking for a sergeant," she said.

"Yes." Godfrey's face paled, losing any signs of mirth. "Lett. Wendell Lett."

She leaned into the desk. "Where is he?"

"He's alive. I can't tell you much more, I'm afraid."

Heloise's stomach quivered, rolled. She retched and tried to hold it in but couldn't. She rushed to the tent door, and vomited out.

A few minutes later, she sat back inside the tent holding a damp rag to her face. Godfrey had given it to her.

"How long have you been pregnant?" he said.

She waved at air, dismissing the notion. Had she told him when her head was spinning? But then some men just knew these things. "Euh, I'm not sure if I am."

"Though you will find out for sure? Won't you? For Wendell."

Heloise nodded. "We love each other." She grabbed Godfrey by a wrist. "Listen, please. You must not tell him."

"You know what I think? I think the man knows what he wants. He just has to finish the job."

"But you must not tell him. I do not want our baby to make him do it. I do not want him to have any regret. He must do it for his reasons. Not for my reasons. Do you see? I only hope, it is not too late. In the meanwhile: You can protect him. Will you protect him? Can you?"

"I'm trying, dear. You have to know that I'm doing all I can."

***

Wendell Lett and the other GIs of X, Y and Z stared down at the mud-caked yet foreign black boots on their feet, deep in thought, letting the road rock and jostle them, their shoulders bumping. They rode in the back of a troop truck. It was December 12, before sunup. They wore German Army greatcoats and tunics, unbuttoned to reveal their GI field jackets. Keeping their true uniforms on underneath was Lett's idea. He had found a GI Field Manual and looked it up. What they called "perfidy"—using dirty tricks in war—could be a war crime. Yet, wearing enemy clothes could be okay as long as soldiers didn't fight in them. It didn't mention what happened to a dogface in disguise on the wrong side of the line, but it was all they had.

Lett had added a German scarf to his disguise. As they rode along, he watched Weber. Weber was shaking his head, muttering to himself. He opened a tin of pills and popped a couple in his mouth. Weber was their only real born *Deutsche*. His German was fluent. He was the only one who could do extended talking. He would have to keep it together.

The troop truck left Lett, Weber and Auggie at their insertion point and moved on. They were to cross over at a gap in the line, at an unmanned portion of the Siegfried Line between the Ardennes and the Hürtgen. Their German jeep was waiting parked just inside the trees. They had picked a Kübelwagen and let the other teams fight over the Schwimmwagen. So what if a utility vehicle could swim? It only attracted attention. They slogged through the underbrush, tossed their gear inside the Kübelwagen, and buttoned up their German tunics and greatcoats.

Their local Belgian guide stood watching at the nearest tree trunk. They hadn't even heard him. He was older and dressed like a farmer in wool and denim. Only Weber could understand his Belgian German dialect. The three got in their German jeep, Weber at the wheel, Lett up front and Auggie in back, and Weber got the engine started after a solemn give-and-take between fuel cock, ignition key and clutch, choke and cranking motor button. Once the engine had warmed up, he pushed the choke all the way in and steered them into the road, driving as slow as he could without stalling. Their guide ambled along the front fender, as if leading a donkey.

Twenty minutes later their guide walked off into the forest, leaving them inside a misty fog forming for dawn. Lett, Weber and Auggie had crossed over into the German lines, though they could only see walls of trees and the two-rut road before them. No bunkers, no checkpoints. Weber kept his eyes on the ruts, both hands on the steering wheel.

The forest receded in fog behind them. Weber drove them through a village. The signs were in German. They really were in Germany. A couple farmer locals chatted, ignoring them. They saw German uniforms ahead, which made them stiffen, and they passed the group—a crowd of teenage soldiers gathered around a horse-drawn kitchen wagon. The soldiers took no notice of them. The sun had come up, and they drove onward, heading east. Lett consulted maps on his lap as cows watched from a field. Passing them the other way were a small troop on bicycles, a couple utility vehicles, a staff car. Alone again, they drove along a trickling stream, and passed over an ancient stone bridge.

They should have been nabbed first thing. Lett's hope had been that they would be spotted and could somehow hightail it back across the border. This had been far too easy, he thought. This was the kind of luck that dropped a guy in a hole. His hands were shaking. He stuffed them between his legs, ostensibly for warmth.

"No sentries? Then there's horses towing a chuck wagon. Horses and boys and old contraptions? Is that really all they got left?" Lett said.

"Yeah, wouldn't that be swell? Which way?" Weber said.

"Right. No, left."

Weber steered them back into forest, and down another narrow road. Soon a layer of hay covered the road, dampening the sound of their tires.

"Why the hay?" Auggie said.

"Search me," Weber said.

They drove the long single road down the middle of ever-deeper forest, the highest stories flocked with snow. Lett looked around, the close tree trunks passing in a blur.

He saw it first. Then Auggie, his mouth open. Weber did too. He inched along, his knuckles tightening on the wheel, the dread stretching his mouth open. "Shit. Shit," Weber muttered.

On both sides within the trees stood tanks, vehicles, artillery, and troops in droves, and more tanks. Machinery. Depots. More troops. Static. All around them. Waiting. An on and on, crammed inside the forest.

The road seemed never ending. The Kübelwagen stalled. Frantic, almost drooling in panic, Weber restarted and continued his slow slog.

Two sentries approached the roadside and waved them along, giving them the universal signal that they're on the wrong road and should move it along and quick. Weber accelerated, the hay kicking up and rustling inside the wheel wells.

They drove through a valley and into another wood, this one empty. Lett and Auggie scanned behind and around them, to confirm that no one was coming or following. They saw a covered bridge up ahead. Weber sped up for it. He braked in the middle of the bridge, his chest heaving, his mouth stuck open. He took deep gasps of air, but it only made it worse. A panic attack.

"What's the matter?" Auggie said.

Weber reached back, grabbed Auggie by his collar. "In German, you hick," Weber said, snarling. He released Auggie. They sat listening to the engine idling, and the stream rushing below.

"Why all the hay back there?" Auggie said in broken German.

Weber snorted a laugh, because he'd figured it out too.

"It hides tracks," Lett said. "Keeps things quiet."

"And for miles. Miles of them. Jesus Christ."

"Let's just go. Okay, Web?" Lett said. "Everything jake?"

"Sure. Sure."

They passed through another village, past more farmers and boy soldiers, horse carts and old trucks.

"That's the thing. They want it to look like this," Lett said. "Like nothing's doing. No checkpoints means no point in looking."

They cleared another valley, its grazing field void of cows. Lett stared at the map, hoping to find a different road back, but these all passed through villages, towns.

"We got what we need, right?" Auggie said. "Right? So let's get back."

"We can't go back that way," Lett said.

Weber pounded on the steering wheel. "Goddamn."

"These German maps S-2 gave us, they're just ancient," Lett said.

They reached the crest of a hill. Slowing, they looked down to see that their road led into a secondary highway. Refugees and retreating German army units moved along the highway in a vast, disorderly stream.

Lett heard something, a clanking sound horribly familiar. He and Weber jerked around to look behind them.

An armored German half-track was coming from the direction they had come.

Lett didn't need to convince Weber. He drove them onward, down the hill. They steered on into the chaotic flow of vehicles and carts and downtrodden, war-weary stragglers. The enemy faces were close, in car windows and open carriages, but no one spoke around them. People focused on the road ahead with sunken eyes. Children stared at them, but right through them. Bandaged soldiers slept, leaning into one another, shuddering.

Snow fell. They managed to get their canvas top up, which kept them secluded and let them speak some whispers of English. "We can't go off this road now," Lett said, the map on his lap. "The side roads could have checkpoints—real ones, with *Polizei*, SS, military police even."

"Know what they call their MPs? 'Chain dogs.' And they got 'head hunters' too—looking for deserters," Weber said. "And who knows what else on this side of the border. And if there's some waiting up ahead? What then?"

"We just keep going for now, keep it moving. It's all we can do."

Weber nodded. "You know we used up all our good odds on this? You know that, don't you? Fuck."

Lett knew it.

For an hour they traveled within the highway stream of refugees and retreaters. Up ahead the horizon darkened. Ashes, gray and black, mixed in with the snowflakes. Lett stuck a hand out and let some fall into his hand. The grit darkened the melting flakes in his palm, like liquid charcoal.

The skyline of a destroyed city appeared on the horizon, burning and smoking. Only a cathedral's two blackened spires stood tall, but smoke billows dwarfed all. Soon they were passing storefronts and junctions, first of villages and then of dim suburbs.

A sign read: "Köln."

"It's Cologne? A big city? Oh, my god," Auggie whimpered.

Lett didn't like it either, but they had to make it work. Heloise had given him the strength to make this work. Auggie and Weber would depend on him now. "We'll get through it, and we'll get the hell back," he said in a strong, staccato voice, as if he was promising Heloise herself.

If anything, they were safer among the untold numbers of fellow lost and weary with nowhere to go, among the orphans and refugees, soldiers and wounded wandering like old goats before them. They drove into the city of Cologne without problem. Somehow. It helped that there had been bombings overnight. The broken cityscape fumed and crackled. Sirens wailed in the distance. They passed through the southern city and street after street of rubble piles, of craters exposing wires and cables and pipes, some half submerged in oily liquids, and of so many skeletal building fronts, their blown-out windows little wind tunnels for grit and stench, the whole city a demolition site, it seemed. Random screams, some muffled, and more rescue whistles told of the many still people under the rubble. And the fetor of decaying, churned-up bodies burned in their noses, making them welcome the smoke drifts that smacked at their faces. Another air attack must have just hit, during the day. Fire crews and police waved them along. No one spoke to them. Just surviving seemed more important than security on the streets they followed.

"Up ahead used to be the Old Town," Weber muttered. "We visited when I was a little boy. Holy shit. It might as well be a rock quarry now . . ."

The Rhine River appeared on their right, the current greasy and black and clogged with wreckage, the grand bridges busted up like balsa miniatures, upended and half-submerged. One bridge still stood. An endless stream of refugees and orphaned military streamed across it in trains. All three knew they had to avoid getting sucked into crossing the Rhine and going farther into Germany or they would never get back. And it was getting dark fast. Lett proposed it was best to hole up a while, out of the open. They parked their Kübelwagen next to others on a square a few blocks from the river promenade, what looked like a makeshift motor pool for soldiers hoping to find their homes or any family at all. There was no check-in, no sentry here, just weary troopers shuffling back and forth. Lett proposed they carry no weapons, to avoid committing perfidy. All agreed. They walked close together, heads down, hands deep in their pockets. Stepping through half-standing buildings, over fallen beams and mounds of loose stones and bricks and crossing cramped lanes, they happened upon a tall and glossy green door with a mighty brass knocker and handle. The building around it was a heap of scorched sandstone. The door opened into the foyer of what must have been a grand dwelling, but now led to nowhere. Inside, stone dust and ash coated the marble, and the ceiling timbers bowed downward, creaking, as if ready to bust at any moment. A perfect hiding hole. It was even warm from some unknown source, perhaps a buried but still functioning radiator.

"We'll have to hunker down here," Lett said. The other two nodded, too exhausted and horrified to speak.

More air raids came overnight, and the horrid racket kept them in their hovel.

The dawn brought December 13, a Wednesday. Outside, a bluish haze from the river had settled within the dips between the rubble dunes. Frost coated the debris. The three of them had slept foxhole-style, curled together for warmth—Lett's latest hole buddies. The tall green door looked out onto a lane in the rubble, the last trace of a street. Auggie kept watch by peeking out into the new daylight, keeping the door cracked open.

Lett kept his eye on Weber. Weber had been sweating all night despite the cold, his face pasty. "So hot in here," Weber muttered. "Why so damn hot?" He had loosened his German greatcoat, which revealed his American uniform. He tugged at it, wanting to loosen it more.

Lett pushed the coat tight. "It's just another panic attack," he said. "Hold on. The sun's coming up. We'll get back by lunch, I promise."

"You keep saying that." Weber raised a fist to his mouth. Lett grabbed Weber and pried open his fist, revealing two pills. "Just pep pills," Weber said, "best Army ration going."

"Those aren't helping you."

"Quiet!" Auggie whispered. "Someone's coming."

Lett crawled over for a look. He saw a silhouette in the fog, then it became a man patrolling the lane, a rifle slung on his shoulder. The man wore an army-style field cap but his overcoat was civilian, the wool so worn it looked shiny. Lett could make out a black armband with red piping and white letters. He was *Volkssturm*, the Nazis' last-ditch home guard. The guard took his time. He looked in doorways and windows, but moved woodenly.

Lett pulled back from the door, trying to think. Weber glared at him, sweating, shaking. The man was in no shape to talk to anyone, much less in German.

Always keep moving, don't bunch up. Or seize up. Keep it moving.

"We can't let that man in," Auggie said.

"Just, stay put," Lett said. "Okay? The both of you."

Auggie nodded. Weber squeezed his eyes shut.

Lett pushed the door open, pulled it closed behind him. He stood out in the lane, and let the guard come to him.

"Morning," Lett said in German.

They stood a couple yards apart. The guard looked to either side, as if at imaginary comrades. Lett could see hints of white hair under the man's cap. He was an old man. The skin hung on his neck and his cheeks showed his bones. "*Morgen*," the guard said, and stepped toward Lett. He had a whistle hung around his neck—

The door flew open behind Lett. Weber rushed out, pushing off Auggie trying to hold him back. Weber's German greatcoat had fallen open, showing his American uniform.

The guard stumbled back, reaching for his whistle. Lett lunged and grabbed at the whistle, snapping its string.

The guard's eyes flashed a brilliant gray. "What is this? Who are you?" he said in German.

Seeing the guard, Weber found his feet and stood frozen. Auggie's American tunic showed now too. Auggie pushed his German greatcoat closed, but it was too late.

The guard backed up, trying to unsling his rifle. Lett sprung at him and seized his elbows. The guard shouted: "Help! Americans! The enemy!—"

Lett slapped a hand over the guard's mouth and thrust an arm behind his back, the guard groaning. Auggie and Weber surrounded him. Auggie unslung the rifle. They closed around the guard and moved him into a doorway arch blocked by debris on the inside. Lett released half a hand, giving the man a chance.

"Please, don't hurt me, please," the guard whispered.

Weber pushed and pulled at his German coat and American tunic underneath. "What's the rule now?" he said. "Which we wearing? Huh, Lett, huh?"

"We're not spies, we're not," Auggie said to the guard.

"We keep them on," Lett said.

The guard watched their panic with increased panic, his eyes darting between them, his breaths shorter, panting, his lungs rasping, rattling. He shouted again: "*Hilfe! Amerikaner! Der Feind!*—"

Lett pressed his hand back over the guard's mouth and the old man struggled, moaning with muffled screams. Lett scowled at Weber and Auggie, his grip tightening. He felt his chest and neck and brain growing hot and red and fierce, violent. The old man kicked and ran in place, stuck.

"You got to," Weber said. "We got no choice."

Lett felt a snap. The guard's arm had broken under pressure, behind his back. The guard shrieked and tried to bite at Lett's hand, the teeth slimy and sliding with nowhere to go. Weber and Auggie stood close, on their toes, keeping watch. Lett tightened his other arm around the guard's neck and clamped down. He kept pressing, pressing. The muffled screams ceased. The gray eyes stopped rolling, still like marbles. The guard went limp and his body heavy, and they lowered him to the ground.

As Lett took point, Weber and Auggie propped up the guard's corpse on their shoulders like a drunken comrade and carried him down to the river wall, the guard's toes striking and bouncing off debris. A cluttered mess of burnt-out autos and trucks gave them cover on the promenade. Lett kept watch, whispering instructions. They tore off his *Volkssturm* armband. They stuffed bricks and rocks into his pockets and clothes. They hustled him down a half-submerged, wobbly boat ramp, using the drifting smoke and river haze for more cover. They used wood scraps and timbers to push him out under the cold water. He sunk fast. A hand remained, as if reaching for the sky. A drifting plank of debris struck the hand, and it vanished under. Bubbles popped at the surface.

The three walked back, Weber and Auggie looking drawn and spent. Lett knew his face still showed the vicious, bloodthirsty scowl. It was slathered on his face, like a hardening plaster. They wouldn't look at him.

They stopped. Looked up.

A little girl stood before them in the rubble-strewn lane. She was no more than ten, eleven years old and had her hair in long braided pigtails as dark as her long black skirt. A white lace collar offset her stark military-style short coat.

She was backing up. "Opa? Where is my Opa?" she said in German. Lett's face hadn't changed. She saw his dark mien. She turned and ran off down the cratered lane. "Enemy! Spies! Enemy spies!" she shouted in German.

Weber and Auggie looked to Lett with contorted, begging faces. He sprinted after the girl.

She was heading for a directional sign that read: "*Zur Volkssturm-wache.*" To the *Volkssturm* guards station. But she had it wrong—she zigzagged around rubble and debris while Lett leapt over it all, stepping off stones and fallen beams for more speed.

He caught up with her. She gasped, tried to scream. He covered her mouth, muffling her shrieks, and came around her back and put her in a hold. After all he'd been through it was all too easy, like snatching up a sickly cat.

***

On Stromville's main street Heloise stood beneath the lamppost, hands clasped at her waist, looking down the road stretching into the snowy valley beyond. The clouds hung low, heavy.

"*Mademoiselle?*" a voice said.

Heloise started, whipped around. It was Doctor Servais, from Malmedy. He stood at her side in a long overcoat and homburg hat. She'd been so deep in thought worrying about her Wendell that she hadn't noticed the doctor walk up.

"Oh. Good day," she said, and her heart raced.

The doctor tipped his hat. "I can tell you that the frog, it produced."

"What does that mean?" Heloise said. "I'm sorry, I don't know."

"The frog test. It's positive. You are pregnant."

***

For Holger Frings, hibernating in the barn near Schmidtheim had been like waiting in the pens before a sortie run. In the dim light, even their utilitarian American uniforms resembled the hodgepodge of S-boat gear. Most of his fellow doomed commandos didn't feel so natural. They sat slumped, with heads bowed as if they were praying. It was late morning. Another night had passed. The barn had grown more damp and cold, the soggy ground seeping through the hay. Frings joined the group of sailors who huddled under the loft and shared the scuttlebutt. They said: In the forester's house nearby that was the command post, their famed leader had supposedly arrived after staying at his Berlin HQ during much of Grafenwöhr. He was none other than SS Lieutenant Colonel Otto Skorzeny. As Hitler's favorite commando, Skorzeny featured in magazines and top Nazi rallies. Skorzeny was the newsreel hero with the frat boy dueling scar, the type who fucked the mistresses of the generals asking for his autograph. Grabbed all the glory and slathered the gleaming metal all over his tunic—the man had more chest disease than a regiment of storm troops. But Germany needed a bold warrior of action, its walking Wonder Weapon, and a poser like Skorzeny had won the part. Meanwhile, the sailors whispered, some of their comrade commandos were receiving special assignments, such as venturing out to assassinate Eisenhower in Paris or to help retake Normandy.

These were all pipe dreams. Frings had only his one pipe dream: He would return, kick the brownshirt Scherenberg's ass and take his daughters back. He knew this would never happen. The end was coming too fast. If the girls were still alive by then, and if the Russians hadn't raped them, their mother and aspiring stepfather would only sneak them off to some final fairytale-land like Bavaria—to commit suicide with the rest of the rotten seducers.

And so it went from the top on down, an imposing and ancient machinery of power-seekers and small-dicked glory-worshippers, the sole of every polished dress boot pressing down on the hair tonic-slick head of another puffed-up seeker-worshipper, and that big head licked the shiny boot, and his boots gave and received the same beneath him, and down and down it went, the boots less polished and the heads more hopeless, until the chain of exploiters finally reached them here, in this barn. Where no more boots could be licked. Where they could only be blown apart. And finally, that morning, the word came down: They could go out any time. It was December 15.

***

On the morning of December 15, Wendell Lett sat in a corner of S-2's requisitioned barn, on his own, his butt down in the straw and dirt and his back against the splintery siding. Lett, Weber and Auggie had made it back from Cologne. They had escaped the city by jumping on a local westbound train stuffed with refugees, foreign laborers and silent, hollow-eyed soldiers. Lett and his two sorry companions looked like all the rest. They evaded checkpoints somehow. They had hitched a ride on a farmer's cart too near the border, and passed back over the American lines on foot. It had taken them all of a day and into the night. The odds kept favoring them, after a sick and grisly fashion. Lett had led the way. All spoke little, though Lett heard Weber and Auggie whispering at times behind him. Near the insertion point the Belgian guide had found them and delivered them to S-2's secluded barn in darkness. They had collapsed in exhaustion and slept most of December 14. At some point during that evening, Selfer had come and taken their statements for a report.

S-2 kept them in the barn. Their German uniforms and gear still lay in a pile. They had a field stove going for warmth. At the long plank table Weber and Auggie sat close together, facing away from Lett. They passed a bottle of rotgut local cider. A single light hung above them, enclosing them within an illuminated shaft of swirling cigarette smoke, as if to spotlight their unified evasion. Pussyfooting. Giving him the cold shoulder.

Lett stared up into the hanging light, letting it burn in his eyes. He seemed to have stopped blinking altogether. Cologne had ravaged all his thoughts, worries. He must have gone over it five hundred times in the day and night and day. He had dragged that German girl to the same doorway as her *Opa*. His combat-hardened senses had hashed it all out in split seconds. At first he had thought there must be some way to take the girl with them, keeping her quiet until clear of the city and then letting her run off, out of some forest. But she wouldn't stop screaming. He had tried to stuff his scarf in her mouth and tie her up with something, anything, but she wouldn't stop screaming. She kicked at his crotch, as if thinking he would rape her. "No!" he shouted. "No!" He tried to shush her. She only seemed to gain in strength, fury, desperation. She spat at him, she punched him. Weber and Auggie had caught up to him. They stood out in the lane keeping watch but hopeless, flat-footed, unable to help. She spat out his scarf and screamed, shrieked. He pushed her back to a column and pressed a hand to her mouth, and pressed, and kept pressing. He squeezed his eyes shut at one point, so he wouldn't have to see her pleading eyes fade. When he opened his eyes again, he saw that her face had gone pallid and her skin had set, like a cooling wax.

Lett had made Weber and Auggie dig out a grave in the rubble but he had insisted on laying her in there himself and covering her up. He had to be sure not to bruise her too much, or cut her, or break anything.

***

December 15, afternoon. Lieutenant Colonel Archie Archibald and Captain Selfer rode in the rear seat of their late-model US Army Cadillac staff car ensconced in leather, velour and chrome. Archie had Z team's after-action report resting on his knees. He squinted at a page. "No one would believe this," he said, but absently, as if Selfer was not there. "Why, it simply does not correlate with any 'Archie's Account' in one iota. Absolutely not. Here."

Selfer took the page and slid it into a folder marked, "Detritus: Non-read."

***

Wendell Lett started awake. The barn door rolled open. The thin light of dusk showed sparkles on the frosted ground, and a few swirling snowflakes. Their sentries were now MPs, with the white-stripe helmets and armbands. They let in Archie and Captain Selfer, who wore fur-lined coats, Archie's in brown leather and Selfer in spotless OD.

"As you were. Don't get up," Selfer said, though no one had tried to stand or salute, not even Auggie. Lett stayed down in his corner. Selfer set a bottle of Johnnie Walker and a box of cigars on the table. Weber grunted.

"Where's the other teams, sir?" Auggie said to Selfer.

"I'm afraid they didn't make it back," Selfer said.

"Why you keeping us here?" Weber said.

"Security. It's S.O.P.," Selfer said. "Don't forget, this all remains confidential."

"So, my good commandos—all the way to Cologne, eh?" Archie said, rubbing his gloved hands together. "That's one fine heck of a marvelous run. You really went beyond the call."

"In a literal sense," Selfer said. "It's far beyond our sector."

Weber and Auggie eyed each other. "We thought we were done for," Auggie said. "But Lett here, he took care of this kraut sentry for us."

"Yeah, the kraut had our number. Lett did what he had to. He really saved our behinds," Weber added.

Each had said their sentences mechanically, as if reading from idiot cards. Lett bristled inside at their omission. Why didn't they just say it? And why had he let them talk him out of stating it for Selfer's report? He had killed a girl. He had done it to save the team. Done it to save his cold behind. The mission nor the Allied Cause had a thing to do with it. He might as well have been John Dillinger covering his tracks from feds hot on his trail. So what did that make Selfer and Archie?

Archie beamed at Lett. "That one over there's a hero," he said.

"Hear that, Lett?" Selfer said. "The Horseback Hero himself is calling you a hero. That's something you can take back with you."

"I heard it," Lett said, to Archie. "You know that German I killed was *Volkssturm*, their civ Home Guard? I killed an old man." He stood, the words tumbling out of him, spittle shooting off his tongue. "And you know what? I was only getting warmed up too, I—"

Weber bounded over and grabbed Lett and turned him away from Selfer and Archie, leaving Archie squinting again, throwing up his hands.

"Very well. No one like a cigar?" Selfer said. "They're cream of the crop."

"If he mentions a medal I'm gonna walk," Lett muttered to the barn siding.

"All right, easy," Weber whispered. "Easy."

Archie and Selfer were whispering to each other.

"Now, listen up, men," Archie said finally, raising his voice. "Your after-action report, it just won't do—"

Selfer cleared his throat, interrupting. "The report, it's simply not complete," he said.

Lett turned back around, and walked over to face Archie. Archie stood tall, with his chin up, but it looked hard to keep it there above all that fur.

"There simply could not be a whole army, division, whatever you saw in that forest," Archie said. "Inside woods, you say? It's so dark in there. Who knows what it was? And you only passed by. So quickly. Did you even go in the forest? They could've been dummy troops, even."

Selfer added: "We're going to let you in on some other intelligence that, you'll be pleased to know, corroborates many of the rumors you've been hearing. The German war machine is finished."

"Kaput!" Archie said. "People are saying it's just around the corner."

The realization hit Lett straight and hot in the face, an imaginary slap. "Hold it right there," he said. "You're sending us back?"

"Oh, no they ain't," Weber said, "Not on my—"

"Shut your snouts!" Archie shouted. "Do you know how many lives this could save? Any idea?" He turned to Lett, and took one step forward. "Some hero, you—it should be an honor, and you question it?"

Lett charged at Archie. Weber lunged and turned Lett around again. "Stop. Everyone, please," Selfer said. "Everyone, just take a moment." He placed a hand on Archie's shoulder. Archie shook it off.

The room was stuffy from the stove, and moldy, the stench of wet hay and grimy equipment mixing with the aromas of too much smoke and over-fermented cider. Auggie had set his forehead to the table, as if wanting to headbutt through it. Weber kept a hand on Lett's shoulder.

Selfer sighed. "You now know the lay of the land over there. We just need our own corroboration. Everything else you told us fits . . . The kid soldiers, the civ sentries. Retreating troops, disarray. It fits—it confirms—all that we know. It's what we would call the truth."

"Horses!" Archie said. "By god, they're using horses. If only we could."

Weber sighed too, but it came from deep down, like a stomach ailment. His hand left Lett's shoulder, and he paced the room as he spoke to Archie and Selfer. "Here's the thing, sirs. We were tired, see. We were drinking schnapps. We made it all up about the woods. We did. We thought it was what you S-2 types wanted to hear. But it was all fairies, gnomes, pink elephants. See? So, there's really no need for us to go on back. We'll corroborate anything you got, sure, any damn thing at all. Tell you what, sirs, get your note pads out toot-sweet and we'll do the deal right here." Weber showed lots of teeth, and it wasn't the smile he wanted. He would have made the worst brush salesman ever known.

Archie shook his head. "Pathetic. Craven . . ."

"You men need rest," Selfer said, as if Weber hadn't said a thing. "Do get some rest. All right? There's hot chow inside the farmhouse next door. It'll be your billet."

"Won't that be fine?" Archie said. "Fine!"

Weber and Auggie looked to Lett with the same begging look they had when they wanted him to kill a girl to save them. Archie and Selfer looked to Lett too.

Lett let them all sweat it out a moment. He glared at them. "I have one request," he said finally. "We would like our own dog tags, from here on out."

December 15: Evening. The farmhouse was a block made of many sturdy stones, easily centuries old. Inside, its unvarnished wood floors and furniture seemed cut from the same knotty tree. It had three rooms and an attic and a cellar. No personal touches remained; whoever had left this place, had left for good. The main room had a tiled stove that heated the whole. Lett sat on his simple wooden bunk in the communal bedroom, staring out a dark window into nothing, his real dog tags hanging outside his field jacket—Selfer and Archie had given them back. He could hear the muffled talk and laughs of Weber and Auggie in the main room.

Lieutenant Tom Godfrey sat at a small table watching Lett. He had his own bottle of Johnnie Walker, and two glasses. Godfrey had found his way to the farmhouse after greasing a few palms at battalion S-2.

Lett hadn't talked much. What was there to say? He was still sorting out the hideous secrets in his head. Weber and Auggie had insisted he not mention the girl, sure. Yet he was the one who let himself be convinced. Why? Was he that ashamed? Or did he think it could hurt his chances of finding his way back to Heloise? He reckoned it was somewhere in between.

He didn't want Godfrey to see him like this. So adrift. Worse than Godfrey ever was. An eyelid kept twitching. A buzzing deep in his nerves had given him another bout of diarrhea after eating the hot chow. The absurdity of it all ate away at his wits, at his reasoning, and wrenched his gut. If he had been able to get that old German guard or his granddaughter to a medical team behind his own lines, then those two enemies he'd had justification in killing suddenly became patients to be saved at all costs. Of course none of it made sense. Heloise was right.

Where could he go? He couldn't confess to the MPs or even Criminal Investigations Division. It would be like turning himself in for murder after combat. He had been on a secret mission for S-2. They'd probably only lock him up for divulging a covert operation, then throw him back into another front-line outfit as a private.

Godfrey threw back another drink. "What am I going to do with you?" he said. "You keep playing the hero, they're going to go and make you one."

Suddenly Lett remembered what he'd seen in the German woods. He rushed over to the table. "Listen to me. Tom. You have to get off the front line. This is all far from over—"

Godfrey held up a finger. "Ah-ah. Loose lips and all that. Besides, I don't like scary stories . . ." His finger was trembling. He yanked it down.

Lett stood at attention. "Lieutenant, I'd like to request transfer into a noncombatant role. I hereby 'formally object to warfare as a means of settling international disputes.'"

Godfrey took another drink. "Cut it out before I split my sides. And sit down."

Lett sat.

"What, you're a conscientious objector? It's too late for that. You know I got no authority here," Godfrey said. "It all goes through division S-2. Besides, you really don't want to go conshie—despite what those Mennonite nuns told you growing up. Back home, maybe. But over here? We got so many master killers in the stockade these days, those sickos make stew with the bones of pacifists."

Lett reached for a glass. Godfrey poured. "Always ready with a joke, aren't you? You got it all figured out," Lett said, shaking his head.

Godfrey let a little smile curl up one side of his mouth. "Your girl is the one who's got it figured. Take it from me."

"Wait," Lett said. "Is that why you're here?"

Godfrey let the smile take over.

"You saw her? She saw you?!" Lett said, bouncing on his chair. "She got to you? She did. Tell me she did. But you can't say anything? Okay, I get it. Loose lips."

"Sometimes, the locals will go and wander into our billet unnoticed," Godfrey said and kept smiling.

"That's my girl. She's got some pluck."

"To be sure. Now. Here . . ." Godfrey slid a card across the desk to Lett. It was an enlisted man's temporary pass. All the fields were left blank, but it was signed. "She said you needed something Army-like to help you get there. Said she'd take care of the rest."

"How is she? Is she well?"

"Positively glowing. You're a lucky man."

The whisky and the thought of Heloise and Godfrey conspiring together warmed Lett's heart. He let out a happy sigh. He picked up the card. "This isn't your signature on here."

"No, I made it up—a Captain Beauregard. I always did want to be a writer."

Lett pushed the card back to Godfrey. "No. You could get the stockade for this. Besides, you don't even know her."

"I know you. And, let's just say that she spoke to me in a language I understand."

Lett took the card. "I'm never leaving her alone again," he said.

"Good. That's good."

"Thanks, Tom. Thanks."

Godfrey poured another, toasted Lett, downed it and stood. "I'll miss your special courier deliveries. If you ever find a good magnum of good prestige cuvée out there? Don't you spill a goddamn drop of it."

Lett stood. He came around the table to Godfrey. "I won't. I mean, I wouldn't hear the end of it, would I?"

"No, you most certainly would not."

Godfrey left just before midnight. Lett stood with him outside, in the doorway, the cold stinging their cheeks. "You know what happens to a German soldier who gets free, even for a short time?" Godfrey said. "Shot on sight, I'm guessing. Not so in this man's Army. At least officially. And that's one of the big things this war is supposed to be about, I guess."

They shook hands, and did so a good long time.

Lett went back inside to find Weber and Auggie playing cards in the main room, their backs to Lett. The farmhouse had a record player too but older than Godfrey's and it had only one record, a gloomy thundering symphony. They kept playing it. Their S-2 prize bottle of whisky was almost empty. It had just turned Saturday, December 16.

Weber said: "Tell you one thing—that Selfer and the Horseback Hero? I run into 'em stateside? Right upside the jaw. If only for all the goddamn riding they give us."

"Way I see it? The krauts put us in this spot," Auggie said. "Making us kill an old man. Know what? I want back over, sure I do, really let 'em have it."

"Then why didn't you say something?" Lett said.

Weber and Auggie kept their cards up, trading worried glances.

"They need intel that fits their need," Lett said. "That's heaps more important than some kraut girl. Wrong place, time, wrong granddaddy—tough break but that's war, right? Fact is, it's why we strangle— for whatever it is they need."

Weber and Auggie lowered their eyes. The record had ended, leaving only the scratching needle to break the silence.

"You're mixed up," Auggie said. "Sounds like the enemy you're talking about."

Weber got up and pulled the needle, turned off the player. "Never mind Auggie here. He's drunk. You were doing it for us. You saved us. That's what a Joe does. You got the guts."

"It's not guts. It's something else," Lett said. "And as for saving you, we don't know that yet."

Weber sighed. He found his seat. He and Auggie held their cards up. After a couple hands, Auggie said, "It's easy. All we do is, we go over like they ask. But we hole up and good. Then we come back and tell 'em what they want to hear. We saw nothing. And it wouldn't even be like lying."

Weber slapped down his cards. "Suddenly you're the expert, kid? Don't you get it? Then we take the fall for sure. That's no way out, not like that."

"Forget it," Lett said, "just forget it."

He knew what he had to do. He went into the bedroom. He pulled the temporary pass from his GI haversack. He opened his field jacket, raised his trench knife, and cut a small slit in the jacket's inside liner. He slid the pass card inside. Then he lay down to sleep. He had most of his gear on, including his boots and gloves, but that was not surprising for a GI near the line.

4:30 a.m., December 16. Lett lay in darkness, his eyes open. Weber and Auggie slept in their bunks. Auggie snored. Weber faced the wall, away from them.

Lett sat up. He moved to the edge of the bunk, and it squeaked. Auggie snorted. Lett waited, till Auggie snored again. Lett slung on his haversack, and his carbine. He tiptoed over to the door, watching Weber and Auggie sleep, inching along so his gear wouldn't jangle.

Out in the main room, a floorboard creaked under his foot. He stood still in the darkness, and heard another creak. He pivoted, in slow motion.

Weber stood in the hallway. "I know what you're doing," he whispered to Lett. "Me, I just can't do it."

"I know. It's all right," Lett said.

"I want to. I'm a coward." Weber stared a long moment, and a look of horror widened and paled his face. Then, as if sleepwalking, he turned and wandered back down the hallway.

Lett cracked open the front door. Some new snow had fallen. He made his way into the forest, moving among the tree trunks and over the frosted underbrush as light snowflakes fluttered down, mixing with more frost from branches above. A few minutes passed. The fog thickened. He stopped at a tree to check his map and compass, making sure he was heading west, toward the rear. Stromville couldn't be too far, but it would be slow going.

At 5:15 a.m., artillery boomed in the distance. The intensity of it made Lett stop, listen. His gut squeezed up. He didn't like what he was hearing. He headed onward, to the forest edge. The booming came closer, and the screeching of rocket launchers joined in. He ran to enter the open field.

Shells ripped through the forest behind him in flashes. Shrieks and thumps shifted the earth. He dropped to the snowy ground for cover. The trees crackled and toppled with horrid crashes. He heard screams and wailing that seemed to mimic the rockets screeching.

The flashes lit up a sign before Lett: "Danger! Mines!"

The sign lined his field. Behind him, GIs fled the forest for the field and mines burst, flinging bodies and parts of bodies and spraying blood and earth through the fog.

Lett rose and leapt beyond the sign and found himself on a road. He sprinted down the road as the forest beside him burned, toppling onto itself. More men screamed and he saw the silhouettes running about inside the bursting inferno as if mad, trapped, held on leashes. Vehicles raced by him, spinning in the mud and ice, some burning. Jeeps and trucks hurtled into one another.

Lett kept sprinting, his chest heaving with pain, his legs burning from the effort. He stopped, stood in the road panting, and turned to face the front lines erupting on the horizon.

What was this? A full counteroffensive? The new boys in his unit wouldn't stand a chance in this. He couldn't get to them, but he could get to Weber and Auggie. It was what a Joe did. You saved your squad.

He turned back for the farmhouse, sticking to the road, crouching low as he made his way.

Lett burst through the front door to find Weber only now scrambling to put his gear on. They had a field radio in the main room. Weber had wasted time with it. It blared static, interspersed with American pleas for help from forward observers, command posts, units on the run. Lett's ears still rang and the sound was muffled, but he knew what it all meant.

Seeing Lett, Weber looked to the ceiling in relief. "I can't raise anyone on this thing."

"Where's Auggie?"

"Passed out. Can't wake him."

Lett grabbed Weber by an arm. "Were you going to wake him?"

"Says the Joe what took a hike," Weber said.

"I'm back, aren't I?" Lett tried the radio. They heard voices in German: "This is group leader," said one. "Cleared the first line. Resistance scattered, weak . . ."

The artillery bursts grew louder. Auggie bounded into the room dragging his gear.

They heard a voice in English, sounding frantic: "The huns closed our rear flank! We are cut off. All retreat. Everyone fall back!" But the voice had a slight accent, and no one said "huns" anymore. The Germans were pulling out all the tricks.

Only now did Lett think of Stromville. Could this reach Heloise? "Let's get going," he shouted. "Weber, disable that wireless set. Listen . . ."

The artillery had let up, to reveal the pops and burps of small arms fire. A faint clanking rumble grew louder.

"Leave it. Follow me," Lett said. Auggie fell in behind him, pulling on equipment, his rifle.

"Where? There's nowhere to run," Weber shrieked.

"We can hide."

"Cellar's no good, too obvious. The attic?" Weber said.

"Of sorts. Come on. And get your gloves on, both of you."

Lett had seen a rain barrel outside his window, near the lowest overhang of the roof. They used it to clamber up onto the roof, pushing each other up, almost slipping on the icy tiles and moss but hanging on, and finding their way to an attic dormer that they clawed at and hugged. In the fog they seemed to hang within the clouds, clinging to a mountain peak.

Panzers and halftracks appeared, dark masses within the blur below, staining the fog blue and gray with exhaust, the engines' growl drowning out the small arms fire. Dark figures passed by, some barking orders in German. Others stomped through the barn and house and attic right beneath them, raving and twitching as if being prodded along by hot irons. The bitter reek of the exhaust hovered over the roof, and the soldiers left a pungent aroma of hard schnapps—heavy drinking was always the last refuge of desperate, doomed infantry. The machines roared onward down the road, the soldiers trailing through gaps in the forest, heading west through the American lines.

***

0515 Uhr, Dezember 16: Holger Frings woke to thumps of artillery. He dove under a cart and covered his head — he thought the shells were incoming. The others in the barn had done the same. Now they wandered outside into the freezing fog, listening. Frings went out. He could hear now that it was their own guns, the salvos landing off to the west. Shaking off sleep, he remembered: Half the jeep teams had been called up during the night. Most of the sailors had gone. They were heading out on sorties, somewhere over the American lines.

Frings made his way over to his American jeep. He smoked his pipe and heard the rest of his team trek through the fog from what had to be their final hot meal. He shined his flashlight on their silhouettes—there was the stocky Florian, lean Kreisfeld, and young Gamm. Florian was a Luftwaffe sergeant, a rear-liner. Kreisfeld was Army, mechanized infantry. Gamm was also Army, in one of those new units formed since D-Day using boys, older men and head cases. Kreisfeld had seen ground combat, and too much shelling. He told Frings about it in a sputter, then clammed up again: He had been at the Falaise Gap when the Allies trapped German divisions with massive flanking movements, all so Allied bombers could bombard them to shreds with a line of bombers so long it reached back to the horizon. The miles of inferno had eclipsed the sun. Many survivors had gone mad or charged the enemy in suicide or lost their hearing. Carcasses of horses and cows outnumbered trees and the corpses swelled in the summer heat, swarming with maggots crawling out, in, out. The ensuing retreat, back to the border where they were now, had been a hopeless and starved-out tragedy. Soldiers shooting civilian families for their food. Soldiers shooting each other for a car, donkey, cart, any way back. It made Napoleon's retreat look like a boy scouts' excursion. Kreisfeld had learned his English from Spaniards, back in a lost golden age when he was a professor. Nowadays he only mumbled to himself. Frings suspected Kreisfeld was much like him—just wanting to expire when he expired. Florian was a special piece of work. He had once been a headwaiter in New Orleans, or so he said. His excellent and surely hard-won *Ami* English had come at a sorry price, though — he spewed claptrap about the threat of American jazz and what he called "niggers" and their general sloppiness and how the *Amis* could still be beaten easily. And then there was Gamm, just a boob of a kid. He just wanted at the enemy. He thought it his mission to save Germany. He had been enrolled in an Adolf Hitler School after his family died in an air raid. Talk about a boy scout. One of his parents had been English, supposedly, so his British-accented English could be a problem. Each had his cover. As Sergeant Clarence Arthur, Frings was supposed to memorize that he was from Chicago, Illinois, but he hardly bothered. Among his fake papers, they gave him a letter and photo from a girl back home. It had probably come from some poor POW or dead GI. He didn't even read it. They had also been given "anti-sleep tablets," or Pervitin, a form of methamphetamine regularly issued to German troops. Frings had avoided using them on the S-boats. They kept a man awake but made him jittery. Now he swallowed them like bon-bons, washing them down with potato vodka for breakfast.

He flashed his light at his jeep crew with Navy signals, a reflex. They looked at him blankly, Florian leading the way.

"Just make sure you're ready to sail, sailor," Florian said. He wore what *Amis* called a Mackinaw coat, with double rows of buttons, a built-in belt and darker wool collar that matched the liner. It made Frings recall the American and Canadian foreman who yelled at him and the stevedores in so many ports. The coat only made Florian stick out. It made him an asshole. Good riddance, and soon.

"I been ready for four years," Frings said to him.

***

By 7:00 a.m., the storm of attack had passed and the din of battle had moved on, sounding like distant thunder claps. Wendell Lett, Weber and Auggie climbed down from the roof. Around the farmhouse the faint daylight revealed a vast mudscape formed from the friction of so many boots, only now covering with snow and icing over.

The three headed west. They followed a creek through forest, trudging along the trickling water choked with ice, tree splinters and corpses.

"What was that?" Weber said.

"I'll take a look," Lett said. The creek ran along the base of a ridge. He clattered up to find a road. Vehicles sat vacant, at odd angles, shot up. German and American corpses lay about. Lett waved up Weber and Auggie. They approached a mess truck, on its side. They started — a GI cook sat with his back against field mess pots, the lids still on, the heat of their cargo keeping the man alive. His stomach looked gutted, shiny with dark blood, and he had been hugging himself to keep it all in. His face was ivory, like a ceramic. Death neared.

"Go ahead, eat. Last chance," he muttered to them.

Lett and Weber opened a pot. A slop of pork chops and beans spilled out, its last warmth steaming the snow. It probably had come from division mess depot, just as Godfrey predicted. They ate what they could and carried the rest, wrapping the chops in newspaper.

They moved on. They found a hayshed and huddled inside to keep warm. Auggie kept watch at the door, shivering.

"Here we go again," Weber said. "Shit. What more could you possibly want?"

"Can we light a fire?" Auggie kept saying. After the fifth time they stopped answering.

Lett could feel Weber's eyes on him again. "So where we heading?" Weber said.

"West. I told you. Find a way around their salient. It's our only chance," Lett said.

Weber's eyes stayed on him. "And then?"

"As soon as we're able? I say we split up. We find a busy junction, get rides, go back to our old units."

"But that S-2 captain said: We go out and come back together," Auggie said.

"We're done with S-2," Weber said. "Times have changed, thanks to Adolf. I don't know. There used to be the buddy system keeping me on the line. No offense to you twose, but I ain't got no buddies left." He set out a bundle of newspaper and ripped it open—the pork chops from the mess truck. "Now let's eat some, before they freeze."

***

0900 Uhr, Dezember 16: Holger Frings adjusted this and that on their jeep like a Number One did. Florian and Gamm joked about it, how this bucket was his vessel now, and Frings didn't bother to tell them just how sad that would be if true. Throughout the morning more jeep teams had left on sorties, ordered out by overwrought officers who rushed over from Skorzeny's forester house. A few jeeps had already come back, one shot up by their own tanks, another chased back by counterattacking Americans or so they claimed, though none were wounded. By S-boat odds, Frings knew that many others out there were already dead.

Then Frings and his three comrades sat ready in their jeep, Florian the pretend lieutenant in his asshole jacket, the other two slumped in back, leaning against one another for warmth. No one had slept. Frings had begun shaking, and his stomach was rolling. His head pounded. So he had popped another pill, and took another slug of cold chicory coffee Gamm had in a canteen. He pulled out his pipe, stuffed it with stale tobacco and sucked on it slowly, softly, like a baby suckling in reverse, nearing his end.

He was their helmsman, as it should be. This would be just like going out on a run for a night of hunting. And yet he was beginning to think that taking the wheel of this skiff on tires would give him back some control over things. Somehow, it just might free him from the chain of the machinelike system. Maybe it was the Pervitin talking, or the vodka. So be it. He turned on the engine at intervals, to make sure the thing still fired up in this cold.

In the fog he spotted a cigarette ember, a silhouette. An SS captain strode out to their jeep and briefed them. They would follow the main road west, on through the Losheim Gap. This road was the only route through the Siegfried Line, along a valley into Belgium. The Allies called this a Gap but in German it was a *Graben*, a trench, which better expressed how narrow it was. The captain handed them German paratrooper smocks, and told them to wear the smocks while going through so they wouldn't be mistaken as enemy. They shouldn't discard them or put on their American helmets until they were clearly into enemy territory. If they met with traffic, they should just go around it. The launch of the Führer's grand and surprise Ardennes Offensive had depended on this shit weather, SS captain said. Crack German forecasters had predicted ideal conditions. The heavy clouds would keep Allied planes grounded. The morning delivered mist and this dense icy fog and midday more snow. With that, SS captain vanished back into the fog.

Frings turned the ignition key and pressed his toe to the foot starter. The engine revved and whined as they found the Losheim road. The way was muddy from all the advancing columns yet crunchy, wanting to ice over, jostling them. A kilometer on, the road was covered with straw but it was matted down, ground into mud, oily. A massive traffic jam appeared ahead, a mess of fighting and support vehicles, trucks and more trucks, artillery, equipment. Throngs of German infantry stood waiting for orders while some vehicles had given up and parked to the side. Frings steered around it all, sliding them sideways a couple times. It was all a jumble in the fog. Frings knew what to look for from years on a fighting boat at night and acted as interpreter for the others who only saw flickers and shadows, heard shouts and clamor and felt myriad tremors. Even Kreisfeld, the *Landser*. The man seemed to have lost twenty pounds overnight. Frings knew that look, too. He'd seen it on survivors in life rafts, the ones certain to die. No one wanted to tell them the truth, or make them trade places with the stronger ones hanging off the side so the stronger ones might survive in the boat. No one had to. Eventually, they knew the truth.

It went on like this for the next ten, fifteen kilometers. Lines of American POWs plodded by, so tired they could only gape at the sight of fake Americans heading up on the line.

"It's all quite a success, that's what it is," Gamm said. "So many of our forces are getting through that we're clogging the road." No one answered him. No one talked about the other explanation—that this hulking and desperate counterattack might already be stalling.

The fog lightened, bringing clarity. Frings kept them moving, steering around more traffic. They saw a staff car parked along the road up ahead. Just beyond it a tall, broad-shouldered man waved his arms. He wore a US Army sweater and trousers and those lumberjack-style boots but also a leather SS officers' overcoat. It was Skorzeny himself. He tried to direct vehicles like a forceful commander, but to Frings he just looked like a novice traffic cop. Why wasn't Hitler's great hero riding right here in this jeep with the rest of them? he thought. He steered around the big man, jerked the wheel in hopes of spraying a little mud, and didn't bother looking back to see if he had.

They had entered Belgium.

11:00 a.m.: Frings took the first road skirting what had been the American forward lines. Once they had quit seeing German soldiers or tanks, they shed their paratrooper smocks and put on their American helmets. They reached the sector assigned to them. Frings tightened his knuckles around the wheel, wishing it had handles like a proper helm. Driving a jeep thrashed his senses in familiar yet new ways as they passed abandoned battlegrounds. A forest burned with orange and black billows. A putrid smoke of burning rubber combined with sour vapors of leaking gasoline. Neither the compost reek of cratered earth nor the pine aroma of busted trees could stifle the pungent wafts of charred and rotting flesh. The four rarely spoke now in the jeep. Every next turn could reveal an unmapped crossroads, counterattacking armor, an MP checkpoint. An American sentry would find more than enough to hang them. Their jeep-boat carried wads of counterfeit dollars, an M1 Garand rifle, an American Thompson submachine gun and two American Colt pistols, a German Walther pistol, a German two-way radio, explosives, grenades, and cigarette lighters. The lighters had cyanide capsules hidden inside. Their team leaders had passed them out in the barn at Schmidtheim with all the ceremony of handing out ration cards. Of course they would never be held as spies. But if so? Always best to be prepared. Frings had tossed his lighter out the side of the jeep. The other three had seen him do it. "Hate to get my lighters mixed up," he had joked, and no one had laughed.

They drove a narrow road. Men appeared in the fog, running, arms flailing. Frings slowed. Blackened and bloody men ran out of the wood and filled the road screaming, grabbing at the jeep like zombies. American GIs.

Frings sped away. The wheels spun, lost any grip. They sideswiped a fence, scraping the posts. Signs read: "Danger! Mines!" Frings jerked the jeep portside but a culvert almost swallowed them so he yanked it starboard and back onto the road. He screamed, his asshole so tight it wanted to suck up the seat itself, fabric, springs, horsehair and all. He turned to the others, and saw three bleached masks with mouths hung open.

12:30: Snow fell hard, sticking to the fenders and swirling inside the jeep around their GI boots. They could see a crossroads up ahead, the few buildings revealing themselves among the flakes. It was a junction, not even a village—an inn and a couple buildings, shops at street level. Three roads emptied into the junction.

Frings let the jeep coast into the middle of the crossroads and steered portside three-fifty, wheeling around in a circle, staking things out. Outside the inn, an American motorcycle sat parked, empty. That was all, one motorcycle. It had two seats. It still carried a rifle in its holster on the front fender, butt upward as if the rider would be able to pull the gun and shoot while riding like some kind of iron-horse cowboy.

A sign read: "Halt! Checkpoint!" But they saw no one. Had they retreated here too? It seemed the Americans had brought their ghost towns with them.

A pole held US Army directions signs pointing to division HQs and command posts, depots and field hospitals and towns in the rear. Communications wires were attached, hanging loose as if strung up in a hurry, stretching off down the road along poles.

"A juicy goose," Frings said.

He looked to Kreisfeld, who nodded.

"So we do it," Frings said. At some point the Number One had become the Captain. No one had questioned it. The other two kept their masks on, terrified.

Frings slowed the jeep before the inn, revved the motor a couple times. No one came out so he parked by the pole, fifty meters away. He had Florian stay by the jeep, to keep watch and make things look normal. He was the fake officer after all.

Frings, Kreisfeld and Gamm strode over to the inn. They kept between the front door and a window. They heard Americans, arguing inside. Frings peeked in a corner of the window. Two *Amis* stood around a table pointing at a map and each other. One was a tall sergeant, the other a stout lieutenant. Why hadn't they come out yet? They had to have heard them.

Frings had Kreisfeld stay by the inn, to stall if possible. "Tell them we're doing maintenance on the signs," Frings said, and added in English: "Say it like this: 'The krauts have been taking them down.'"

Kreisfeld nodded, and did a little bow.

Frings and Gamm headed back to Florian standing at the jeep.

"You got to look more natural," Frings said in English. "Here, take my pipe."

Florian slid it between his lips and leaned against the jeep fender, one leg up, casual like.

Gamm already had the crowbar and rubber mallet out, the wire cutters. They got to it, working fast, their breath pumping steam. Frings peeled off his overcoat so he could move better, then his scarf because he was hot, leaving only the field jacket over his German tunic.

They switched the signs. Higher up waited the wires. Frings grabbed the cutters. "Cup your hands," he said to Gamm. "Hold me up."

"One moment, Clarence," Gamm said in hopelessly British-sounding English. "What if they're using these cables inside, for a field phone or what have you?"

Smart kid, Frings thought. He might keep them living a whole extra half day.

"Just stand there, hold me up," Frings said.

Frings stepped up as Gamm, wobbling, held him as he clipped the wires, one, then two. Frings jumped down.

Florian was facing them, clenching the pipe in his teeth, his lips drawn back in horror.

The two Americans were walking Kreisfeld over. One may have been stout and the other tall, but both slogged through the mud and snow with effort. Both had holstered sidearms. The stout one had a Thompson gun, but it was pointed down, hanging off his bent arm. Kreisfeld had no weapon.

Frings had his Walther in his lower right jacket pocket, loaded, safety off.

"Stay here," he said to Gamm and Florian in English.

He walked out to the middle of the circle to meet them. The *Amis* eyed him. They had a little too much flesh on their faces for combat soldiers, and not near enough stubble.

Kreisfeld flashed a sickly grin. "I have told these gentlemen here what we do," he said in English, "but they wish to see it."

"Uh-huh." Frings kept his face hard.

Florian stepped out behind him, his hands hooked onto his belt. "We got orders," he said, his *Ami* English dead-on. "Maintenance, see. Fixing that signal wire there; she's a little too low."

The answer was also nonsense, Frings thought—adjusting wires in the middle of a devastating counteroffensive?

"Yes, sir," the tall American sergeant said and, eyeing his lieutenant, added: "We were just thinking, since you boys know gadgets and the like you could come on inside, just have a quick look at our wireless set while you're at it."

For too long a moment, no one spoke. Frings had stopped and Kreisfeld stopped and the Americans stood between them, eyeing them, Gamm at the jeep with Florian and his pipe and Mackinaw coat. Kreisfeld moved to the side with a slight step, pretending to look around.

"Got to get moving, boys, sorry," Florian said to the Americans. "We're rapid response."

"That's all right," the sergeant said. "No one to reach anyhows." They started back toward the inn, moving faster, having no trouble with the mud-snow now.

"Tell me something: Are you two alone here?" Frings said to their backs. He could hear his own accent. He didn't give one shit about it.

They pivoted, slowly. The lieutenant nodded. "Not for long. Just holding the fort a spell."

Frings pulled his Walther. He fired. The first missed. He fired and fired. He shot the sergeant in the head, the lieutenant in the chest. The sergeant dropped. The lieutenant swung up with his Tommy gun and sprayed around in a circle as Frings kept firing, emptying the magazine, the lieutenant's head bursting open.

Florian and Gamm froze at the jeep, too green to have hit the deck. The head-shot American lay lifeless, the dark blood pooling out from what remained of his skull. The lieutenant lay in a ball, his gangly arms at such odd angles they seemed longer than his legs. Both dead. Not even a twitch.

Frings ripped open his *Ami* field jacket, revealing his German uniform.

"Geneva Convention," he said.

Florian and Gamm stared at the bodies, steaming, and shared a look of horror that combined to glare at Frings in anger. Kreisfeld only gazed at Frings, and nodded.

"Let's go." Frings jogged over to the jeep. "We keep going. We keep it moving."

***

2:00 p.m., December 16: Lett, Weber and Auggie trudged onward. The day had stayed gray, more snow fell, and they heard German vehicles so had to zigzag their route. They followed a road southwest, stopping often, listening.

They only had a couple hours before the sun went down and they would have to hole up somewhere. Lett told himself: If they didn't split up soon, he would leave them during the night. But he needed them safe. He didn't need these two sorry sacks joining the rest in his sick dreams.

An American sign read: "Halt! Checkpoint." They had found a crossroads, a junction with an inn where an American motorcycle and scout car sat parked, the motorcycle covered with snow. Out in the road lay two corpses on their backs, arms and legs frozen at grotesque angles, bent back, pointing up. The heads were blown half away, the remains of brain frosted over. Lett, Weber and Auggie squatted in a roadside trench near the corpses, to decide how to handle the inn some forty yards away—just go around it, or case the joint? Weber downed another pep pill.

"You there. What are you doing?" shouted a man from the inn, an American.

Lett, Weber and Auggie lowered their heads. "We're friendlies," Lett shouted back. "Trying to find our units. We got scattered—"

The American showed himself in the doorway. He had a white-striped MP helmet and armband. He shouted over to them: "Question: Who had the most hits last year?"

"Huh? What's the big idea?" Weber said.

The MP turned to others inside. "They don't know, don't know it," he said.

"Snuffy Stirnweiss!" Auggie shouted back. "Wait, no, it was—"

"That's American League," Weber said. "Stan Musial? Wait, which league?"

The MP aimed a Colt. Two MPs rushed out past him aiming Thompson guns.

"*Sprechen Deutsch, ja!?*" one shouted as he reached the trench.

"Unfortunately we do," Weber said in German.

It was a test, Lett saw. "Wait, no don't, stop—"

"*Hände hoch!*" shouted the other MP. "Stay down! Said, hands up!"

Auggie raised his hands and began to step up out of the trench.

The MP pushed the butt of his Thompson gun into Auggie's gut, knocking him back down.

Lett and Weber got their hands up.

"Let them stand," said a voice. "Let them out."

The MPs stood back, letting Lett, Weber and Auggie step up out of the trench.

The voice belonged to Captain Selfer. He marched out from the inn wearing his fur-collared coat and a new helmet. He smiled at Lett. "Somehow, I just knew you would make it."

Selfer had Lett, Weber and Auggie driven back to Archie Archibald's villa in a heated staff car. They passed scores of American units regrouping after retreat, working to beat the coming darkness. The three were led into a grand room refitted with maps and file cabinets, desks and telephones and wireless sets—S-2's own war room. The grubby, bone-tired threesome faced Archibald in his version of combat dress—a short Ike jacket and riding pants with glistening boots. All he needed were the chrome pistols. Without speaking, Archie waved them to sit in metal chairs before his large metal desk. Battle maps stood on easels, showing the Germans' approximate advance that had come within mere miles of the villa before swinging north. Selfer stood to one side.

Archie sunk into his chair and sighed, squinting at all of them.

"So. Here we are," Selfer said to Lett, Weber and Auggie. "The Germans, they took us all by surprise."

"They're mad," Archie said. "The very thought of it—disguising themselves as good Americans to trick and kill our fine boys. It's downright criminal. The fifth column."

"It's true, men," Selfer said. "We've now learned the Germans have been running a so-called 'false flag' operation—sending out commando teams behind our lines dressed in our uniforms, using stolen jeeps. At that crossroads, for example? They switched the signs. A couple locals saw them do it."

"And the swine killed our two Americans there," Archie said. "Those were artillery men we lost. They could have been me or you," he added, looking to Selfer. "People are saying these sneaking krauts are out to kill Ike himself. Can you imagine?"

"Thus the baseball quiz," Selfer said. "Passwords, trick questions are being implemented all along the line. It's a strict order now, no one's immune."

"Was it Stan Musial, sir?" Auggie said.

"Shut up," Weber said.

Lett took it all in. Biding his time. On the way back to the villa that afternoon, their driver had filled them in on the bigger picture. The Germans had gathered up all the military punch they had in the West for one last great offensive and thrown it at the weakest points in the American lines. The brass should have known. Intelligence should have known. It wasn't the dead's job to know, but as always they were dying in droves for it. It was madness.

"The good news is, we've captured their plans," Selfer said. "We now know solid clues that give them away . . . One—they travel four to a jeep. We rarely do that behind our own lines, as you know. Two—their jeeps have the slit-style blackout headlamps we don't bother with up on the line. Three—they put a red stripe on their bumpers, to identify each other."

The maps loomed above Archie. He pointed at them. "Second Division caught some of the bastards there, and they're getting the firing squad."

Weber was rocking in his chair; he'd popped more pep pills on the way in. "Meanwhile here in our sector, you haven't caught any of the bastards, have you? You need your prize catch."

"That's out of line!" Archie shouted. "This is war, if you haven't noticed. I can hear it from this window." He pounded his fist on the desk.

"Sir, they're rattled," Selfer said. "It's understandable."

"Not on my watch," Archie said.

A knock. Selfer met a man at the doorway. He had a camera and wore a war correspondent armband.

"The colonel ready?" the war correspondent said. "Really like some photos out by the new tanks, before we lose all the good light."

Archie slapped on a shiny helmet. "You three are heading back out. You'll be guarded till then," he said and stomped out, the war correspondent following.

Auggie slouched. "Heading back out?"

Weber shook his head. "For what now?"

Lett felt like someone had punched him in the kidneys. He'd guessed at the new plan. They were going to trick the tricksters.

"Wolf in wolf's clothing, is that it?" he said to Selfer when the captain came back.

"That's right," Selfer said. "We'll get you close. Details to come. Dismissed."

Weber and Auggie shuffled out. Selfer stood before Lett, halting him, just fingertips on Lett's elbow. He waited till Weber and Auggie were out in the hall. He showed Lett a casual smile. "Those correspondents outside? Why don't you come on out? We'll nab a few candid shots with the Horseback Hero that we can hold for later."

"Is that an order?" Lett said.

"It's an opportunity. Truth is, those German commando teams are doing us a favor by creating a good panic. On the QT? They're amateurs, looks like, picked because they were supposed to know some English."

"Sounds familiar."

Selfer held up a hand. "Unlike you? They're not very good, and only two, maybe three of those jeep teams are loose in this sector. But they're sure worth their weight."

"A wise investment."

"Now you're talking."

"And a way to make up ground."

"Sure. I won't deny it," Selfer said.

"I'll come out, if you tell me one thing," Lett said.

"Shoot."

"When did you find out about this?"

"Come again?"

"You ignored our report because it didn't fit. What else did you ignore?"

Selfer stiffened, and raised his chin. "You're dismissed," he said. "Go rest up."

"No."

"No?"

"Listen to me," Lett said. "I want you to listen to me good and well. I will head back out there for whatever you cooked up because I have no choice. But I won't kill for the likes of you. Not anymore."

The door was still open. Selfer walked over and closed it. "Is that fair to your fellow soldiers? You can't have it both ways, sergeant."

"That's my problem, isn't it?"

Selfer smiled again, but it was a different kind, like that of a man watching a bloody cockfight. "You going 'conscientious' on us, is that it?

Or is this the much-rumored battle fatigue? I must say, I saw quite the opposite in you. You don't seem like the God-fearing type to me. Listening to nuns. So you were raised Mennonite or what have you. Fair enough. But any Catholic will tell you how well that old game works."

Lett shook his head. "I believe in one thing: The Golden Rule."

"Ah, yes. The old 'Do Unto Others.' I know it well," Selfer said, and walked out, leaving Lett standing all alone in the war room.

***

Heloise had hidden in her Stromville cellar since the German attacks began, staying close to her aging father Jean. While down there, Jean had told Heloise he knew all about what had happened to her Paul; and if she didn't want it to happen again, to her and them, she should move the contents of her secret drawer into the cellar where it was safer. He had known about the drawer all along, it seemed. Heloise didn't protest, and only chuckled in surprise. Jean kissed her cheek. In between bombardments, they had gone upstairs and put the passports, ID papers, and forging supplies into a pouch, which they inserted deep inside a sack of lentils stored in the cellar. Jean had never mentioned her Wendell by name, nor did she, but he knew her plan. When the attacks came nearer, they had taken in the neighbors without cellars, those without houses any more, and anyone else who fit. By the evening of December 16, the booms of battle flashed in the high cellar windows. All had hoped to sleep. They had been trying all day, but they had so little to eat. At one point Heloise had stomped up the stairs and out her front door in her father's overcoat and boots, glaring at the flashing sky and listening in horror, hugging herself not from cold but from her powerlessness. An American jeep had zoomed by full of bloodied men and almost hit her, sending her back to her front steps. She curled up there a while, fighting stomach cramps. More American vehicles rushed down the main street and in both directions, honking and almost colliding, the men shouting and arguing about which way to flee. Wounded men clung to trucks and tanks with limbs dangling, like so many killed deer. Heloise could only stare, stuck on her steps in pain for so long that the snow on her hair began to freeze. She had worried for her Wendell, but also for the ache in her stomach. For once, she hoped it was hunger.

She went back down. As night came to the cellar, the booming stopped. A vehicle roared by outside. Another.

"American," said a neighbor boy with thick glasses, Ruben. Ruben had been calling out vehicle types since their cellar refuge began, and most welcomed the information more than they were annoyed. "American . . . also American." Ruben went on like this.

Jean raised a tall bottle of beer, toasted Ruben, and drank.

More vehicles roared by. "American."

Another roar, this time a deeper sound.

Ruben looked to Jean, who looked to others, but they could only shrug and shake heads.

"American. It's American," Heloise said. She had no idea, but it would have to do.

***

1130 Uhr, Dezember 17: Kreisfeld was dead. He had died riding in the back seat of the jeep that morning. Gamm thought Kreisfeld was sleeping. He had spoken so little that no one noticed at first. At one point he had leaned forward, folded over as if to fight nausea or stomach pain, and just stayed that way. By the time they noticed, he was hardening up with rigor mortis and freezing through. They had ripped open his overcoat and jacket and found no blood, no wounds. His pulse had quit long ago. He had just stopped. An autopsy might reveal a heart attack or a massive stroke, but Holger Frings knew better. Death would not come soon enough, so the talented Kreisfeld had somehow summoned the old godfather.

They had needed to secure Kreisfeld, Frings saw, so they had wrapped twine around his waist and tied him off at the seat post to keep him in his spot. They didn't keep him along for the ride like this because they were humane comrades. They had talked about it: They thought it might look suspicious to be riding around in the jeep that wasn't full. Their masters in Grafenwöhr had insisted on that. And with all the chaos going on, all manner of GIs needed rides. On top of that: Having a dead comrade might win them sympathy from a checkpoint—they could claim they didn't want to leave a fellow GI out there to be consumed by the snow.

It was nearly noon. Frings drove them onward, Florian up front, Gamm in back next to Kreisfeld. Over the last day and a half they had changed more directions signs, removed signs for mines, cut communications wires. They had passed abandoned checkpoints and command posts and found little to report back. They had run into no Americans with fight left in them. They had holed up for the night in an abandoned workshop, complete with the jeep. Gamm was their radio man. He had reached Skorzeny's command post through a hiss of static. The gruff officer on the other end ordered them to press onward, to keep probing. Kreisfeld had been listening in. "I've done my duty," he had muttered. It was the last thing he had said.

The snow had piled up, covering the mud and trees up high, the flakes thicker, the ice harder. Frings drove yet another fire lane cut through forest like a part in thick hair. They still hadn't found any radio stations or information posts to sabotage. They could hear bitter battles to the north and south, but in their sector the roads were empty and most crossroads unguarded. Up front, Florian had maps on his lap. They weren't even sure they were in their sector any more. With the snow it all looked the same. The compass only got them so far.

"We're going the wrong way," Frings said.

"Shit," Florian said. "I'm afraid you're right."

Kreisfeld kept leaning onto Gamm, who pushed the corpse back.

"I know what it is. The signs we've seen, they had to be wrong," Gamm said after a while.

Then it hit Frings. He punched at the dash, making the gauges jump.

"What?" Florian said.

"Another of our jeep teams could have switched them around already. We could have been switching them back, even at that crossroads yesterday. That's what those *Amis* there were doing—trying to figure out where in the devil they were."

All fell silent, as the jeep rolled in low gear over new snow, crunching along.

"We're all responsible. None of us noticed," Frings said. He shook his head. He had expected this all to go down so differently. They would find themselves amid thousands of fuming American soldiers. They would be found out. Frings would go down shooting, firing from the hip with a gun on each arm like the Americans in their movies, just like his instructors wanted. It could still be done. They only had to keep going west, until they found those who would take them, kill them. The sector be damned.

Florian stabbed at the map with his gloved finger, wiping away snowflakes. "I found another road. Up ahead. It runs a little steep and winding, but it meets a main one eventually."

"To where?" Frings said.

"Well, east or west. It cuts through the sector, gets us back to Germany or further into Belgium, depending on the compass."

"So we take it," Frings said.

***

December 17. 11:50 a.m.: Wendell Lett, Weber, and Auggie rode in a jeep with a square-jawed Army Ranger assigned to help them hunt down the enemy false Americans. Archie and Selfer had sent them out at first light. They'd been at it for hours after receiving various leads and pinpoints from forward patrols. Like hunters hoping to see further, they traveled along the tops of the Ardennes' many ridges when the roads let them. This almost seemed more dangerous than running into secret German commandos since the roads were icy, winding, and ran along precipices. Atop one ridge, Lett crouched with the Ranger at the rocky edge with binoculars, scanning a snow-covered valley below. The snow and ice crunching under their feet, knees. The Ranger wouldn't give his name, but that didn't stop Lett from talking to him. He'd have to scrabble as much information as he could from here on out.

"Why they send you?" he asked the Ranger. "And spare me the gung-ho Rangers bit."

"S-2 said four to a jeep," the Ranger said, shrugging. He parroted what Selfer told them. They would hunt down the fake Americans by making themselves appear equally fake. The German jeep teams had signals they were to use, to identify themselves to possible fellow jeep teams. Then, when close enough, they would lure in the fake Americans with their German.

"And the tight-lips bit," Lett added. "Spare me that too."

The Ranger sized up Lett as if he was a gun to be reassembled. "Okay. You want to know? I was at Aachen."

Lett remembered: In Aachen, S-2 told them when explaining their own false flag recon mission, crack Army Rangers directed by OSS had helped US units conquer the city by infiltrating the enemy line disguised as Germans. "Tough going?" Lett said.

"Yes, and not really. Didn't know what hit them. Killed a pile of them. Funny thing," the Ranger added, "the Germans are doing the same to us now. You?"

"Cologne. It was Cologne."

"Don't think I've heard of that operation."

"No, you wouldn't and never will, I'm guessing. Tell me something: You Rangers, did your brass make you wear fake GI dog tags going in?"

"Not a chance. That there would be selling us down the river. No saving a guy."

"Yeah, that's what I thought."

At their backs, their jeep sat parked on the narrow ridge road. The jeep had the telltale blackout headlights and a red strip on the bumper.

The canvas top was down. Weber sat in front and Auggie in back. They were all lure, but they were also sitting ducks for friendly fire. Selfer had given them a password that was supposed to save them from friendly suspicion, but who knew if they could get close enough to give it? The other catch: They wore no German tunics underneath their American uniforms, unlike the German commandos. That was just too close to the real thing, even with safety passwords.

They drove on and found another high ridge, with Lett in back next to Auggie. The jeep inched along the icy road, its tires spinning with horrid whirls like nylon ripping. A cliff ran parallel to them, spiked with snow-laden trees at odd angles.

"I can't look down," Auggie said.

"We're decoys, they says. What a load of shit," Weber said and popped another pep pill.

The trees receded, the road ran out into the open, and they approached a steep, downhill grade. The Ranger slowed to another tricky stop, the idling jeep perched like a roller-coaster car about to plunge. They looked down the road descending ever lower.

At the bottom was a shape. It was a jeep, also slowing to a stop. It was like a mirror image of theirs. Was this really happening? They half-stood in their seats.

The jeep had blackout headlights on, they saw.

Weber lifted binoculars. "There are four of them. And it's got red on the bumper."

Auggie and the Ranger reached for their compact new M3 submachine guns. Lett grabbed at their barrels, pushed them down. "Put those away. Listen. Maybe we can talk them down."

"One has binoculars," Weber said. "They're watching us too."

"There's that special signal they use," Auggie said. "Selfer told us."

"I got it," Lett said. He stood tall and removed his helmet. He turned it upside down, and held it up high.

"They did the signal. They did it back," Weber said.

"I saw it," the Ranger said.

"Should we go back, find a squad somewhere?" Auggie said, his voice squeaking.

"You heard S-2—we're on our own," Weber said.

"We walk on down there, we're too exposed," the Ranger said.

"Well, they're not coming up here," Lett said. "We'll have to make the first move."

"We got to keep it moving," the Ranger said. "Let's just coast on down, best I can."

Lett nodded. "Okay, but nice and easy."

"You need a native. What the hell do I say?" Weber said to Lett.

"Nothing," Lett said, and whispered in his ear: "Don't do anything. I'll take care of it."

The Ranger released the brake, but slowly as if counting to ten, and let the jeep roll on, downward. The jeep coasted straight but picked up speed. They grasped at handles, held on. The Ranger shifted down, the jeep veered and the Ranger corrected the wheel one way, then the other.

The jeep slid onward, veering to one side. The Ranger couldn't correct it.

The other jeep sat in their path, like a magnet attracting their own. Its driver scrambled to back up but the rear tires only spun, whirring on ice. The other jeep spun sideways.

Lett's jeep T-boned the other jeep. The crash jolted them, boxing their ears.

Both jeeps slid along, locked to one another, steam hissing from a radiator.

As they slowed to a stop, piling up icy snow, the Ranger stayed slumped forward. Weber nudged him and shrieked. The Ranger's face had smashed into the steering wheel, crushing his nose inward. Blood gurgled from his eyes and mouth and the hollows that used to be his sinuses.

Weber and Auggie scrambled out of the jeep, Lett climbed over the side and out, all of them panting with fear. Three of the enemy had scrambled out. A fourth stayed in the back seat, not moving.

Weber and Auggie stepped out in the road holding their M3 guns, aiming at two of the enemy out in the road just as the two enemies did the same. Their boots slithered on the icy road and all nearly stumbled, like some sickly comic standoff in a western.

Lett had a Colt handgun. He kept it lowered. He stayed next to his jeep, keeping the smashed vehicle between him and the road. The enemies' third man kept to the opposite side of his jeep, his Thompson gun lowered. Peeking over, Lett could see his face, hard-set and stoic.

The radiator whistled and died out, empty. Silence.

"*In Ordnung?*" Lett shouted to all. "Anyone hurt?"

Nods and head shakes all around, from both sides.

"What's with your man there?" Lett said to the enemy, about their back-seat comrade.

"Dead since yesterday," said one of the two in the road. "Froze up stiff."

Weber had blood on his forehead. He wiped at it.

"You hurt?" one of the enemies out in the road said to Weber.

"I'm fine," Weber said.

They were speaking German. For a moment, they seemed all Germans and fake Americans. Situation stabilized, Lett thought. But how would he persuade the Germans to give up without a fight? Surely they knew they'd be shot.

The enemy by his jeep had moved around toward Lett, but keeping a corner of his own smashed vehicle between them. "Who are you really?" he whispered to Lett. "What side you on?"

The words jolted Lett. What could he say to this? "I'm no one," he whispered back. "I'm neither."

The two enemies in the road, still keeping aim on Weber and Auggie, began to pull back their American uniforms. German uniforms showed underneath, one Luftwaffe and one Army.

Auggie gaped. Weber struggled to breathe, hyperventilating, another panic attack.

"What's wrong with him?" said the German from the Army.

"He . . . he's sick. Can't breathe," Auggie said in broken German.

"Show us your tunics," barked the Luftwaffe German. "Show us now!"

Auggie and Weber shook their heads. They squatted lower, still aiming.

Lett and the German by his jeep eyed each other, the German giving Lett a faint shrug and a look that seemed to say: He cannot stop his comrades, they do what they do. Lett nodded back.

"Stand down," Lett shouted to Weber and Auggie. "Calm it. At ease."

"What's he saying over there?" the Luftwaffe German said. "Stand up, you there!"

"You do it! Hands up!" Auggie shouted back.

"All of you, no," Lett said. "Stop, listen to me—"

Shots burst from both sides. A German went down, Auggie fell. Weber and the other German staggered and fell back, ripped with bullets, bleeding.

"They're *Amis!*" one bloodied German in the road shouted, "it's a trick—"

The German near Lett fired at his comrade, laying him out dead.

Lett had ducked for cover behind his jeep. He glanced over. Weber lay in the road, his chest and stomach ripped open and disgorged, his entrails creeping across the snow, steaming. Two Germans lay dead opposite him, the snow growing red around them. Auggie lay curled up beyond Weber, moaning. The German near Lett positioned to fire his Thompson at Auggie—Lett could see the barrel through the mangled jeeps, then the man's face. The German scowled, fighting a bloodlust that Lett recognized too well.

The German pulled up. He aimed at his frozen comrade in the jeep. He fired high into the air, to empty his magazine.

Lett bolted out and around the jeeps, aiming his Colt.

The German raised his arms. He still had the scowl. He still held his Tommy gun. "Shoot me. Put me down," he said.

Lett walked around him, still aiming but keeping his distance.

The German set down his Tommy gun in the road, and raised his arms again. "You do it," he said. "Put me down. Do it! They make you the big, big hero."

They glowered at each other, the German looking as sickened yet curious as Lett.

Lett groaned, lunged and pressed the barrel to the German's temple.

"Good. So many medals you'll get . . . and girls." The German laughed, a screech from deep in his gut.

Lett pulled back. "Check out my men," he said. "Go."

The German sighed, shaking his head.

The German stood over Weber as Lett followed, kicking rifles and M3 guns off the road. Weber had died with a grin, his face already turning greenish from blood drain. "Leave him like that," Lett said. "First time I ever seen him really smile."

The German nodded with his lower lip out, as if approving. He moved over to Auggie, and knelt next to him. "This one lives, maybe," the German said.

"Get him off the road."

The German removed his US Army overcoat, which he wore over a GI field jacket, and Lett glimpsed the gray-green of a German tunic under that. The German lay the overcoat on the ice next to Auggie, rolled him carefully onto it and dragged Auggie over to the nearest tree trunk, tossing the overcoat aside. From his GI web belt, the German dumped out the contents of a small US Army medical kit. Auggie had taken a couple in the arm, Lett saw, and one in his hip. The German doused the wounds with wet snow to clear away the blood, but the flow kept coming, running off the strands of torn flesh, muscle.

"Try his pockets. We all carry spare socks."

"Good idea." The German found Auggie's extra wool socks and fashioned a tourniquet from them. Auggie's eyes opened, he yelped, and he passed out again. The German poured sulfa powder on the arm wounds, and stood back to review his work. His hurried patch-up had left all of Auggie mottled with blood swipes and blotches, even on his face.

"Good," Lett said. Keeping aim, he reached in a jeep and grabbed an Army blanket, and another. He tossed them to the German, who placed them over Auggie, wrapping a corner of one up and around his head.

"He makes it, if someone finds him soon," the German said.

Lett could only hope someone would. A patrol could not be far. "Back up, over here," he said. The German faced him, out in the road. "Take this road uphill. Start walking. Right on up."

The German eyed the path upward. "It is very . . . *steil?*"

"Steep. Yes. Too bad. Go."

The German lunged, to provoke Lett into firing. Lett feinted, the German slipped on ice.

Lett threw the German his OD green American overcoat. "You forgot this."

The German, sneering, got back up and, pulling on the overcoat, started his slow slog up the road with his back to Lett. For traction he used his boot toes to dig into ice and soon moved to a side of the road, using the packed snow for more traction with one foot. The man knew what-for. The German looked back over his shoulder, to see Lett still aiming at him.

Almost halfway up, the German looked again to see Lett still aiming. He nodded, as if understanding that his time had come. He kept slogging, upward, with measured steps. Maybe, Lett thought, the man was hoping he would get a little ride in death—he'd slide right back down the hill. The German kept climbing. He stopped looking back at Lett.

Lett turned away. He ran. Sprinted off the road. He galloped through the snow for the nearest tree line. He vanished inside the forest. As he ran, pushing branches aside and gaining speed over the underbrush, he imagined the German reaching the top of the hill. Near the top, still expecting to be shot, the German would have stopped, and turned, and seen:

No American.

Lett was gone. Lett was done. Lett was out. He ran through forest, clutching his compass and map, the haversack hanging off him full of the few rations he could carry. Just enough. He smiled, gaining speed. He jumped over streams and logs and through the new snow.

***

Holger Frings stood at the top of the steep, icy road. He looked out from the ridge and remembered he still had his binoculars around his neck. Navigating the stiff, snow-laden shrubs, he moved to the cliff and scanned the valley with the binoculars, training them on the forested edge. He saw birds flutter among the treetops, and a shadow moving among the trunks below them. Could it be the American? He hustled out to the road, plopped down on his behind, and let himself slide back down the steep grade.

Down at the jeep wrecks, the only thing left upright was his frozen-through *Kamerad* Kreisfeld, poised like a gargoyle with a frosted-green contorted face. Frings went back to the tree, to the wounded American. He was just a kid, as young as any replacement seaman. He sat with his back against the trunk, pale and helpless. His eyes popped open and rolled around to widen on Frings. "You? You saved me?" the kid said in his kid German.

"Nothing saves you," Frings said, and turned away.

He grabbed the Thompson from the side of the road. He rummaged through both jeeps, ignoring weapons, extra ammo and their worthless field radio for maps and their wads of counterfeit Allied money.

He marched off down the road. He found the fleeing American's footprints, and followed them into the forest. Hearing muted voices, he crouched to watch an American patrol tiptoe from tree to tree toward the jeep wrecks. He kept going.

***

Wendell Lett had stopped running, to save energy. The new snow was too deep. He heard nothing but birds wrestling with branches far above. If that German was smart and lucky, he thought, he'd strip down to his German tunic and keep on marching with hands up till he met the nearest American patrol. But who was lucky, let alone smart?

He reached a village that had been pounded by bombings, from both planes and artillery judging from the horrendous destruction, and moved along the edge of a burning street using a garden wall for cover. He found woods again. He checked his compass and map and fingered his current spot, tracing its distance from Stromville. He was maybe twenty kilometers away. The adrenalin from the altercation and from fleeing had faded inside him, and his legs grew heavier, his thoughts blurry. He'd only slept a few hours in the past few days.

Heloise had always told him: If he decided to do it, he should take his time. The game of going underground was a long one, and going without rest would only get him lost or caught or worse.

He found a clearing in the forest. At one end lay an elongated heap, what looked at a glance like a stack of logs grown over, under a drift of new snow. He guessed better. He made his way over and kicked away snow and underbrush to discover an entrance, through a canvas flap. He hadn't smelled anything foul, a good sign. He drew his Colt, pushed up the flap and stepped down inside a timbered hut built into the earth, the roof made of logs and grimy railroad ties. It was like something out of the Great War. It had probably last been an observation post, once the Germans' and then the Americans', abandoned again when the Germans attacked. The underground room was buttressed with logs and boards, and the floor had a ground cover of US Army tent material. As trench huts went it was luxury, a weatherized cabin about eight by five. No corpses but no food either, just discarded field ration boxes, cans and wrappers. Booze would have been too lucky, but someone had left a bedroll. Lett stooped inside and could almost stand. A couple empty crates standing on ends served as seats for the observation holes looking out into the clearing and forest beyond. Dirt specks covered everything, likely from the bombardments that had sent the last tenants fleeing. One crate was empty, but the other held a couple thick candles certainly plundered from some nice family's dining room.

***

Holger Frings tracked the strange American by following footsteps in the new snow. He found a burning village, and some dark instinct made him detour down the main street. He kept one arm up to shield his face from the infernal heat, and his other hand held a rag to nose and mouth to block smoke. He came around a slight bend. A German panzer-soldier with a bandaged head slogged toward him lugging two gas cans. The soldier was too close to the flames, his uniform steaming from the heat, his eyes squeezed shut. Frings sprinted around him to get clear.

The explosion engulfed the soldier in flames, the soldier not even squealing, simply lowering to his knees, then dropping forward like a burning signpost.

Frings pressed on, the black smoke swirling in his face and his sweat gushing hot and cold. He heard muffled screams and saw local civilians moaning and wailing, staggering and tottering, some with lacerations from broken glass. They had gathered before a pile of smoldering rubble. Frings pushed by them and saw corpses laid out in rows and scorched black, still emitting little blue flames. Some of the corpses were small.

Rage and tears fought for control of Frings, the tears streaming down but evaporating from the heat on his cheeks. The bombed building facades loomed like gargantuan black skulls, spitting hot flames and turning the dim sky into night. He couldn't stop staring at the flames, like a boy so horrified and yet attracted that he wanted to jump right in the fire. What if he just sprinted right into that blaze? Would the searing of his flesh make him stop?

He backed away, and ran off, back toward the forest.

He picked up the American's tracks. He found a clearing. He moved along the perimeter using the tree line as cover. He could make out a rectangular heap of snow, reminding him of a set of torpedoes frosted over on deck. Just some logs or something more? He sat under a nearby tree, casing the scene, listening. A stray chicken wandered up, pecking at twigs. What strange luck. Frings snatched it up, snapped its neck, and stuffed it inside his GI overcoat. And he watched, and he lay in wait. *Lauerstellung.*

The sun went down, but Frings had hardly noticed. His eyes had adjusted just like on the boat. The heap of snow was a trench hut, he saw. His father had probably spent time in one like this before the mustard gas and shrapnel claimed him. But the American was smart to choose it.

The chicken had long gone cold inside Frings' overcoat. He faced a choice. He could go find his way back to his lines, the only survivor. Or, he could take this further than he ever had before. Follow his death wish. He could go in there and deal with this *Ami* right there and now.

Hours after dark, Frings knew what he had to do. He pulled his gloved hands from their warm spot between his legs, released the safe lever on his Thompson gun.

***

In her cellar on December 17, Heloise and her father held each other as they listened to another battle within reach. The neighbors huddled around them. They had heard Americans shouting outside for much of the afternoon but the voices had faded, and all had gone silent. Now they heard more shouts outside—German voices, and the roar of more vehicles muffled the shouts. The neighbors looked to Heloise and the neighbor boy Ruben, but Heloise and the boy could only glare back in fear. Her father Jean put a finger to his lips, shushing all.

When dusk neared again, Heloise couldn't take it anymore. She and Jean climbed the cellar steps, tiptoed into the front room, and peeked out a window onto the main street. She had to smile, at first, at all the Americans marching by. But these grimy front-line GIs were trudging eastward with hands on their heads, and many were wounded. Germans marched them along, looking in little better shape than the Americans.

Young Ruben and other neighbors emerged from the cellar. Heloise and her father shushed them again and shepherded them back down.

Heloise went back for another look. Most of the GI POWs had passed. German vehicles clogged the road, bumper to bumper. Motley German troops gathered to drink and smoke, their faces gaunt and leathery. Others set upon a few straggling American prisoners, pulling off their boots and warm gear, their cigarettes, their weapons. Another group siphoned gas from abandoned American vehicles. The empty gas cans stood like dominoes, needing to be filled.

They couldn't last long needing so much gas, Heloise thought. What then? They would know they had lost, finally. They had already lost that sense of order so dear to them. They were half-naked, wild, desperate beasts now. So would they go down moaning, or foaming at the mouth? And amid the chaos, would Wendell find a way back to her?

***

December 17: Evening. In his trench hut hideout, Wendell Lett woke with a start. He sat up on the bedroll, in the darkness. A chill shot down his neck. He sensed something.

A light flashed before him. It was the flame of a lighter.

The German sat on a crate—the German he'd left stranded. The man lit a cigarette from a red pack—a Pall Mall. His US Army overcoat and field jacket were open to show his gray-green German tunic. He had a Thompson gun resting on his knee, pointing at Lett.

Lett didn't jolt or cower. He sat up straighter, his back against the skinny birch logs. He should have known. The last thing he remembered was lying down after he'd cleared snow from an observation hole, to look out. In his sleep he had thought he heard a chicken, and smelled American tobacco, but had dismissed these as hunger and the usual dreams of dead buddies.

The German had a square face with deep lines—more like a Russian than a German, Lett thought—but thick reddish brown hair. "I thought you never wake," the German said in accented English.

"How did you find me?" Lett said.

"Fog is like darkness. Snow is so. It only shows what is important."

"I thought it was the melting part you had to worry about."

"This is also correct," the German said. "Why did you let me go? Are you not on a mission anymore?"

"I told you. I'm not on any side."

For a time, Lett and the German sat facing each other. They had a good staring contest. Lett studied the Germans' tunic. It was strange. The insignia and buttons were yellow-gold, the buttons bearing little anchors, and the right pocket sported a shiny oval badge with a speeding boat on it.

"You could have sent a unit here," Lett said. "How do I know you haven't?"

"You do not."

"Aren't you just going to shoot me? How do I know you won't?"

"You do not. But I repeat myself."

"You could have stopped them," Lett said.

"You could have also," the German said. "Your jeep rammed us, do not forget."

"No. That's not what we wanted. What I wanted. Far from it."

The German shrugged. "I did what you wanted, yes? I killed one of mine."

"No." Lett kicked at the bedroll. "I didn't want anyone to die. I was going to—"

"What? What was there to do? Talk them all out of it? And then what happens?"

The German had a point. Did Lett really think it could have turned out any better? All the more reason to walk away from it, from all of it. The German stared at him, his head cocked, waiting for something like an answer.

"You did some fast work on Auggie back there," Lett said.

The German shrugged. "You made me do this. Auggie?"

"His nickname. August is his name," Lett said, and winced inside. Ever the incurably cynical dogface, he had never asked Weber or Auggie about their hometowns, or their families. "What's your name?" he blurted.

The German narrowed his eyes. He shook his head.

"Come off it. Who am I going to tell?" Lett said. "Military intelligence?"

The German smiled, showing the browned teeth of a veteran. "My name is Frings. Holger Frings."

"Is that a Navy tunic? *Kriegsmarine?*"

"Yes. I'm a sailor."

"What's that rank there?"

"*Obermaat.* This is much like a Petty Officer."

Lett could only shake his head. A thin smile had spread across his face.

Frings produced a dead chicken from his overcoat, and set it on the ground cover.

Lett's eyes widened, as he imagined the feeling of a warm full stomach. "You can't cook down here," he said. "We shouldn't even have a candle going."

"No. Not until it's safe," Frings said.

Lett, nodding, pulled out a bundle of wool from his pocket and tossed it at Frings—Weber's spare socks. "Take 'em. Me, I still got my own," he said.

***

In Stromville, Heloise couldn't take hiding in her cellar one minute longer. At dawn on December 18, a Tuesday, she went upstairs and outside and stood in the icy road. Much of the battle wreckage had been cleared. German military field police wearing crescent-shaped metal gorgets on their chests stood around a command car and a fold-up table. It was a temporary checkpoint. She saw something, a figure, crushed flat and frozen into the road. Two German soldiers dug away at it. They popped it out of the ice. It was as flat as an ironing board, its head intact. The soldiers laughed and held it up. "Boar schnitzel!" one shouted, his words slurred from drink.

The German soldiers saw Heloise out in the road. They showed her the boar, holding it above their heads like a prize fish. She forced out a smile, and waved. These types won't be digging up squashed animals for long, she thought. Soon they'll be searching cellars.

"You must be careful around here, please," said a voice in French.

Heloise whipped around to see a young German captain, his gloved thumbs tucked into his wide and shiny black belt. His French was respectable, but she would never tell him that. "Oh?" she said.

"Indeed. The Americans laid mines in the valley all around you. Only the road is safe. Please do beware. It's really best to remain in your cellar. We will come for you."

***

Morning, December 18. Out in the classical gardens of their villa billet, Archie Archibald and Captain Selfer strolled paths among heroic statues of Neptune, Mercury, Athena. They had a broad view of the horizon that was flashing and showing towering billows of black smoke. The constant thuds of battle sounded in the distance. Selfer and Archie walked with hands clasped behind their backs, looking like relaxed philosophers.

"The German spearhead has to stall sometime," Selfer said. "They don't have the gas. They don't have enough of everything." He waved a hand at the thinning clouds, and returned to his philosopher stance. "And when this weather finally breaks?"

"Allied air power," Archie said. "That'll teach 'em, really snap their spines."

Selfer lit a cigarette. They strolled on, further from the villa, and from any who might hear.

"You know, we got some damaged hooves here," Archie said.

Selfer shrugged. "We're not alone. Officers all along the front aren't looking so swell."

"True. And we're not the ones heading to the glue factory. Say: Any contact with Z Team?"

"Be a miracle if there was, sending them out like that."

"Oh, don't go all mushy now, Charlie. I was just thinking—have we sent out the latest 'Archie's Account'?"

"We were holding it back—considering the situation at hand."

"Let's do one," Archie said.

Selfer stopped, pulled his cigarette, and turned to face Archie with a raised eyebrow. "I really don't advise it," he said. But then Selfer saw the hard look on Archie's face, the one that at crucial times always helped the Horseback Hero ride over the next hill. It was rare, this resolve, but also why Selfer had stayed on Archie's staff. Theirs was a long game.

"I see. You mean, make it backdated?" Selfer said.

"Updated, we'll call it. It will include those first findings from Z team that I, we—"

"Findings? What findings, sir?" Selfer knew the answer, but Archie always liked it when he drew it out like this. It was the closest Archie probably got to foreplay, Selfer thought.

Archie grinned. "Oh, you're good, Captain. Smooth as they come, like cream on butter. The findings that I, that we, put on the back burner. I tell you what. Put your own name on it. How about that? About time you got some credit for AA. And give it a zippier title, something like, 'Germans Readying Large Movement in Sector.'"

Selfer couldn't say getting the byline didn't delight. "That's not bad," he said, playing along, then doubling down like Archie liked. "Knowing what we know, I have an even better title: 'Archie says: Captured Intercepts Indicate Combined Enemy Counterattack and False Flag Operation.'"

"Ooh, there you are. Now these, I did read. We saw this coming. We saw it all the way. Best thing is, some historian gets his hands on this in fifty years? He will know so too." Archie strolled off, squinting with delight.

Yet Selfer, for once, felt a twinge in his gut. Could it be he was reaching some sort of limit? He told himself he wasn't. Limits were for sops and milquetoasts, his father had told him. That's how old dad had given the Great Depression the slip and came out a winner. No matter that his father was a con man. A man had to climb his way up, from a city sparrow to a slicker. Selfer drew his chromium flask from his jacket and took a long, slow, burning sip of vintage Armagnac. He looked out over the horizon, and all he saw was that black smoke.

***

During the night that became December 18, Lett had wanted to leave the trench hut, but Holger Frings made it clear that it wasn't safe in the darkness. Lett was stupid to go now, Frings stated, a veteran soldier should know better. Lett found himself believing Frings, even though he wanted to hate the German. He hated the Germans' blatant frankness. The Mennonite nuns and elders had been the same way. Of course, they would contend that they were only doing it to help. Why hem and haw like the English? It only invited misunderstanding. Tragedies.

The trench hut was less cold with two people inside. Outside, Frings' chicken lay tucked under the new snow ready for cooking, just in case. Frings had his own bedroll. One slept while the other stayed awake for watch, slumped on a crate, peering out the peephole at the vacant, murky clearing. They hadn't talked about sharing watch shifts; they had simply done it rote like the old soldiers they were. At some point in the night, Lett woke and saw Frings on watch. Just enough light came in through the peephole to make out contours. A pipe hung from the German's mouth, unlit. He didn't blink for a long time. He had the thousand-yard-stare—the bulkhead stare for a sailor. He twitched back to reality, and opened a tubular tin. It held pills.

"No," Lett croaked from his bedroll.

"What? Why? It's only Pervitin," Frings said.

"Uncle Sam gives us pep pills too. They make you jumpy."

"Are you my wife? They do not make me jumping."

"Whatever they're doing, it makes you exactly the way *they* want you to be."

Frings, nodding, put the pills away. "It snowed again. Good for us. It covers us up."

"You got a death wish, don't you?" Lett said.

"How do you mean?"

"I just mean. Clearing off like you did. Your side hangs you from hooks for that alone."

"And you? What about you?"

"What about me?" Lett said. "It's my turn for watch, that's what."

Frings straddled backward off the crate. He sprawled out on his bedroll in the opposite corner, his jacket falling open to reveal his German tunic. The boat badge showed again.

"That's for combat," Lett said.

Frings looked down, and touched the medal as if he'd never seen one before. "This is what we get when we don't die soon enough."

"When you're beating the goddamn odds, more like."

Frings grunted. "Yes. It comes with the death wish."

"Is that some kind of PT boat?"

"Yes. A *Schnellboot*, we call it."

"It must have been rough," Lett said, watching Frings' stare drift off, miles out to some dark sea. "Were there sharks?"

"No. There was us. Humans."

"And now look at you. Under ground instead of water. Say, why are you wearing your tunic underneath?"

"The German thoroughness," Frings said. "My commanders, they studied the Geneva rules of warfare and determine we keep our uniforms under the American costume. In this way we are not spies, in principle. But there is one difficulty—to fight as the rules permit we must first rip off our *Ami* uniforms."

"Now he tells me."

"It is silliness, if not suicide," Frings said. "You know these rules?"

"Not in the way you do. But we're silly too."

"I tell you—know where we got the idea? This war trick? You Americans did it."

"We weren't the first. Armies been trying it since the dawn of killing each other."

Frings punched at a log, shaking the roof. "You listen! I'm talking about right now. In this war. It was in Aachen, in September. You sent your soldiers over in our uniforms. It was, how do you say? An attack by surprise. *Aus dem Hinterhalt.*"

"An ambush?" Lett said. This Frings had obviously heard stories. And he knew from an ambush. "What do you want me to say? Join the club? It wasn't me."

Frings grunted, calming, staring at his reddened knuckles. "Perhaps that's the future way—your true action man of fascism. Anything goes. Yes? Time will tell us for certain. In any case, it's your Americans' world now to cock right up."

"I was a trickster, too," Lett said. "But, we were in Cologne."

The words had come out before Lett could stop them. His sorrow about Cologne, and his failure to deal with the jeep face-off, it all pushed him to say and do dangerous things.

"You?" Frings pointed. "This, I don't believe."

"It's true. Just days ago."

Frings glanced at his Thompson gun leaning next to him. "Shut up," he spat.

The German didn't have to know details. He only had to imagine the ghastly deeds his black propaganda wanted him to. Lett tightened up at the prospect, cocking his arms close to him. Frings' neck had bulged red, thick veins pulsing.

Frings jumped at Lett, knocking him back and holding him down, his knees digging into Lett's armpits. Lett could smell stale tobacco and that metallic reek of despair. Frings clenched his thick hands around Lett's neck and started to squeeze, grimacing, panting, the drool slinging out in strings.

"This, it's exactly what they . . . want you to do," Lett wheezed.

Frings sucked in air, held his breath. He let go of Lett's neck, released his breath with a pop, and crawled off of Lett. "So many medals I'll get . . ."

"That's right."

Lett sat up, catching his breath. Frings sat back, catching his. Minutes passed.

Frings sighed. "We once sunk an LST with GIs aboard," he said. "No survivors. This was not the only time."

"You know how many young *Landser* I've put out of their misery? Just boys, too. You do not want to know."

They shared a grim smile. Frings raised an imaginary beer mug, with a closed palm. Lett did the same, but with fingers out. His beer was a bottle.

Frings chuckled. "A beautiful city, *Köln*. Did you have a nice time?"

"Just lovely. The Rhine, it runs right along Old Town," Lett said.

"Indeed. So let's drink to that."

They pretended to drink.

Lett tried more of his German on Frings. Frings grinned. He spoke in German to Lett, laying on the Kölsch dialect. Lett had to chuckle—from continents and probably centuries away, their dialects sounded similar enough in spurts.

"Your German is terrible," Lett said.

"Yours is not better."

They laughed. It was probably too loud. Their smiles faded. They sat in silence, trading thousand-yard stares.

"Me, I got to thinking that maybe the war would be over by Christmas. What a sap," Lett said.

"As in your Hollywood movie, yes? You *Amis* so much like to dream. Your life there keeps you dreaming too much."

"We all dream, in our own ways."

Frings nodded. "Listen. I'm sorry I attacked you just now."

"It's understandable."

"Yes." Frings' eyes flashed in the dim light. "I'm trying to trust you, but really I wonder if I should just shoot you and move on."

"Maybe. We might be better off," Lett said.

Each should have laughed again. They could only shrug.

In the morning, more snow fell and helped cover the trench hut's log roof, making it look like any other snow drift. As Lett sat on a crate keeping watch, his legs began to cramp and his toes went numb. Worries of trench foot and frostbite hounded him again. He pulled off his boots and rubbed at his toes, squeezing and pulling them. Frings had woken and sat up, watching Lett work away.

"I have to get out of here," Lett said. "I don't care how risky it is."

"I think it's time," Frings said.

They gathered their gear and combed through it, discarding what they didn't need. Lett had a plan, but he hadn't told Frings. The unspoken agreement between them had become clear: They would stay together until it didn't help either anymore.

They heard distant artillery, like a drum corps gone mad. They heard shouts from somewhere in the forest. Frings grabbed his Thompson gun and Lett his Colt, his pulse thumping. He shoved his feet into his already cold boots.

The shouts grew closer.

Lett and Frings peered out, their chests pressed to the log wall. They heard the shush-shush of footsteps in snow, the rustling of brushed branches. They heard a shriek, right outside. Figures appeared in the clearing, darkened against the snow. Lett and Frings scanned the silhouettes for telltale contours, their eyes adjusting.

Six German guards in a mishmash of uniforms herded about twenty American POWs into the clearing.

Lett saw Tom Godfrey among them, exhausted, grimy. He didn't even have head cover. "Oh, God," Lett muttered.

"You know them?" Frings said.

"One."

The POWs bunched up. They kept Godfrey in the middle. Lett didn't see rank insignia on Godfrey. He had on a GI overcoat. Were they hiding that he was an officer?

The German guards kept the POWs in a tight group, stomping and pointing their guns. Haggard and panicked, the guards chugged from flasks and canteens, chomped on cigarette butts.

The battles sounded closer. A few more Germans rushed into the clearing and shouted orders as the POWs screamed back, pointing in rage and waving fists.

The German guards argued, pointing their guns at each other.

Godfrey and the POWs gathered around tight, in a huddle. They faced the guards. The guards howled warnings at the POWs, some kneeling to aim their guns.

Godfrey yelled "go!" and the POWs rushed the guards.

The guards fired.

"Tom!" Lett shouted.

The shots flung snow and splintered the roof logs as Lett and Frings ducked.

An immense heat rose up through Lett, and he glared at Frings with his scowl. It made Frings stand back. Lett grabbed the Colt with both hands and rushed the exit. Frings grabbed Lett by the calves and pulled him back, pinning him to the ground cover.

Outside, the shots slowed to periodic pops.

Silence returned.

Frings sat up on a crate and looked out, wiping away snow and wood shards. Lett came over to look. The Germans had moved on. Out in the clearing lay the murdered POWs, looking like so many snow angels if it wasn't for the blood and claws for hands.

Tom Godfrey lay on his stomach, his eyes still open and directed right at them.

***

In Heloise's Stromville cellar, the incoming artillery screeched on and they didn't even know whose it was anymore. Heloise hugged her father. She didn't know what else to do. She had tried everything to keep this war from her home, even praying, but no one was listening. Shells pounded the world above them. The cellar rocked and shook, sending so much thick dust and slivers down that she feared the beams themselves were coming apart. It wasn't a crazy thought. She could hear the rafters crack and split under the pressure.

One neighbor, then another couldn't take it. They ran screaming up the cellar stairs and out. A whole family, the Boudains, followed and shook off Heloise's and others' grabs at their coats. The neighbor boy Ruben used the diversion to make a dash for it, too, but her father Jean tripped him and Heloise grabbed young Ruben. She hugged him while her father whispered to him that it was okay to cry.

After the shelling had stopped, Heloise went upstairs. Opening the cellar door brought in a wash of open morning daylight, dust and grit and smoke. The other half of their building lay in rubble. Her room was gone, collapsed onto itself, the dresser smashed. Her father wanted a look, but she pushed him back. He seized her by both arms and gave her a stern glance—the first she'd seen from him since before her mother had died.

"You let me go up," Jean said. "I've seen this before. So has your grandfather. And his. So you let me go." His old arms shook, but he held her even tighter.

Heloise let him out. Hand in hand, they stepped over debris and entered the street.

Their village was a smoldering terra of rubble drifts and fires and black smoke whirling. Birds flew low and wildly, as if crazed. Animals wandered, domestic and farm. Neighbors wandered by, some burnt with hair gone, others cut all over, all coated with dust and soot. Heloise touched them as they passed. How could she console them? What was there to say? No one was listening.

Her stomach churned, the cramps stabbing at her. Her father squeezed her hand, held her up. One lamppost still stood, she saw. She staggered over to it and they used it for support. She couldn't see down the road into the snowy valley. A heap of rubble blocked her view.

Where was her Wendell? she thought. What have they done with him now? What kind of a sick world was this?

"He'll come back, dear, he will," her father whispered into her ear.

***

Morning, December 18: Lett and Frings waited for their chance to make their break. Outside, enough snow had settled into the folds and crevices of the corpses to make them look like underbrush. The frozen stiff that was Tom Godfrey had become just another white drift.

Lett hadn't spoken much since Frings kept him from rushing out. Frings used the silence to gauge the location of faraway battles. "The action moves east now," Frings said. "We wait a little longer. Then we go. All right?"

"Sure," Lett said. He felt like talking, suddenly. He told Frings about Heloise, about how she waited for him. He showed Frings her photo.

"Pretty Belgian girl," Frings said. "Lucky man."

Lett hadn't told Frings where she lived, or her name, and Frings didn't ask. But Lett told this stranger things he had only told Heloise: "I saved Tom Godfrey's life. I guess you could call it that. We were clearing this street. Tom lost it. Wailing like a widow. He wouldn't be right out there now if it wasn't for me," Lett said.

Frings stared at Lett with one eye screwed up in pain. "I killed two of your fellow soldiers at a crossroads. Personally. I did that."

"The crossroads, near St. Goff."

Frings nodded. "Yep. And I did not take off this American uniform to do so." He tugged at his US Army overcoat. "So my jeep comrades? They only followed my example. That's why they fired at you."

"What the hell's a sailor doing here anyway?" Lett said.

"Lost. I can tell you. I grew up on a river. I'm from a city once called Cologne. Perhaps you know it?"

An ache rose up Lett's his throat, chest. He tried to swallow down the grief, but it only swelled hot. "Oh. I get you now."

"I could fight more on the land," Frings said. "Kill more. It had nothing to do with the Fatherland. I wanted to kill. Battles at sea, that is another story of horror you do not want to hear."

"We dogfaces got our own horror. In decades from now, I'm sure they'll say we Joes were all noble, every one of us grimy but patriotic cherubs. Because we won a war. Back home they already do think it, thanks to the publicity teams, the ads, correspondents, censors. I'm not buying it. If we have to come here and fight to do away with your Hitler and the sorry mess he created, then people ought to know just how much the effort sucks all our souls. That way, maybe no one will try a war again." Lett grunted. "Oh, now I don't doubt that our fight, this Allied Crusade of ours will prove to be worth something. Fighting the likes of you. You will probably turn out to have been worse than we thought, worse than the Japs even, and with more horrid secrets. We'll find out, once we get into your Germany."

Frings stared into his lap, his hands loose, limp. He shook his head, but he wasn't disagreeing.

"We should be over here," Lett said. "I'm just not the guy to do it anymore. I did my bit. If I do any more, I'm done for. But with my girl, I can be someone else. That's what she tells me."

"She is a smart one, your girl." Frings pushed off his American overcoat and field jacket and pulled off his German tunic. He had a GI sweater on underneath. He tossed his Navy uniform to a corner. He reached into his overcoat. He pulled out papers. Photos. They were smoke-damaged, burnt on corners and larger, frame-sized, showing crease lines from folding. He held them up. One was of a slight but cute woman with dark hair. It had to be his wife. Another, of two young daughters who had Frings' fuller face and almost could be twins. In the third, Frings posed with his wife and daughters as just babies. Frings didn't give names, and Lett didn't ask. Frings fired up his lighter. One by one, he fed his photos into the flame. He looked away as he did so, unable to see them burning up. The embers sprinkled the ground cover as ashes.

"My wife left me. My parents died in air raids. My sister died. My wife fled Cologne with my girls. She was afraid of the air raids. Afraid of being afraid. I wasn't there." Frings yanked out his pipe; he jammed it back in between teeth. "She left me for a Nazi pig. But it's not the pig's fault. Everyone loves pork. Pork is a comfort."

"I'm sorry. You could have kept the photos."

"No. I cannot. I can't carry anything suspicious."

"I guess not," Lett said.

"So. What are we talking about here?" Frings said.

"You have nothing left in Cologne," Lett said.

"Cologne has nothing left in Cologne."

"And I got nothing stateside. We're already on the lam."

"So? We break the chain of this goddamned gear-machine."

"Because it's a swindle. Let someone else lick their shiny boots. Bloody their own, I say."

"Exactly. This is what I am thinking."

"So let's make it official-like."

They crawled out of the trench hut, scanning the forest. They stood. Out in the clearing, they stared down at the American POW corpses buried under drifted snow and ice. One German lay there too. Caught in a crossfire? Tried to stop it? No one would ever know.

The contour of Tom Godfrey looked as if he froze while still crawling, clawing along. "Godspeed, Tom," Lett whispered.

"I could use better boots," Frings said, seeing the iced-up, bloodied footwear.

"Couldn't we all?" Lett said, and marched off.

Frings pulled out his S-boat War Badge, having retrieved it from his tunic. He flung it toward the dead, where it sunk into the snow, and followed after Lett.

Lett and Frings trudged through thicker snow in thicker forest. Lett had the chicken in a haversack stuffed with ice. They crossed a small trickling creek, stepping across rocks. "Remember—anyone asks we're lost, looking for our unit," Lett told Frings. "We escaped Germans just this morning. "We can't help your accent, your oddball English, but there are lots of accents in this man's army. Still, we can't have anything else that's fishy. Deal?"

Frings, nodding, pulled out his Pervitin pep pills and tossed them into the snow. Lett patted him on the back.

Together they climbed a muddy hillside, slipping and banging against rocks and limbs. Panting steam. They navigated an icy creek as the thuds of battle sounded, far off. They stopped to gnaw on hard tack, and sip from their canteens. They followed a secluded and narrow forest road, which led them to a junction. An old stone bridge was the only way to the other side. They cased the junction from the edge of the woods. The bridge was empty, but across it US Army trucks were parked at random angles, some towing light howitzers. Yet no one was around. It seemed lucky to find no checkpoint. They had expected one.

"Well? Either we walk over, or swim across," Lett said.

"I was a sailor," Frings said, an attempt at a joke.

The bridge was the only way. They walked out into the open and started across the bridge, walking fast. They cleared the bridge and headed for the forest opposite, trying not to look at the junction and vehicles. A couple heads popped up from the vehicles but no one bothered with them. A GI was working on the tire of a truck. They were steps from blending into forest again.

"Hey! You two!" shouted a voice.

Lett and Frings stopped and turned around. Lett smiled, and Frings mimicked him.

A thick-waisted American strode out to them from the trucks. The man was an older lieutenant and maybe Regular Army, Lett thought.

"Do I salute?" Frings whispered from the corner of his mouth.

"No, not for this lug. We're front-line Joes."

"What unit you guys?" the lieutenant said, stopping a few feet from them.

"Hundred and Sixth Infantry, Four Twenty-second," Lett said. "We broke out."

"You guys are a ways off." The sergeant gave them a once-over. "You troops took a beating, we're hearing." A couple of his GIs strolled out, to back up their looie.

"Yeah, we did," Lett said, making sure to stare at the ground in turmoil. "Just trying to get west, find a reassemble point. We don't know no passwords, if that's what you're thinking."

"Course not, son. How could you?" the lieutenant said.

His GIs unslung their rifles. From a corner of his eye, Lett could see Frings' fingers creep onto his Thompson gun. Lett stepped in front of Frings and said, "We just want to get back, you know?"

The lieutenant looked to his GIs, and back at Lett and Frings. "Question first. What's Gary Cooper's latest picture?"

Lett figured they'd get trick questions, but this was a tough one. "Jeez mac, I been up on the line a while. 'Story of Dr. Wassell', I guess? Wait, no—'Casanova Brown'?"

The lieutenant pursed his lips. "You get one more try."

"What's the big idea anyway?" Lett said. "Who you take us for?"

"No idea. We're just talking," the lieutenant said.

"We been through the goddamn wringer," Lett added, but the lieutenant looked to Frings.

"You mind that, son?" the lieutenant said to Frings.

"Nope," Frings said, shaking his head.

"So tell me: What's the capital of Maine?"

"Who's gonna know that? You?" Lett interrupted. "Not unless a man is from there."

"Not talking to you," the lieutenant said.

He and Frings shared the same gritty look, their crows-feet all tightened up.

"Augusta. It's Augusta," Frings said.

The lieutenant swung around to one of his GIs, who nodded. He turned back smiling. "Hell, and I thought it was Portland."

"Nope," Frings repeated.

The lieutenant nodded, still smiling. "We're heading east or we'd give you a jump start. Use some rations? Camp stove? Name it, boys."

The lieutenant's GIs loaded them up with rations and a Coleman pocket stove. They spared the chitchat, luckily.

Once out alone on a valley road, Lett and Frings were able to stroll looser. They gnawed on chocolate D-Bars.

"Capital of Maine, huh?" Lett said.

"I was a merchant marine sailor too. Ports up and down your East coast."

They reached a farm. Animal carcasses, stripped of meat, lay in the iced mud around the main yard. The house was a jagged, sooty pile of wreck. The barn was untouched. They hunkered down inside. Frings stripped the chicken like a veteran butcher, leaving feathers and entrails in a neat pile. Lett did his best to make a spit out of sticks, perching it over their cylindrical little stove. After they ate Lett and Frings relaxed on straw, sucking the meat and fat off their fingers, and kept warm around a kerosene lamp.

Frings stared at Lett, and Lett knew why; Lett's face had gone pale and stretched with worry. A wave of despair had fallen over him. How the hell was he going to make this work? Create a new identity? Even if he made it, someday, someone would find out and take him from Heloise. When he least expected it. What was he even thinking? This all assumed that Stromville still stood, that it hadn't been devoured by bombs and flame like Frings' Cologne.

Frings, humming a tune, reached deep in his haversack and set out a wad of money. Lett gazed at it. There were big British pound notes, and crisp compact dollars.

"It's tip-top quality," Frings said. "We have expert counterfeiters."

"Thank you. It might help."

Frings reached over, placed his big hand on Lett's shoulder, and squeezed. "Wendell, you must listen to me. It will be there. She will be. I know this like I know that mine is not anymore."

"Thank you. Maybe you're right." Lett sat up. He fingered inside his field jacket, and produced the enlisted man's temporary pass. He held it up for Frings to read. He told Frings how to fill out the rest, with only a name, date, and place. Using a typewriter was best.

Frings smiled.

"Now, it's not as useful as it could've been before you guys attacked," Lett added. "No one around here's on leave, not till the war moves further east. That's why I haven't used it yet. But, soon. And I will need a typewriter."

Lett saw Frings averting his glance, like a boy up to no good. "Wait—you saw the pass?" Lett said.

Frings nodded.

"How?"

Frings smiled. "You're a deep sleeper for a land soldier. I had to be sure that you are who you say you are. I had to know, that you really are like me. That you really do break the chain."

***

December 18. Afternoon: In a well-equipped infirmary tent just close enough to the front to be called a field hospital, Auggie lay bandaged up on a bed surrounded by cots of horribly wounded men. He had found himself in a morphine fog, wasn't sure when it would end, and wasn't sure he cared. He was missing one arm, the blood still soaking through layers of gauze. The morphine somehow made it fine. He was alive, and wasn't it wonderful?

The next time his eyes opened Archie Archibald, Captain Selfer, and a two-star general stood over him. The general looked old and kindly. Auggie stared up at them. Archie squinted with excitement, while Selfer eyed Auggie like a discerning doctor.

"Now here's our good man," Archie said to the general. "The one in my latest field report."

"Huh?" Auggie looked to Selfer, who smiled and nodded. Roll with it, son, he seemed to be saying. So Auggie did. He smiled back.

The general placed a hand on Auggie's surviving arm. "You did well, son. Real well."

"He took out the kraut spy team," Archie said, touching Auggie in the same spot. "A true hero, he is."

Selfer said, in the general's ear: "These were kraut spies, let's not forget, who were gunning for Ike himself."

The general sighed with relief, and shook his head. He placed a Purple Heart and a Combat Infantryman Badge next to Auggie's head on the pillow. "There's a citation in the works for you," he said.

Auggie didn't remember. He only recalled bullets coming at him. "I don't remember. Did I?" he muttered. He tried to think but the morphine stoned him. No one answered him. Through a haze he saw the general and Archie move on, a proud smirk on Archie's face.

Selfer stayed with Auggie. He leaned down close to him, waited till he came back around. "They're sending you stateside," Selfer said. "How about that? A publicity team will cover you."

"Someone helped me. Saved me," Auggie said. He could see the man. A square face, and stern. "Was he a German?"

"No. Listen. You helped yourself. Hear me? Now there's a good fellow," Selfer said.

Auggie remembered the night would have to come again, and his chest tightened up with fear. "I have dreams about it—nightmares," he said.

"Those will go away," Selfer said. He took a good look around the room. He whispered into Auggie's ear: "Where's Lett? Do you know? You can tell me."

"He's gone," Auggie said.

"Gone how?"

"Lett, he tried—he had us all talking. No one shooting . . . Then? I can't remember. I just got shot, I guess."

Selfer was patting him on the head. "Okay, okay. Just, forget about Lett. Forget all about him. Lett's gone. We'll be back to talk about exactly what you did. You did more than you think, son. A hero's work, to be sure. You heard the general."

"Me? A hero?"

"Sure. Why not you?" Selfer said, but he was gone before Auggie could think of any good answer.

***

The light between the trees grew dark as dusk neared. Lett and Frings walked a high road. They came to a sign battered with scrapes and bullet holes: "Stromville, 3 km."

Lett grinned. He couldn't stop grinning. "It's right in the middle of this lush little valley. I've never seen it with this much snow. Come on. There's a ridge this way, we can look down in. Say, you know what we're gonna do? Most deserters live for the moment, just to live. Not me. I'm in it for the future . . ." He couldn't believe how hopeful he sounded.

Frings nodded. He had gone quiet. As they marched through forest, Frings said, "That pass you have is enough? You don't need more?"

Lett shook his head. "We GIs travel light. The company clerks, they keep our papers, paybooks, personal goods near the rear."

Frings stopped walking. "Wendell, I didn't tell you something," he said. "I have no American dog tags. Sure, they taught us how to act like you—chew your gum even. But they gave us no dog tags. So much for the thoroughness. Our plan could never work. The other three in my jeep? Hopeless. And the one I shot, he probably deserved it."

"What about Ike—General Eisenhower? Were your teams really sent to kill him?"

Frings smiled. "We? This is a joke, correct?"

"I'm sorry it's not. Listen, don't worry about dog tags. They look for those when we're caught, injured or dead, and we'll be none of the above. What I'll do is, I'll go in first. You'll hole up nearby and we'll sneak you in. She has contacts, knows forgers. Got me? *Vive la Résistance*."

"Very well. But when she hears me? Sees? A German . . ."

"She won't care who you are. I promise. As long as you're with me. You helped me. Us."

They found the ridge. The tree trunks spread out and let in the remaining light as they scrambled up a rise. They looked out. For a moment Lett thought he'd found the wrong valley. He saw a snowy white plain almost a mile vast, pocked with craters and the lumps of destroyed vehicles. The one road cut through the valley, but it led to a blackened, flatter version of Stromville. "Give me those," he said to Frings, who handed over his binoculars. Lett focused on the dark and smoldering village. Most red roofs and spires were gone, replaced by gray rubble mounds and black charred patches. People and details weren't clear from this distance. He thought he could make out one of the lampposts still standing.

His face had slacked, in dread. Grief. His chest thumped and wanted to burst open yet compress down tight. Frings watched him with a pinched face. No way to sugarcoat this. A battle had raged at Stromville.

Lett had to run. If he didn't move his heart would explode. He tossed the binoculars at Frings and took off down the ridge, pushing off tree trunks and trampling over bushes and rocks, and reached the lower road into the valley. The snowy meadow stretched out on either side of him. Signs lined the road: "Danger! Mines!"

Frings had followed. He caught up, walking step in step with Lett. "I'm supposed to hole up," Frings said. "Wait for you."

"To hell with that. Who knows what will happen."

They marched along the valley road, the village less than a half-mile off, a ragged horizon before them.

"Her name is Heloise," Lett said. "Remember it."

"I like this name. Yes, I will."

Lett jerked to a halt. "Listen. Hear it?"

"I hear it."

It was the whining drone of a US Army jeep, coming up the road behind them.

Lett's despair yielded to a hardness, infusing him. That machine-like purpose kicked in, forged by combat. He sensed no panic in Frings. His comrade still matched his stride. They had the focus.

"So it's just like before," Lett said. "We're two Joes—we're lost. Same unit."

"Got it," Frings said.

The jeep passed, an MP jeep, its two occupants wearing the white-stripe helmets and MP armbands. The two didn't look back at Lett and Frings.

Lett and Frings kept an even pace. The jeep pressed on, nearing the village.

The jeep stopped. It was turning back around.

Lett felt Frings seize up a little, falling out of step.

"No shooting," Lett said. "Then they really have us."

"What about the money? We could use it," Frings said.

"Only if we have to," Lett said.

Up ahead the jeep slowed, turned at an angle and parked sideways, blocking the road. The two MPs stepped out and stood tall, waiting.

"This is not good," Frings said.

But they had to walk onward. As they neared, they saw that the MPs were young, a private and corporal, the corporal wearing only a Colt holster and the private a carbine slung on his shoulder.

Frings picked up his pace. He walked ahead of Lett. Lett couldn't stop him. What could he do? It would look more suspicious. Lett strode faster but only caught up with Frings as the German approached the MPs smiling, his arms out wide as if to hug them.

The MP corporal had his hands clasped around his belt buckle and was so young his smooth neck could have been a woman's. "Afternoon," he said, in a voice that imitated the gruffness of a father.

"Afternoon, boys," Frings said. "But it's evening."

"No—'afternoon' what?"

"Ah, it's a password?"

Lett had stopped just behind Frings. The MP private eyeing Lett had a boy's face full of teenage freckles. "Afternoon," the boy MP said to Lett.

"Fellas, lookie here," Frings continued. "I'm trying to find my unit. I don't even know this Joe here with me—we just met. But he keeps hangin' on."

Lett bristled at Frings' sacrifice but couldn't stop it. What could he say? It would only confirm Frings' accusation.

"What's with your accent?" the MP corporal said to Frings.

"Mine? What's with yours?" Frings said.

"The man's an immigrant," Lett said. "What's wrong with that? It's what we're made of, remember?"

"A daily password's been issued all along the line," the MP corporal said. "If you came from that way, you should know it."

Frings stomped his feet. "Man, I hide out from krauts for three days, this is what I get? Hell."

"Listen, I can vouch for this man," Lett said.

"I thought you didn't know him," the boy MP said.

Frings had used his stomp to move to the side, putting him at an equal distance to the jeep as the MPs. They had left the jeep idling, Lett could hear.

"We'll have to run you in, vet you," the MP corporal said. "That's the drill. They'll get you back to your unit. It's what you want, right?"

"Just one second," Frings said. "I think you dropped this." He held out a wad of American dollars, his eyes pleading.

The MP corporal and boy private exchanged looks.

"That's a lotta dough," Lett added. "Maybe, you dropped more even."

The MP corporal drew his Colt.

Lett pushed the MP corporal off the road, out into the snow past the mine signs. The Colt fell away. Frings knocked the private's carbine loose and pushed him off into the whiteness, the private tumbling backward.

Frings sprinted for the jeep. Lett followed fast behind.

The private and corporal stumbled to their feet, found their weapons in the snow. They lumbered back toward the road from either side, trying to match their footsteps. They raised their weapons.

A crack split the air, the earth rocked. A mine exploded and hurled the private in shreds.

Frings revved the jeep, slammed down the clutch. Lett reached the passenger side. He glanced back. The corporal had hit the deck. He aimed and fired at them, three flashes.

A bolt of pain seared through Lett's torso. He felt nothing a moment. Then his insides seem to erupt and boil, like a hot lava.

***

Heloise's fellow villagers managed the destruction as best as they could. Piles of salvageable belongings lined the street of half-standing buildings, a heap of clothing here, a cluster of furniture there. They had rescued some of their townsfolk from rubble but a few were still missing. Surviving farm animals stood watching from a makeshift pen of chicken wire, while cats and dogs stayed close to their owners' ankles. Heloise stacked loose bricks. Her father helped. Young Ruben did his best. They heard the chug-chug sound of an engine. Ruben stopped to listen, looking to Heloise.

"Belgian," Heloise and her father said at the same time, daring a little laugh. An old tractor entered the street and, as neighbors directed it, pulled up to a mess of debris.

As sundown neared, Heloise was lugging pails of water from a well. She made her way down the main street, past the town's one remaining lamppost, the heap of rubble blocking her view.

A boom and three pops ripped through the air. From out in the valley.

She stopped to listen as neighbors emerged from ruins and doorways. Her father joined her.

"What was it?" she said. She had set down her pails.

"A mine blast? It has to be. The front's moved on," Jean said. "Probably just a stray cow."

"I mean the shots. There were shots. I heard three."

"Poachers? GIs hunting? Here, you should not carry these." Jean ambled off with the pails.

Heloise's feet felt light, drifting, as if on shifting sand. She hugged at the lamppost. She threw up again, but this time it wasn't from the baby inside her.

***

The MP's shots had propelled Lett into the jeep, slamming him against dash and windshield, unconscious. Frings pulled Lett all the way in and linked his right arm tight under Lett's to keep Lett in as he sped on out of the valley. He drove on, down narrow forest lanes and crossing firebreaks, steering them deep inside woods and away from any patrols, pursuers, predators. He kept driving on the narrowest lane he found, just two mud-filled ruts, navigating the plunging, rising path that lurched and jostled them and made Lett moan. The lane led to an abandoned forest shack, its plank siding gray and mossy. The jeep's motor clunked to a stop, the radiator pinging. Frings found the first aid kit behind the starboard seat. He grabbed blankets.

He hauled Lett into the shack. He lay Lett on the floor, ripped open his field jacket, saw dark blood, and tore at packets of sulfa powder. He doused the wounds with canteen water to clear blood, located the dark punctures, and dumped on the sulfa. Lett groaned. Frings slapped on bandages, and ripped apart a blanket and wrapped a strip around Lett to compress the bandage tight. He was no *Sani*, no medic. It was all he could do.

He glared out a window of the shack, his combat senses still set and buzzing inside him, making him hyper alert and ready for more. Outside the stolen MP jeep sat empty, the windshield shattered. Blood had smeared on the starboard side, and as handprints on the fender. Frings went to work. Soon he had fir boughs and branches covering the vehicle. Any new snow would help blanket the camouflage. He had done such concealment many times. It was how an S-boat hid along a rocky forested coastline or moored next to their camouflaged tender ship.

He wanted someone to scout him out. He would take them on, and make them fix Lett. Put them down if he had to. But this shack was too secluded. It bordered a steep ravine, the sky all but blocked out. Evening had fallen early here.

Lett lay on the earthen floor, his torso swathing soaked through with blood. Lett's face was white. His eyes, still closed. Frings knelt next to Lett, to check his pulse. Lett's eyes opened. Frings started.

"You thought . . . I was dead," Lett said, his voice a thin creak.

Frings held up a canteen for Lett. Lett, somehow, raised an arm and pushed it away. Frings tried again. Lett pushed it away. "Save it," Lett said.

"Okay."

Lett stared up at him, his eyes glossy yet cloudy too.

"I'm sorry," Frings said. "Those MPs, they weren't going to let you get to her."

Lett lowered his chin, a nod. "My dog tags. Get them," he said.

Frings felt his throat seize up, and constrict, like someone was choking him. A heat burned behind his eyeballs. He swallowed down his sorrow, if only so that Lett couldn't see it.

Frings shook his head, no, no.

Lett reached for his dog tags at his chest but let out a piercing wail. His arm dropped away. Frings lifted the tags from around Lett's neck. They came up red and glistening from blood.

"And, the pass," Lett said.

Frings wanted to slap Lett for being so obstinate, but he could only nod. "This means, you forgive me?" he muttered.

Lett nodded. "Don't hide out too long. Soon they won't even bother looking. Our tanks will be over the Rhine soon enough. A month should do it easy. Use a typewriter if you can. Can you do it?"

"Okay. Yes."

"You know what? I was so . . . I was so scared that she was dead. And now? I so wish that she could be."

The heat behind Frings' eyes blurred his sight. Tears rolled down his face, and he let them.

Lett fell silent. Frings kept checking his pulse. He got another blanket from the jeep and lay it over Lett. He sat next to Lett and stayed there as night fell.

Later, Lett began groaning, and moaning. He whispered something in the darkness. Frings leaned in close to listen. Lett said:

"In Cologne, in your city, I killed . . . an old man . . . I killed a little girl. I had to. Don't tell her. Don't you tell Heloise."

Frings pulled back. His throat constricted again. For a moment he thought he might suffocate. He expected a fury to take over, the kind that had made him kill men, but his heart only ached.

"*Niemals*," he said. Never.

"Tell her . . . She convinced me."

Frings nodded. "You convinced me."

In the middle of the night Frings sat alone, in a corner. His tears had left cold tracks on his cheeks. At one point he had pulled Lett's dog tags from his pocket, still sticky with blood. He had gone out and cleaned them off in snow, wiped them dry, placed them around his neck. He didn't touch the rations in the jeep. He would need them. Over in darkness, Lett lay on the floor. Many times Frings had thought of pulling off Lett's blanket to wrap around himself. He would have to. He was shivering. He didn't. He resisted the thought, the truth and the reality, that Lett's odds had played out.

He crept over to Lett and, aching in the hope that Lett had not gone cold, moved beneath the blanket with Lett. The man was still warm. Frings stretched the blanket tight over them. It was how they did it in foxholes, trench huts, boats if they had to. They were warmer together, at least for a time. Frings could feel Lett's pulse throb, weakly. He closed his eyes to sleep.

The jeep started up, somehow. It was just before dawn. Frings had lowered the windshield to help hide the shattered glass and MP markings on the lower frame. Ice and snow had piled up on the fenders and bumpers, covering other markings. He had flushed out and wiped down the starboard side, in and out, to remove any obvious blood. It was cold and gritty work, but he'd done worse on a boat in a North Sea winter.

He lay the two blankets in the back seat. He hauled Lett out of the shack and loaded him in the back, facing up, and swathed him in the top blanket. He tied off the bottom blanket's corners to handles and seats, forming a makeshift hammock to keep him steady and cradled. Lett's lower legs hung over the side, bent at the knee, but it would have to do.

Frings drove fast and as far west as he could, stopping often to listen for battles. He drove toward any combat he heard, trusting that the chaotic, ever-changing front lines made roadblocks pointless and too dangerous. He drove through two firefights. One raged in a forest, directly starboard. He zigzagged along it, ducking as low as he could while driving. Bullets and shrapnel clattered at tree trunks and metal, ricochets striking the hood, his helmet. The other was a battle for a crossroads. Frings steered right into the line of fire and gave it full throttle, passing anti-tank guns, mortar teams and covering grunts from both sides. GIs and *Landser* alike stopped and stared. A few rose even, shaking their heads. What they saw was a madman. And yet here was the only thing that had made them stop fighting, if even for a moment. Frings laughed at them, hugging the wheel as he sped onward, westward. If his odds ran out like this, then what better way?

He passed a burning barn portside and saw a medic hovered over a howling wounded GI, the medic tearing open sulfa packets and ripping open clothing. Frings slid to a halt.

The medic, seeing boots hanging out the back, gestured west and shouted, "Aid station 'bout a kilometer!"

Frings hit the accelerator. A pistol shot rang out, zinging close to his ear. He looked back.

The medic was screaming, "Wait! Wait!"

Frings slammed on the brakes, shoving up a wake of snow.

Medics didn't carry weapons, but this one had a Colt. The medic tossed the gun off into the snow, glaring at it like it was a grenade ready to blow and he stumbled over to Frings' jeep, panting, smothered in blood, his hands steaming.

"You gotta take this one, hear? I done all I can, just done all I can," the medic said.

"Okay." Frings and the medic somehow piled the wounded man onto the front seat, his unconscious weight like a stack of sandbags. The poor bastard was a captain and older than Frings. The captain groaned. Lett groaned from the back.

"*Verdammt noch mal,*" Frings muttered and drove on.

He entered a village overrun with frantic, bustling American troops. He saw a red cross—the aid station tent stood in the courtyard for a bombed-out church, as if that was going to save them. Wounded had been massed under the end of the church still standing. Medics, make-do orderlies and civilians rushed in and out, handing off litters and hauling supplies from a truck. Frings pulled up as far as he could, only stopping before a line of bodies. Lett and the captain had gone silent. Frings jumped out and shouted, "Help! Help here!"

No one came. Frings glared at those rushing past. He grabbed a medic by his sleeve but the guy shook it off, kept going. Frings took a deep breath, and went to check on Lett in back. His blanket cradle had held up. He had a musette bag for a pillow. His eyes had been closed so long a crust had formed between eyelids but his face wasn't green, a good sign. Frings touched his neck splattered with dried blood—still warm, pulsing.

A German POW came at him. A German medic? He wore the armband with red cross. Frings grabbed him by his leather belt as he passed. "You! You have to help these men," he shouted in English.

The German medic had swung around, eyes wild and cheeks sunken from exhaustion. He saw the jeep. He held up his palms.

"So no English?" Frings said in German, lowering his voice. "Then you listen to me. All right? You hear me good now?"

The German straightened up, and nodded.

Frings whispered: "The one in back—promise me you'll go get him help. If you do, good fortune will come your way. And, you never saw me. Clear?"

"Clear. I promise. As ordered, sir!" the German said and ran off for the tent.

Frings bent down to Lett. "Thank you," he said, and kissed Lett on the forehead. "I'm sorry, but I have to leave you."

He turned, studying the scene. Beyond the church, to the West, he saw more treetops. So he headed around the church toward the woods, leaving the wheel of his craft for good.

***

Wendell Lett's eyes opened. He floated, was floating. He jolted, was jolted, but only knew it as such, as one would in a dream. He dreamed he was suspended on a litter, riding on a medical truck, and the cold stung at his face but he only recognized the sensation as a notion. He saw the sky, and it was blue, which made him know this had to be a dream. If this was real, the grayest clouds and blinding fog would be bearing down on him like iron and lead, ice and snow.

With time, the dream grew surreal. He smelled salt in the air, as if he was near the sea, and the dream told him the truck waited at a port, lined up with many such trucks in the neatest file the Army could imagine. This made Lett giggle. He laughed out loud. Still he felt no pain. Of course this was one long dream. That was why he floated. No weight on him. Like this, nothing horrible had ever happened. It was like being on water, yet lighter, as if the water itself was flowing through him, carrying him along as it did so, he was the water flow. He could keep flowing like this forever. He would find Heloise in the flow and hold her hand and carry her along like this, forever. All he had to do was not mention his real name to them, or hers, and her hand would find his and flow into his. As they floated.

***

The sky shined blue. American planes passed high above, roaring on to hunt down the enemy columns retreating farther back into Germany. Holger Frings, in full and sloppy American battle dress, rode into a US Army transit depot in the back of a jeep. He had hitched another ride. The driver was a courier, which Frings noted with irony. Frings had perfected his GI costume with items he had picked off the dead he'd come across during his weeks on the lam, including an almost new field jacket, good leggings, a wool helmet beanie and another GI sweater. He had spent Christmas alone in a cellar, but the abandoned house above him had given him a gift: a portable typewriter, left out on a writing desk. His feet felt good and warm. He was wearing Lett's spare socks.

An MP was directing traffic. Frings saw lines of wall tents, including latrines and showers and a mess hall. The courier stopped for Frings to jump out onto a walkway of plywood over the mud and frost. "Thanks, mac," Frings said. He found the check-in table in a heated tent that Frings could have warmed in for days. He waited on a bench. Someone had left the latest front-line edition of *Stars and Stripes*, dated January 17, 1945. "Nazi Spies Executed," read a headline along with a photo of three enemy impostor American soldiers moments after being shot by an MP firing squad, tied to posts, their heads hanging far forward as if their necks had been snapped for good measure. Had Frings been able to see the faces he surely would have recognized at least one Stielau commando, and probably a comrade sailor. The story said that more caught spies awaited trial. He didn't need a photo to tell him what it meant for them.

He slid a stick of Wrigley's gum in his mouth, and smacked it.

When his time came, he approached the table and handed his temporary leave pass to the clerk, a frail-looking corporal. Reading the pass, the clerk gave Frings a sorry look. He handed back the pass. "I hear your outfit took a beating out there. Sergeant Lett?"

"That's right," Frings said, swallowing the last "t" like Lett had taught him, for less of an accent.

"Well, make the most of this, will ya?"

"You bet I will."

***

All was white. Wendell Lett saw an eternal whiteness, cold and fixed. For a moment the overwhelming whiteness made Lett think he'd finally bought it. This didn't scare him. It could only end this way for a dogface up on the line too long. Sergeant Lett of the Army of the United States had been used up and wrung out for all a man could give.

Then the white he saw around him took on layers and textures. He saw rumpled white blankets and thick white gauzes, white walls with hard angles and protruding bolts. He saw white bunk frames. Men lay under the blankets and gauze, the blankets held down with straps, the gauze oozing reds and yellows.

He was strapped in. He looked up. Another man lay above him, the mattress wanting to press through thin metal slats. He had a lower bunk. The stacks and rows of bunks went on like this down the aisle, unending as if mirrored.

Something hit his nostrils. He smelled odors mixing together— sharp antiseptics and the fumes of cleaners, the sweetness of blood and sourness of urine, gangrene, a general rot.

He couldn't keep his head up. The fog inside it was too great, the weight on him heavy, and on his eyelids. It was how the morphine lingered in a man.

His heart jolted, thumping. His eyes popped back open. Sweat poured out of him, cold and slimy.

He remembered Heloise. He had almost made it back to her. He was so close, almost free.

He remembered: The German Frings had helped him get away. The last thing he remembered after the MPs got a shot off was lying on a cold damp floor in a dark forest, and shivering. But Frings was there, too. Frings somehow had kept Lett warm.

Lett did not forget that he must never, ever speak the German's name. Yet nothing explained how he got here to this infirmary. The few small windows were high, between those bolts and buttresses. Was it some sort of armored hospital? A bunker maybe? If so he could still be in Belgium, near the line, still close to Heloise. He could hope.

The medical gear was US issue, he could see that. He peeked his head out, and saw a nurse in white pass down the aisle. But Army nurses didn't wear all white near the front. And his pajamas were white? This place was too damn white—too spic and span and all spruced up.

At least he had nothing stuck in his arms. He pushed off his blanket down to the strap around his hips and tried to reach down and unbuckle the strap, but his back rippled with pain. Did he have broken ribs? Or could something be wrong with his spine?

Then it hit him, sharper than any busted rib: What if they knew about him, and knew just who he was? He felt down under his pajamas, but couldn't feel dog tags. They were still missing. Good. Did it mean Frings had done just like he promised? Had Holger made it to Heloise?

His heart jumped again, like someone had punched it. What about Captain Selfer? Did that bastard know his location? If so the game was up. Or was Selfer still out hunting for him? A man like that would never rest until he nabbed the prize, but no reward would ever be enough. Lett felt a chill in his chest. He thought: What if Selfer had him sent to this place, to keep an eye on him, to heal him up for what Army intelligence had in store for him next?

The patient across from Lett was out of it, mouth open, thick bandages covering his ears like kids muffs. Lett pulled himself to the edge of his bunk, looking out.

A man came shuffling up the aisle wearing pajamas and one arm in a cast.

"Hey, buddy," Lett said, his voice creaky.

The patient kept going, almost past Lett. Then he stopped and pivoted around, his slippers swishing on the metal floor. The man looked right through Lett. It wasn't from a sedative. He had the look—this sorry case was a beaten-down GI.

The patient seemed to see the same in Lett, giving him the slightest nod. "Whatcha want, bud?" he said, sounding like he had sand in his throat.

"You got to get me outta this fix. Help a Joe out?"

The patient scanned the ward, casing the room as if it was a wood hiding a German flamethrower pillbox. "We got to go careful-like, but we keep it moving," he whispered.

"There's no other way," Lett whispered.

The patient, grunting, undid Lett's buckle with one hand and pulled Lett up to sit on the edge on his bunk, the blanket falling away.

"You know there's no flying this coop. You know that, right? There's only one way out, and it's a long way down."

Anger rose up in Lett, wrestling away the pain, and he let it take over. "What's that supposed to mean?" he barked. "Huh? Just what?"

"Ease up. Just giving you the lay of things. You should be happy as hell. You're heading home, sure enough."

Home? What home? Lett's rage had helped him stand, the patient hanging on to him, but now his chest burned and his legs ached, sapping his breath.

"What day is it? Month?" he said.

"Don't know the day. It's middle of January thereabouts. Nineteen forty-five."

Less than a month had passed. "All right. Sorry," Lett said and pushed away from his bunk, one foot in front of the other, using other bunk frames for support. He had to catch his breath. A little nausea crept up his throat but as he steadied himself he realized it wasn't his head gone spinning. They were moving—the whole damn ward was. Was this a hospital train? He couldn't hear or feel the click-clack of tracks, and the room was too wide. And the floor wasn't swaying like a train. It went up and down, it rose and fell.

"Dear god, no," he muttered. He moved on, grasping at bunk frames.

"Go get em!" a patient yelled from a bunk. "All da way ta home base," yelled another and raspy laughs echoed through the ward.

He kept going, out a narrow doorway and down a corridor, passing under caged lights and more buttresses, then past doorways for narrow exposed metal stairways going up, down.

Lett looked behind him. A nurse was coming after him, with two male orderlies jogging up behind her.

"Stop there, soldier," shouted the nurse, her voice hard.

Lett charged forward, pushing off the cold iron walls. The nurse had caught up to him but slowed, her palms out as if ready to catch him. He wasn't sure why she let him go on. Maybe it had something to do with the hot tears splashing at his forearms.

An open door showed daylight. His legs jittered, sending jerks of pain up his torso, but he kept slogging. He'd been in far worse than this, sure he had.

He stepped through the doorway. A blast of cold fresh air smacked his cheeks. The two orderlies were already outside, having flanked him from another door, their arms out ready for him. The nurse had fingertips on his shoulders, calming him, stroking him like a mother would a boy's too-long hair before cutting it.

"Can't hurt to let him see?" one of them said. "What can it hurt?"

Lett had to squint though it was barely light. Before him spread a vast sea, the dark shifting water soaring into peaks like mountain ranges, then descending into deepest canyons. Beyond the dim horizon, and all above, loomed a sky laden with impenetrable low clouds of the same dark gray as the metal on his M1 rifle.

"What is this?" Lett said. "Just what the hell is this?"

"English Channel, friend," one orderly said, trying to sound chirpy but not pulling it off.

The three stood around him, holding him up, hair whipping in their eyes.

He had to test them. "Do you know my name? Do any of you?" he said.

"You came with no tags," the nurse said.

So Frings really did it? Could he have made it to Heloise? Lett couldn't help smiling.

The three eyed each other. "But, we'll get to that in due time," the nurse added.

Lett remembered: He had woken up like this before, as if it was the first time waking. Then he always adjusted. He knew his name, but acted like he couldn't remember. Combat exhaustion taking its toll, they would assume. The missing dog tags helped and his wounds didn't hurt either. The main thing was, he couldn't open his mouth until he knew the play—until he knew just where Captain Selfer and his goddamn patron Lieutenant Colonel Archie Archibald lurked, looking to sink their claws back into him. Only when he was good and clear could he find his way back to Heloise.

He thought of her, and his tears came back. One of the orderlies was shouting for a litter. "They'll kill us, they'll kill us all," Lett ranted, spewing whatever nonsense came to him, his mouth contorted, stretching, drooling. His legs felt warm, squishy—a reddish-brown liquid ran out his pajama pants onto the wooden deck.

"Dysentery case," the nurse said.

"Get a litter, dammit!"

They moved him back into the hallway, pulled the door closed. Someone was wiping at his legs so they could get him on the stretcher. "I can't go back on the line, I can't," Lett shouted.

"Don't worry. There's no Germans where you're going."

"It's not just them! Don't you see? Can't you see the ones that done it?!" He grasped at their collars and glared into their gleaming eyes wanting to care—the looks of those who had never been anywhere near the line, for which they should eternally thank whoever it was they thanked. "They take it all out of a guy, see, stray dogs got it better, rats do," he went on, figuring they would stick him with something any moment.

He felt the prick.

"That's all right, pal," an orderly said, "that's all right now."

Lett's legs seemed to have faded away, as if they had lowered him into a warm tub, and his head felt heavy, foggy again. He smiled, and held out his hand for Heloise. She would find him here.

"There. Now, now. Not the first time a soldier caught a little trouble…"

Just before he went under, Lett winced at a realization. That sorry case thought he had wanted to jump overboard, and the man wanted to help him do it. That's what he meant by a long way down. That's how wrecked they all were, and there were so many of them.

Lett would never jump. They would have to kill him first, he thought as his dream of Heloise washed over him.

***

March 30, 1945: Holger Frings rode a bicycle through the valley that led to Stromville. He wore simple civilian clothes, an old corded suit jacket and a gray overcoat that was sparse and vaguely military like most cut during the war. A leather cap. Back in January, the temporary leave pass got him to Brussels. His time there as Sergeant Wendell Lett had made it easier for him, just another veteran GI on a deserved rest, to spend and trade his counterfeit money. If anyone asked about his accent, he told them he couldn't help it—he grew up in a German-speaking Mennonite sect in Ohio. No one cared much now that the front had moved on into Germany. He had spent a good month or more bouncing between Brussels, Namur, and Liège, dealing with *marché noir* types and the assorted mobs of dead-end American deserters so desperate they'd turned to crime to survive, trading and selling everything from heavy troop trucks to parachutes for the ladies' stockings to be cut from them. He had used the profits to finance going underground. From that point on he had made (and imagined) himself a wayward Belgian German and he kept to the countryside of Southeastern Belgium, always on watch for the slim chance that he'd find Wendell Lett making his way back to Heloise. He had to wait until Stromville was safe enough, until he had nowhere else to go. Cologne was an exhausted moonscape, overwhelmed and occupied. The Hindenburg Bridge had finally collapsed from air raid damage and the burden of endless retreating in panic, he had heard, the suspension span tumbling into the Rhine and taking untold fleeing civilians and soldiers with it. In every corner of the defeated Reich, stray German soldiers—and whatever so-called spies were among them—were sure to be rounded up. In the East, masses of Red Army troops had entered East Prussia. They would soon set upon Brandenburg and Berlin. In Frings' darkest moments, a part of him hoped his girls would be persuaded, sensibly, to commit suicide. For the coming Russian retribution will have to sicken even Godfather Death himself.

The snow was gone, at least for this day, the valley spiked with early weeds that hinted at lovely meadows returning. He heard the roar of a truck coming up behind him and kept riding, head down. The truck passed him. It was Red Cross. Frings raised his head and eased off the pedaling.

On Stromville's streets, the locals worked on rebuilding. The only cars and people were civilian. Riding along the main street, Frings saw the Red Cross truck pull into a square across from a building, and locals gathered around.

He saw her. She had to be Heloise. She was even prettier than her photo. Her stomach showed a small bump, and her long blouse hung from it. She didn't gather with the others, Frings saw. Her gaze had fixed down the street, right at him. She walked over to a lamppost and stopped at it, still gazing at him.

He got off his bicycle, and walked it the rest of the way. Within steps of her, he doffed his cap and removed it. He stood before her, holding his cap with both hands.

"*Mademoiselle?*" he said.

"Yes. What is it?"

"It's about Wendell," he whispered in English, but he choked on the name.

Heloise shook her head at him. She stepped backward, glaring at him, and held onto the lamppost.

"Please, listen—"

"No!" Heloise fell to her knees. Frings dropped the bicycle and rushed to her, holding her shoulders as she cried, and she howled, pounding at his sides.

"But he might be alive," Frings said in her ear. "This is what I want to say. Do you hear me? There is always a chance."

She didn't seem to hear him, or want to. She moaned. Wailed. She grabbed at her stomach. Blood trickled down her legs, from between her thighs, spattering the earth.

***

April 30, 1945: Allied officers in best dress uniform—American, British, Soviet—sat smiling at a V-shaped table bearing lavish food and drink, whole hens, caviar, whisky, vodkas. A sign in English read: "Victory Soon! Archibald Barracks Welcomes You."

A former SS barracks near Germany's border with Czechoslovakia had been requisitioned by the US Army. A victory party had filled its grand hall. An American Congressman stood to speak, his expensive wire-framed glasses not doing enough to offset the slickness of his pencil-thin mustache. He said:

"Just when the war was thought won in the West, events took a dark, menacing turn. The enemy even resorting to a fanatical squad of assassins who dared wear our good uniform! A false flag operation! And yet there were those who understood the threat and held to that truth, even when it wasn't popular. I bring you one of those great men tonight. Yes, my Allied friends, it's a sublime honor to introduce you to the Horseback Hero himself—General Archie Archibald!"

The applause resounded in full force as Archie took the stage in his new general's uniform. He bowed and bowed but the applause and hoots wouldn't stop. Selfer applauded from his prime spot at the table. Another general approached Archie, holding up a medal. The Congressman took the mike again and shouted over the applause: "Our Archie, he'll do just fine back home, now won't he? Now won't he ever?!"

***

The celebration roared on. It had started the day before, when a sole nurse had rushed through the metal hut, then two and three and more, shouting, "It's over, boys, it's all over!" Locking arms and jumping up and down. Doctors and orderlies had joined in, and they moved on to the next hut, and all who could filed on outside to the grassy common area. Today, a Tuesday, they had put tables out on the commons before noon. Champagne appeared and bottles of strong cider the

English called "scrumpy," and some guy with a banjo of all things, and then an administrator man brought out a guitar that looked like a mandolin and a refugee fellow a violin. All stomped around, singing and playing, patients and staff and civilians alike in the spring sun. It was May 8, 1945: Victory in Europe.

Wendell Lett had stayed inside, poised on the rickety chair next to his bunk. His was no hospital bed anymore. Getting over the physical injury had proved routine. The bullets had busted ribs and hit nerves but somehow missed major organs. The strap on the hospital ship, simply a seagoing precaution. The problem came after. The hospital ship had delivered him to this hospital in Southern England, near Folkestone on the coast just southwest of Dover. A hospital stay of a month or so led to convalescence in this Quonset hut, what the Brits called a Nissen hut. They had built a hutment of them, all lined up in a vast camp. The rounded, corrugated one-piece metal roof with a few tiny square windows was like being inside a cargo plane. It was cold when he first got here, now starting to heat up in the spring.

He could hear them outside, really singing now, but he couldn't see it. He wasn't lucky enough to get one of those little hatch windows near his bunk.

He didn't know how long he could keep this up. For a long time he had thought the hospital ship was the worst part, when he had broken through his morphine and who-knew-what haze on that ship, not knowing at first it was a ship, stumbling out onto that chilling deck in pajamas of all things until the nurse and orderlies and dysentery found him. Seeing the sea surge and want to swallow them like that was a horror in itself. He couldn't imagine what Frings had been through out there. After his injuries were sure to heal, he told them he couldn't remember much. He knew he had been in battles, and that D-Day happened, and a surprise counteroffensive had really walloped them in the Ardennes, and that was it. The doctors listened. They asked questions. He kept it simple. He gave them a few discoveries. He suddenly recalled his rank, a sergeant. He was platoon leader. He believed his name was

William. Last name of Long, Lamb, something like that. He so wanted to find out who he was, he said, and the doctors had seemed to take that as a good sign. It wasn't a surprising occurrence. His was a fugue state, they called it, brought on by dissociative amnesia, reversible in theory but it was never clear how long it would stay with a man. Extreme battle fatigue had triggered it. It had stricken hundreds of thousands of GIs, if not millions. Lett had seen it up on the line. Guys just blanked out, all out of change. It was the only, final way to block the goddamn horror of the endless grind. A few were faking it but most were full-blown cases and the Army had far more than the War Department had bargained for, even after what they'd learned from World War One.

He had used this monster they created against them. Time was running out, though. For now, no one knew where he was. He had quit sending any letters stateside well before the Ardennes Counteroffensive, what American papers were now calling the Battle of the Bulge. He hadn't even dared getting a letter to Heloise. The censors could get wise to that tactic, and he didn't want to break her heart with the promise he could not keep. It could all shatter in an instant. He could always run into a dogface who knew him, or they could send him back to a hospital in the states at any time. And if he suddenly copped the miracle recovery, he was theirs too. He was a veteran platoon leader, a rare breed that they still needed. Of course they would send him back up on the line. VE-Day didn't matter. Sure, it was a good party for the rear and the home front but who were they kidding? He hadn't lost sight of the truth and he repeated it to himself as his sacred counsel, as if old Sheridan was right there whispering to him in the dark under ground: This was for the duration plus six. They would send him to the Pacific, where the Japanese would fight to their very extinction. If it wasn't Asia, they would take aim at Joe Stalin sooner than later. The German POWs had talked about it all the time. Don't get too comfortable, Joe, for soon we will join forces against the Bolshevist hordes aiming to enslave Europe, and Amerika was next. He got a constant reminder of where he was heading right here in the hospital. Some sobbed whether asleep or awake, while others could not speak or had taken on warped, warbled, stuttering voices like deaf men unable to hear themselves. One man burst out screaming at random and it was like artillery shrieking every time. Another went catatonic, eyes open like some undead mummy, and they rolled that one away, never to return.

A couple of the nurses passed through and urged Lett out to share some laughs but he stayed silent, as he was wont to do. Down the line of bunks, a couple of the hard-done cases lay on their beds, facing the corrugated metal, arms folded up. And the guilt washed over Lett again, like the icy rain in the Ardennes. He was using up a precious bunk. Other Joes needed it.

He had been waiting for the right time. He would make his move any moment. Outside he heard laughing, chanting. The whole hospital center had to be out there. Inside his footlocker, he had secondhand civilian clothes, a simple sweater and a peacoat, corduroy pants and brown brogues, a workingman's cap. Other patients had handed down the civvies when leaving. He had bought the rest of the items on one of the excursions the nurses led into town and no one had lifted an eyebrow. Yanks bought and traded for everything these days, so why not civvies? They had a little allowance for such trips. He saved what he could. To augment his stash, he had tried his hand at the card games in the hut. He had always hated cards. Maybe that was why he won so much. It all helped.

The Quonset hut door had been left open. In rushed a spring breeze with hints of the sea and a musky scent of chestnut trees. Keeping an eye on the doorway, Lett opened his footlocker and pulled the clothes on over his pajamas.

One of the remaining three had turned his way, sat up, and stared at him. His name was Thatch. Thatch had the boyish face like Lett and even the curly hair messing with his forehead but he sported a glare that made him more Jimmy Cagney that Mickey Rooney. Thatch had been up on the line. Thatch had been in the Hürtgen. The man never got near trees without screaming, howling, curling up in a ball. A guy like Thatch would have to live in the desert back home. Yet they were sending him back—he'd gotten orders to report to a repple-depple near Namur, Belgium.

He had tried to postpone redeployment by pricking his finger and draining the blood into a urine sample, complaining he had pains. The doctors knew that old trick. It only convinced them he had been faking all along.

Late one morning two days ago, Lett had found Thatch outside alone on a bench in his pajamas, no robe.

Lett had sat with him. "Everything jake?"

Thatch had nodded. "I knew you'd find me here," he had said after a couple minutes.

"That a fact?" Lett had said.

"I saw your face. When I just mentioned the word 'Belgium.'"

Lett wouldn't deny it. He had felt his face empty right out. Thatch noticed everything.

"You just did it again," Thatch said. "So listen up, see. Here's what's going to happen: You're going over for me."

"Look, maybe I should go get your robe for you. That or a doctor. You might have a fever."

Thatch glared at Lett. "You're not fooling me. You know exactly who you are, and you been eyeballing a way to get out of here."

Lett didn't say a thing. He sighed and stared at the chestnut trees, at lush green clusters of branches swinging and swaying like the gear on a GI hoofing it.

"They issued me new field ODs," Thatch said.

Lett moved to get up, but Thatch latched onto his wrist with surprising speed and grip. He had probably saved a snafu or two at the front before they ruined him.

Lett lowered back down.

"I got my ID card, paybook, travel docs, immunization sheet, the lot. Best thing is, I got a pass to that repple-depple in Namur."

Lett should have been smiling. He felt his face go numb, his skin like a layer of tinplate.

"There's that face again. You got a will and a way. You just gave me your answer. So come to me when you're ready to hit the gas."

Lett looked around the grounds. They still sat alone. Was it some kind of test? He had to be sure. This might be too good to be true. It could mean the stockade.

"Hell, we look enough alike," Thatch said. "Just promise me you're not really going to that repple-depple."

"Okay. I promise."

With that, Thatch had slapped his palms on his knees like a man who'd just enjoyed a nice lunch.

"What are you going to do?" Lett had said.

"Don't you worry about me."

"What about your dog tags?"

"Ah. Excellent question. I can't give you those, soldier. When they do find me, I want these bastards to know just who they got."

Now Lett stared at Thatch, sitting up on his bunk in the Quonset hut. Now it was Thatch whose face had emptied out. Lett had given Thatch a chance to back out when they'd heard the war was over, but Thatch had only shaken his head. The man had his own way out, and who could blame him?

"Well?" Thatch said. "Come and get it."

Thatch eyed the door for Lett as Lett emptied Thatch's footlocker. "Keep your eyes open. Keep moving. And don't you look back," Thatch whispered to him, like a platoon looie to a man about to lead a night patrol. "If I see you come back here, Willy or whatever your name is, I'll fucking kill you myself."

"Yes, sir."

"Then go! Get. You got those poker winnings to boot. I'm almost jealous. Go."

Thatch's small duffel was march-ready, half full with ODs and the documents. He had also left Lett a plaid civilian daypack he'd bought in town.

"I just can't do it," Thatch said, as Lett slipped the duffel inside the daypack. "It's a hell of a thing."

"You remind me of a Joe I knew," Lett said. "A couple of them, now that I think of it."

"Sure I do. And I'll bet they're dead too."

Lett nodded. "Thank you."

"Forget it."

"But, why?"

"Why you? Because you seem like a fellow who would do the same. We hole buddies look after our own, am I right? Now go."

Lett went. He had it all planned out. He took the far paths on the rear of the hospital grounds, where there was a civilian entrance— a little stone fence with iron gate like for the cemetery of an English country church. The guard there was dancing with another guard as three nurses cried with laughter. They drank scrumpy from thick glass handle mugs; it trickled down their chins and glistened in the sun. Lett had his cap down low. He grinned, big and brightly like a civ, and they waved and he waved and they kept on dancing and laughing because the main thing was the war was over and done, friend.

He kept grinning as he strolled right out the gate.

The whole world around him had fooled itself into thinking that war was over. It made things easy at the moment. He walked into town, listening to the revels and music along the way. Waving and smiling. He passed the rail station, and his heart thumped. Two British MPs stood around a jeep, shooting the shit but not quite grinning like the rest. Good thing he wasn't taking the train.

He had eyeballed his route on their various trips into town and farther up the road into Dover. It was a few hours' walk there, half a day if he had to play it safe, but who was looking to hassle a chap on VE-Day? The Dover Strait was the narrowest passage across the English Channel to France, no more than thirty miles. Requisitioned ferries were running troops and certified civilians across, as were LSTs. He remembered that Holger Frings himself had helped sink one or two of these ships. Frings had told Lett he knew the Dover Strait as well as St. Martin's Quarter in Cologne, the way it used to be.

The narrow inland roads ran little wider than one large sedan. Lett walked to one side and felt naked not to have a dogface tramping along the other edge. Hedges lined his route for long stretches, so close the tendrils and twigs brushed his hips and grazed his cheeks.

It all looked a little too much like Normandy hedgerow country. Every few minutes his lungs pressed together so bad he had to hunch down and peek around shrub lines and scan the next hedge coming. He walked on. He passed junctions and heard more singing, music, laughing. The road opened up again. A delivery truck slowed to pass. A couple girls on bicycles rode by, ringing their bells at him, who to them might have been just another birdwatcher or farmer. He started to breathe easier, loosen his step. He passed a farm.

A crack-pop rang out. He dove between skinny trees along the road, hit the deck and scrambled over to hug a tree trunk, his heart thumping, his vision blurring, going dim.

His eyes sprung open. He had blacked out. He didn't know for how long. Minutes maybe? He was crouched inside a small wood. He looked out. Across the road, a woman in a work smock was chopping firewood behind the farmhouse. This was all it had taken to knock him down—one piece split.

He let out a sigh, brushed off dirt, and strolled onward. He let his arms flap along and he smiled at a little bird following him, hovering and darting, teasing him. Sidewalks and houses of red and brown brick and timbered white stucco, then two-story buildings began to line the way on the back road leading into Dover. A man approached on the sidewalk. He wore a regular British uniform with gaitered ankle boots and short jacket, but gray hair showed from under his sidecap and he had an old rifle slung. A civilian overcoat was draped over his shoulders, and a whistle hung from his neck. He was one of the Home Guard, nicknamed "Dad's Army." Walking beside him, doing her happy best to stay in step, was a girl of about eight in a flowered dress, a granddaughter surely. She smiled at Lett, and the old man smiled, but Lett could only glare. His face had scrunched up, and filled with heat. He hustled around them and off behind a brick building. He hugged the brick wall there. He cried. He wailed. His fingers dug into the gaps between the bricks, the mortar creeping up under his fingernails, his fingertips scraping until bleeding.

***

In Stromville's only park, a simple open green behind the battle-scarred church, the trees and flowers had bloomed and the sunlight bathed all in its glow. All the village and surrounding district had gathered. Jaunty music played, Belgian in spirit but sounding like a Dixieland tune. The people danced and kissed, and US, British and Belgian flags waved. It was May 8, 1945. Many of the people had left the area during the last years of the war, some as early as when the Germans first invaded in 1940, and were now returning to celebrate the end of all they had missed.

Heloise sat on a bench with the man once known as Holger Frings. Frings held her purse and a basket while Heloise rested her hands upon her pregnant stomach. When Frings had come with the news of her Wendell, she had expected the worst. The trauma contributed to a "false miscarriage," as Doctor Servais called it—a bit of bleeding but nothing to worry about. She was lucky this time, he said. She still wanted to despise Frings for the news he brought, even though it contained hope, and yet the man had offered to stay near her and help her recover. She and her father needed the help. Frings stayed in the cellar of their destroyed building, guarding the remains while she and her father moved in down the street. He vowed to watch over her stash of passports, ID papers, and forging supplies, and he would take the fall. He told her more about his time with Wendell, about how Wendell had talked Frings out of destroying himself. He told her that if her Wendell turned up alive anywhere, anytime, he was prepared to help bring her man back to her. Even if Wendell was in a prison. Frings demanded the duty. He had nothing else. He still didn't know if his daughters were alive. A part of him didn't want to know the truth. He doubted if he could ever get to them inside the cursed rat cage that was now defeated and occupied Germany. He was the orphan now.

A car slid to a halt and released four young men wearing armbands of the Belgian colors. More patriots. There were those who served Belgium, and those who served themselves. The latter now roamed the countryside fingering wartime traitors according to a criteria they only seemed to know, and had the full support of those citizens who had just returned. Heloise knew better, and recognized most. Many had only just joined the Secret Army when a winner was assured. A few had been in the leftist Front of Independence, and some the fascist *Légion Belge*. Some were just independent operators. No matter their current team, all the new boys had been scrambling to report any tip-offs and catches to the British and American authorities before their MPs and intelligence corps decamped for Germany.

"Harvest time," Heloise said to Frings. "Took them long enough."

Frings knew what to do by this point. He slipped another stick of Wrigley's in his mouth and leaned back, legs spread—the casual Yank.

Two of the patriots marched over to the bench. The lead one was tall with long arms, like a goalkeeper. He stood over Frings. "Who are you? A goddamn German maybe?" he said in French.

His apparent deputy stood with fat little hands pressed into his plump hips. "Speak!" he shouted in French.

Frings grinned, and held up his hands as if he didn't understand.

Heloise stood, got in their faces. "He's American," she whispered in French. "He was, in any case. The gendarmes checked him out."

The patriots backed up a step. The goalkeeper crossed his arms at his chest, and plump deputy jammed his cigarette back in his mouth.

"He's more than clean," Heloise said and stepped forward. "The Resistance cleared him too. The Resistance who risked it all for you. Were any of you in the Secret Army when it meant something? No? No?"

"Very well . . ." The two patriots backed off further, making for the crowd. They argued and pushed at each other, and once inside the crowd began looking for others to harass.

"They won't do a thing about you," Heloise whispered out of a side of her mouth.

"For now." Frings still leaned back, but she saw his fingertips had pressed to the bench planks as he eyed the men puffing themselves up in the crowd. He cased the periphery and horizon, as if still aboard his old fighting boat.

***

Wendell Lett sighed in relief, the fresh air filling his lungs, and his chest just about exploded from the force of it. Stromville was still there, he saw. He stood on the ridge, crouched between tree trunks, sizing up the final stretch to the village through the little valley. It was green again.

He had walked the same route as he and Frings before—up a high road, cut through forest, and his steps had lightened in the underbrush, his GI instincts taking over. He wore his civvie sweater, corduroy pants and workers cap but hung the peacoat on the daypack. Dust and road dirt had worked into his clothes, and they smelled like exhaust from all the cars and trucks that had passed him as he walked. It was May 11, 1945. Crossing over from England had been the easy part, thanks to Thatch. In Dover he had recovered from seeing the old man and girl and pressed on, into town. The British and American MPs had a presence there as always, but they were celebrating V-E too. The pops of champagne and howling, the parading, lurching vehicles' engines whizzing like 88s—it all threatened to make him cower and on the street they must have thought him the old man the way he hobbled along. At one point he sat in a dark corner of a pub and could only drag himself back out into the world when the publican closed for the afternoon. He had changed into the ODs in a back alley, and stuffed the ID and papers in his pockets. Thatch had indeed led a platoon, as a field commission looie. Lett had looked at his ID card and realized Thatch was smiling in the photo. Like this he looked more like Lett, or at least like Lett before the war. It would do. The travel papers were for tomorrow so Lett booked a cheap hotel, partly as a way to test his papers, and the front desk didn't even ask. He stayed in his damp room the whole night, ignoring the parties roaring on and memorizing what he could from Thatch's documents in case an MP or clerk went asking. The man was married, with children. Not even such a thing as them could keep the man going.

The next morning Lett strode down into Dover harbor wearing the ODs with looie bars and a pair of flyboy sunglasses Thatch had thrown in, the duffel hanging off his shoulder stuffed with the daypack inside. Checking in was a breeze, the surely hung-over clerk hardly looking up. Lett had simply walked onto the requisitioned military ferry as directed. Along the way he had been ready to show his papers, holding them out, but the guards only kept everyone moving. On the trip over he had sat by himself on the open deck, pretending to be seasick if anyone got too friendly. The boat tossed and rolled enough as it was, and it made Lett think of Holger Frings again, what a guy like that must have gone through out here on the open sea.

The ferry delivered him to Ostende, Belgium where, Frings once told him, the seaman had hunkered down in bomb-battered S-boat pens. Lett took a crowded train to Brussels that afternoon and switched for Namur, and the sight of so many lights coming on for another evening of peace jolted him. GIs from the repple-depple roamed the glowing streets probing for any fresh action, the *poules* and hustlers luring them in, the MPs tracking them. In his looie getup he might as well have been a baby snug in a buggy. He found a shitty *pension* above a shitty cafe, the type where they water down the booze for drunk GIs on leave. In the morning he changed back into his civvies, rode a tram till it ended and walked out of the city. He headed southeast, sticking to the side roads and small towns. Sometimes he mixed in with columns of refugees, but never too long, and other times just went it alone and no one bothered him. It could have taken him only one long day if he pushed it but he didn't push it. He had found an abandoned bicycle and rode that until the chain busted, at which point he had handed it off to a passing refugee boy who was overjoyed to have it. Lett, in his wandering daydreams, had imagined the kid growing up to become a designer of sleek motorcycles as long as the next war didn't claim him. That night he had slept in an abandoned farmhouse. He ate country eggs and pears right from trees. In the morning he had started recognizing the countryside and the roads. He had passed through British troops milling along the road once, and a good number of their jeeps had passed him, but still no one had bothered him. This peace business was a damn fine thing, he had told himself. People should work for it as hard as they went to war.

His dogface nose kept him up on the ridge above Stromville a good while, casing the valley until he knew every bird, every flower. He had to talk himself into pressing on, tricking and charming and promising himself. Finally he walked down the ridge, finding the same way he had run down before. He walked through the valley. His heart pinched and his veins pulsed, his neck swelling with emotion. He heard a droning sound like a spotter plane and it was all he could do not to dive along the side of the road. Mine signs still stood here, and he saw craters that he might have caused himself. Up ahead in the village, billows of dust rose into the air where, he could only hope, the people were rebuilding. He kept going, step after step, his legs and joints as if detached, like a puppet's wooden legs he had to keep moving and bending with his hands and it wore him out.

He entered Stromville. He flanked the main street and his feet found the cobblestone of a village lane, his hands as fists, packed with anticipation. A couple people passed. He thought he recognized one elderly lady from his days around here but he kept going, and he felt her watching his back as he continued on.

He neared Heloise's building. He came around a corner and

thought maybe he had the wrong lane. It took him a moment to understand that the pile of rubble standing there had been her house.

His lungs emptied out. His legs wanted to give way. He picked them up, onward. He rushed inside the remains of the house and squatted down, the piles of debris and bricks surrounding him. He peered around on his haunches, panting. The door to the cellar still stood, and some of the frame. Not much was scorched, a good sign. But he couldn't go down in that cellar. He peered out down the main street, squinting at the light sparkling on the cobblestones and dancing in the dust, just like a Joe looking for snipers.

So where to now? Did he even want to know what had happened to her?

All energy had left him, like it did a Joe after making it back from another hairy patrol. He lowered himself to his butt and his fists opened, palms up on his lap. He might have passed out.

Someone was hugging him. At first he thought it was a child, because he heard a mix of sobbing and giggling and he felt what seemed like a play ball.

She hugged him. Heloise was hugging him. She looked up at him with the same expression he had, somewhere between utter horror and outright laughter. The play ball was her stomach. She was pregnant. He saw it. She nodded.

They held each other. She cried. He had not stopped.

Her face went hard. She shot up and grabbed his hand with the strength of a BAR gunner. "We can't stay here," she said, and led him away.

"So very good to see you, old boy," her father Jean said using one of his stock English phrases, as if he'd just seen Lett a couple days ago. Heloise had led Lett down the main street and into a newer building with few shrapnel pocks. They had a second story apartment, with two small bedrooms and a view onto a back courtyard, but its sparseness revealed it was borrowed. It had a narrow balcony. Jean left Lett and

Heloise out there. They sat on little metal chairs, facing each other so close their knees interlocked, cradling each other's warm hands. She hadn't spoken the whole way over.

"I can't believe I'm here," Lett said. "I can't believe you survived that bombing back there. I can't believe we're expecting. Me and you." He held her by the shoulders, his gaze fixed on her bump of a pregnant stomach. "You're going to have to start calling me a new name, *chérie*, whatever you got for me, and I can't wait to learn French the way you Belgies speak it, and . . ."

Her head had slumped to one side. She stared at the balcony railing, at the rusting metal bars.

"What is it?" He leaned toward her, resting his forehead on hers. "Listen, I know, we've both been through so much, the town's taken a big hit, but it's like a funeral around here."

Her chin quivered.

He perked up. "Wait. Where is he? Is he here?"

She started to speak, three times. The third time, she said, "He was here."

His eyes welled up hot and searched the sky. He glared through the glass at Jean inside. Jean sat forward on a sofa, hands hanging between his knees. He shook his head at Lett.

"Holger came here," she said. "He made it. He tells me everything you two experience. He tells me about poor Tom. Wendell—do you know, I almost lost our baby?"

"But you have it. Look. Feel it. You have it."

She nodded. She perked up now. Her eyes widened, wild. She felt at his back and ribs, fingers probing, as if searching for a wasp gone down his shirt. "What about you? Your wounds, my god, are you all right?"

"Yes. Don't worry about that." Lett had stood. He grasped at the railing, looking out, but all he got was the courtyard and more walls like theirs. "Where is he? Do we know? What do we know?"

She sat up straight. "We do not know. He is just gone. *Allé.* He lived in our bombed house. In the cellar. He wants to guard it. We don't know what happened to him. He is here before a couple days ago. All was normal. He was happy. Always he talked about the day he finds you again."

"But he would have told you if he left."

"Yes, of course. His things are still there. It is as if someone steals him—like a person steals a baby. *Soudainement.*"

"So suddenly. Just like that."

"Yes," she said, shaking her head again. "But I should not get upset. The doctor says it. It upsets my stomach."

***

Holger Frings knew: He had been a fool to let himself believe, for one moment, that peace might save him. This peace was only war by other means. Until they could figure out what the next war would be exactly, a sorry bastard like he remained a seditious menace and a firestorm to be snuffed out at all costs, if only to rally the war-weary.

He was back in an American uniform, but this time it was OD prisoner fatigues. The *Amis* called his prison a "stockade," which sounded like something out of the Old West. As the US Army moved him farther into Germany wearing handcuffs and heavy iron leg shackles, first in a jeep, then in a prisoner train car, then in the back of a heavy truck surrounded by four thick-shouldered MPs, he knew, with a sick smile creeping across his face, that they were taking him right back to good old Grafenwöhr. They had followed the route of the US advance. The few times Frings got to see out he wished he hadn't. Germany looked worse than he heard, all rubble and black smoke high into the sky, sometimes blocking out the sun, the elderly begging for food with heads down, children wandering with no one to wipe their dirty faces. The familiar stench of rotting dead and a gritty dust kept scratching at his nostrils.

"What the hell did we all expect?" Frings had muttered in English.

Two MPs told him to shut his kraut trap, but one said: "You give a lickin', you get a lickin'. Everbody gets got, Fritzie."

The prison was a former barracks with a half-timbered framework and that light yellow stucco of Southern Germany. The only iron was in the cell doors and cell windows. It was a glorified barn stable and nothing like the villas they surely kept the bigwig Nazis in, nor like those sprawling, exposed, disease-ridden POW bivouacs for the millions of nearly starving Wehrmacht regulars. Theirs was a special place for special types, like an asylum for deviants, sadists and sociopaths. He imagined another wing for former concentration camp guards, another for former Gestapo henchmen.

Back in Stromville he had let down his guard. He should have kept a better night watch. Those Belgian bastards had nabbed him in the middle of the night, right from his position down in Heloise's former cellar. They tied his wrists with a thick, grating rope and stuffed an oily rag in his mouth and heaved him into a car trunk like Chicago mobsters. Luckily they hadn't found Heloise's stash; they were too full of piss and vinegar and dark ale to take time searching. They had delivered him to a US Counterintelligence Corps team sweeping the area. Those boys were German emigré Jews and didn't want to hear stories. So Frings told them a lot of truth. During the Battle of the Bulge he had taken part in what had become known as *Operation Greif*. He had deserted after his jeep crashed. But, he had gone on the lam all on his own, he said. He left out the part about a GI named Wendell Lett and a Belgian gal called Heloise.

It was nearing the end of June. He had his own cell, about the size of his S-boat wheelhouse but with walls of cold, damp stone and that thick iron door painted gray. His plank for a bed swung down from the wall but inclined slightly toward the floor, always giving him the feeling he would roll out. So he slept on the hard stuff, like a tired seaman coming off watch without a bunk. They had let him write letters. He had written to Christiane's family's address in Brandenburg but nothing had returned, not even his own letter, and he did not expect it to come. He wrote to Christiane's sister, Hedwig. That letter had just come back undeliverable, stamped by German and Allied authorities. "Dead letters," the *Amis* called such mail, almost sounding like Germans in their fitting grimness.

He recognized fellow inmates from his Grafenwöhr training and from Schmidtheim on the Belgian border last December. The US Army had rounded up a couple dozen of the Stielau Unit commandos and stuck them here. Most had been in custody for months, others since the mission itself. When allowed fresh air out on the walled-in courtyard some promenaded the perimeter as if it was intermission at the Bavarian State Opera, a few even arm-in-arm as they debated like two-bit philosophers, others arguing gently like small-time barons and mistresses, all envisioning just what the victorious Allies were about to do with them. They were fools and they were tools. They thought that peace would save them, just like the Führer's Wonder Weapons were supposed to have delivered them. Frings knew: The Allies could give a shit about them any more they could the shot-up German tanks and planes already rusting across the land. They were so much scrap metal. They were walking dead, a disgrace, an embarrassment even to those few hysterical sows who still clung to Nazi views.

Meanwhile, others had crumpled. They gathered at the courtyard table, heads down, shoulders slumped and hands out, the most pathetic *Stammtisch* ever known. They could barely look at each other. They had told their own fortunes. So they had been drafting appeals and writing group petitions of mercy to American generals. They had been duped, they said. They thought they were to become interpreters. They could not refuse the duty or would have been shot. And they could only act when it was almost too late, when they were already on the mission. Some claimed they had driven their jeeps right to such-and-such US headquarters and surrendered themselves, but no one would believe their innocence. Some had only gone over and hidden, or done as little as possible and returned to Skorzeny's command post. The promenading true believers wanting to slit this group's throats, if they ever had the chance. The poor bastards, all. None of it mattered. The fact was, they had all crossed the enemy front line, and the enemy had won. It didn't matter who made them, what made them. It only mattered what uniform they wore.

Some were former *Kriegsmarine*, in both camps. Frings didn't mix with his fellow sailors now. He kept to himself. Besides, he suspected the Americans only let them congregate so they would talk—and could be listened in on secretly.

He asked around about one matter only, and he got his answer from a diehard still wearing a squared-off Hitler-style mustache. The man told Frings that, the way he heard it, the former Gauleiter Werner Scherenberg had committed suicide in rural Austria. He didn't know about a wife or any daughters, and looked surprised that Frings expected him to know.

Frings knew how this would play out. Suckers like them didn't get to survive wars intact. Only the pawns were sacrificed. That was why they had never seen their leaders. Just like before at Grafenwöhr, vaunted SS commando mastermind Otto Skorzeny never ended up in this prison. The reasons why should have been made clear enough when, as they watched the movie allowed them once a week, there came a newsreel in which appeared none other than former SS Lt. Col. Skorzeny himself. It was in a story about prominent Germans captured. The image only lasted a moment. Skorzeny was under guard, but he was smiling along with his MP escorts in dress uniforms of white gloves, white belts and white gaiters. The entourage was exiting an Alpine villa. The newsreel mentioned trials to come. Surely Skorzeny would have a limousine take him there.

Frings had stood before a make-do military court they had set up here, a C-shaped tribunal of wooden schoolhouse tables. The judges sat facing him before the backdrop of a large American flag on the wall. The lawyers on both sides probably called each other by first names as Americans did. Their uniforms were crisp and clean and loaded up with ribbons and decorations ("fruit salad," *Amis* called it), and Frings got a whiff of hair tonic and mothballs. They gave no witnesses or testimony. The point was to add him, the latecomer, to the rest of the defendants. A formality. Then a stern Army lawyer in horn-rimmed glasses entered waving papers and announced that he had news for him, for all of them: The ongoing appeals had been halted based on conclusive new evidence that would be provided to defense lawyers.

The gist: Sentencing would be carried out the next morning.

The news hit the others hard, even the hopefuls. Fantasy Land had run out of sugarcoating. Intermission over at the opera. They moaned, shouted, sobbed in their cells. They retreated inside themselves.

Frings had no more retreat left. He had come to understand, finally, the machinelike system that had haunted him on the S-boat when he had manned the wheel but felt no real control. There was no secret, no solution, no release from the cold horror. He never could have had control. He was an implement; he was implemented by orders. The machinelike system should have never given him comfort, and certainly not a feeling of freedom, for this was precisely when it had been allowed to reap its worst damage. Powerlessness was simply his natural state. From his position, he could have never preserved his family. He never could have kept them safe. He should have never promised them, and no one should have expected him to survive. Christiane, in her cruel pragmatism, was the wisest of all in realizing the truth of it.

He requested his last meal: A big steak. Surely they had one like he had remembered from America. The thin slab of meat he got was tough and gray inside, like stew meat past its prime.

In the morning, the names were called out. Three men at a time. Cell doors squeaked open. Some men shrieked, while others said nothing. Frings had sat on the edge of his plank bed most of the night. Like on the S-boat, he had watched the sun come up. The light streamed through the window in vivid rays cut by the iron bars, at first the color of salmon fresh from the Rhine, then golden like the fruit gum dancing bears he loved as a boy. He waited to be called. He clucked his tongue, letting the vial in the back of his mouth roll between molars and flesh. A few days before, one of the sailors had shaken his hand out in the courtyard—and slipped a vial into his palm. Frings knew the drill from *Operation Greif* itself: the vial contained cyanide. A few of the vials had been making the rounds, provided by a sympathetic defense team translator, it was said. But they were getting passed along like they were steaming hot iron. His comrade *Matrose* figured Frings for a willing taker, considering that he had not been so during the mission itself.

Frings couldn't believe his good luck. This was the only thing close to deliverance. He had choice now. He had the control.

"Frings, Holger!"

They led him and two others out to the rear side of the building. He saw the wall pocked with bullet holes, the shards of stucco on the ground. Some ten meters before it stood three poles, stained dark red. Walking alongside them were two MPs each and one Army chaplain wearing a black cossack and an OD sidecap with captain's bars. The sun had risen over the treetops, blinding with sparkle and casting golden patches on the short mowed weed-grass at their feet. He saw a few onlookers on the fringes, smoking, chatting. No cameras, no reporters, and certainly no newsreel.

A squad of MPs stood farther out, the sun bouncing off their polished helmets. The brightness made the men squint and look like they were wincing at what they were about to do, but Frings didn't buy it. They were a firing squad, just as he had been an S-boat wheelman. The first line knelt and the second stood like ranks of infantry from the days of Napoleon, as it always had been, back to the Thirty Years War. Tiny stars of light danced on the shiny barrels of their rifles. The two MPs grabbed his wrists, pulled them behind his back and around the pole, and tied them off. At some point a circle of white paper had been pinned to his chest. His brain couldn't follow it all now; the more he tried to focus, the blurrier things became until the perimeter was only a gold-rimmed whiteness of sunlight. Then the Army chaplain was speaking to him, first in English and then in a wooden, formal German but it was like Frings could understand no more human language. He only shook his head. He thrust his back against the pole, letting it dig into his spine. A hood came over his head, black fabric that still carried the metallic scent of another man's desperate spittle. This triggered some drastic lever in him and his pulse kicked in, racing full ahead. He heard the rustle of feet out before him, the soft clatter of rifles held to aim. The squad leader shouted: "Ready!"

Frings bit down, crunch, and the poison burned inside his mouth and brain, searing, expanding. He couldn't breathe, got no oxygen like he was drowning, and he wanted to flap his limbs as if to swim up to the surface but his limbs had seized up, and his lungs, and the whole of him squeezed up, compressing into nothing.

It was so dim he could only make out his hand. He held it up before his eyes, pasty white and glowing. Dark sea surrounded him. He floated. He was underwater. He floated without needing air, without breathing at all. He sensed something looming above him—the hull shape of a boat, about 35 meters long and narrow and almost sleek. He looked down. A black abyss waited below his feet, far, far below. He felt a chill from it, rippling up his spine, but then he realized that he wasn't descending. He wasn't even treading water to stay in place. He didn't have to.

The dark water began to lighten, in one spot far off yet growing brighter, whiter, wider, at first like a diving light and then, fantastically, like a star beneath the dark sea.

Two little figures floated before him, the white light illuminating them.

"Elisa, Kristina," he said, able to speak even though he was so far underwater.

Their faces brightened. They flapped their arms as if treading water, in that way they liked to play. He flapped his arms for them.

They grinned. He grinned. A profound warmness filled him. Whatever held him there in place released him, he felt it. He moved toward his Elisa and Kristina, just by thinking he could.

They moved on away from him but facing him, smiling still. He followed. As they traveled along he reached out to touch them but it only made them rush onward in a spurt, like keen and perky fish. They led him to the light this way, the water brightening them, growing ever whiter, warming them together.

***

"*Fire!*"

Lett jolted awake. He'd had another nightmare. This one was different and new. He was up on the line as always, but Heloise and the baby were huddled in his foxhole with him. It's night. Enemy artillery shrieks down from above while friendly mortar fire thunks from the rear, all of it finding his line. He covers Heloise and baby with his body, hugging them underneath him. Shrapnel zings past, striking his helmet, tearing at his web gear. Daylight comes. Men shout. They yank him from the hole, leaving Heloise and the baby exposed, reaching out for him and screaming. The men are MPs. They drag him away kicking and punching at air and they stand him to a post. A chaplain comes, in black. He ties Lett's wrists behind him and to the post. A firing squad faces Lett. Dead men, already executed, lay between him and the firing line, like so many olive drab bedrolls and packs but they're bloody, ripped through with bullet holes. Tom Godfrey lays there, and Thatch, and all his GI buddies. They're dead but they watch him. Then, Holger Frings is there. He stands watching from the side, on his own, with a serene look on his face that Lett has never seen, what he imagines as Frings before war. At the chaplain's command, the MPs pull a black hood over Lett's head ...

It was the fourth time that night Lett had shocked himself awake, as far as Heloise knew. The truth was, he had been awake most of the night. It was only when he fell into something like a sleep that the nightmares came. It was the end of June 1945 now. They had come so far. He had long burned all traces of Thatch's identity that he had carried, and Heloise had helped create a new identity for him using her stash and her Resistance contacts, some of whom had drifted back into crime now that war didn't require their expertise. His papers were intact, though some would not pass dedicated scrutiny by a crack detective from Criminal Investigations Division or even a hawk-eyed MP. It was enough to get started. They had even made him fake discharge papers. His name was now John Macklin. John Macklin had been in a unit like Lett's, up on the line since Normandy, so he wouldn't have to pretend to be someone too far from what he was. The best part was, John Macklin now had a proper Belgian *carte d'identité*. If he could only get on with his new life. The day-time wasn't always easier. Too many noises rattled him. Confessing things to her had helped. He had told her he felt like a criminal, but not like a common deserter. He felt like he had gotten away with something sick, like a murderer. Other times, he told her, he felt guilty about all the other guys who bought it. Why not he? Why a good man like Tom Godfrey?

"What is it?" Heloise whispered in the dark. She brushed back his damp hair with her fingers. His sweat was cooling, chilling his neck and messed-up ribs. She had moved closer to him, warming him with their baby in her tummy.

"He came back," he whispered.

"Who came back?"

"Holger. In the dream. He was there. I saw him."

He thought about Holger Frings all the time. He wouldn't be here without the German. He wouldn't be alive. Frings had even left Heloise a bundle of francs, for them. Lett had to repay the German. Many times he wanted to head out and find Frings, but Heloise wouldn't let him. It was too risky. Lett knew about risky. He worried that the phony Belgian patriots would come back or finger them to the Americans, but Heloise assured him that they certainly would not. This was a kind of stalemate. In grabbing the defeated enemy Frings, they were only looking for easy booty, something they could use to move up in the world, to prove them-selves to the Allies. Fingering her was too bold for such men. She and her Paul had been in the Rèsistance while they had cowered and some even collaborated, so she could always hold that over them if they ever tried.

"This does not sound like a nightmare," she said.

"No. I know. It started out like one, and then it wasn't one at all."

In the dream, with the hood on his head, all had gone black. He heard the firing squad ready their rifles. Except he could still see Holger Frings through the dark fabric, his silhouette shining through it as if illuminated by a bright light. The squad leader had yelled "Ready!" But Frings had only smiled for Lett.

Once Lett's sweat had dried, and his breathing eased, Heloise rolled away from him to get something from the side of the bed. She came back grasping it, just glints in the near dark it was, but he recognized the soft jingle it made. As his eyes adjusted he saw the thin metal rectangles hanging on a ball chain like some sick joke of a rosary. She held them up dangling, catching a little moonlight through the windows.

His dog tags.

"Holger wanted that I keep these," she said. "I couldn't throw them away."

"Good man. It's okay."

"I did not know if you wish to see them. If you want them still, for yourself."

He stared at them a while. They were probably his only way back to his old life. "Of course not. I don't want them. Don't be silly, *chérie*."

"I feel I must give you the choice. For a one last time."

"We'll throw them away. Bury them deep, melt them down, whatever. Tomorrow."

"Very well." She watched him, one hand caressing his chest and one hand feeling her belly, linking all three of them.

"What did he say to you?" she said. "In the dream."

Lett turned to her. "How do you know he said something?"

"The look on your face. You look something like happy. Maybe this is you before the war."

"I don't think I can ever be like before. But, you got a good eye. What he said was, we were going to be all right. He didn't say it out loud, but I heard what he was saying just the same."

AFTERWORD

I thought I had finished writing about everyday soldiers forced to impersonate the enemy and endanger themselves as spies during the Battle of the Bulge after writing a novel (*The Losing Role*) and a brief nonfiction history of the Germans' notorious false flag operation (*Sitting Ducks*). And yet the story found me again. Acting on a tip from a friend, I had the honor of interviewing an elderly American, loved and respected in his community, who had a secret to tell me. In 1944, he revealed, he was called up to take part in intelligence missions similar to Wendell Lett's: one was with a frightening recon patrol disguised as German soldiers that somehow ended up in bombed-ravaged Cologne; another mission, conversely, was a decoy operation to hunt down Germans disguised as Americans roaming behind American lines in Belgium. At the time of my contact's mission, S-2 had told him never to speak of his duty for a good fifty years, for it would remain classified. Despite speaking to me, my contact wished to remain anonymous. I searched for records of such missions nevertheless, and kept finding dead ends. My contact may have had some details mixed up in his old age, though one thing was clear—the emotions he expressed to me lay bare horrid memories. I doubt I'll ever know the whole truth.

Fiction allows a writer to mine deeper truths. As it turns out, my fictional story takes a different path. The man I interviewed would have never considered deserting, and Wendell Lett is a much differ-

ent character who did worse deeds. Nevertheless, the wanton recklessness of such missions made me wonder what could drive a man
to his limit.

The answers lay in the combat experience. The true horrors
of front-line duty—and S-boat warfare, to be sure—are difficult
to express and convey, even though I based mine on actual conditions, operations and mental states. Truly, one can't make up such
degrees of organized savagery without sounding far-fetched. As for
the combat GIs, a small segment of the US Army did almost all the
fighting without break and died for it in droves. They had signed up
"for the duration," an open-ended if not hopelessly endless stretch
before tours of duty became common. Some could only perform
so much duty for a big picture war effort they rarely saw or appreciated. By 1945, the number of AWOL and deserted soldiers in
war-torn Europe had reached tens of thousands. Only some were
considered active criminals. Others certainly chose to quit fighting
in a war that they knew didn't match the publicity back home, a
war that only they could know intimately in its horror and unique
capability to consume lives and souls in increasing numbers. That
war has been mythologized ever since, providing the ideal alterna-
tive for the United States' involvement in more recent campaigns.
By its nature, myth lies far from reality. In the words of one who was
there: "The Allied war has been sanitized and romanticized almost
beyond recognition by the sentimental, the loony patriotic, the ig-
norant, and the bloodthirsty," wrote historian, professor and World
War II frontline combat veteran Paul Fussell in *Wartime* (1989).

The surprise German counteroffensive of December 1944 fooled
American intelligence and ignited the Battle of the Bulge—a grim
wintry bloodbath that could have been avoided. In the notorious operation mentioned above, Germans infiltrated American lines in US
jeeps and wearing US uniforms. The Allies prosecuted their commander, SS Lieutenant Colonel Otto Skorzeny, in the Dachau trials
of 1947, but key defense testimony from Allied officers revealed that

such tricks had been attempted since the beginning of war (and certainly continue today). Indeed, it's been suggested that Hitler got the idea for the operation after hearing that American Rangers pulled off a similar ruse to help capture the German city of Aachen in September 1944.

For me, preserving the sanctity of uniforms fit for killing exposes the absurdity of war. I'm not placing blame here, not saying World War II should not have been fought, but rather I hope to remind. Morality does not endure in actual war, during close combat, so let's quit claiming that it does. Let's honor a man or woman who was there, but never a war itself and those who start it. Those who lead us to war continue to perpetrate a profound failure of humanity, and all too often a heartless crime against all of us.

ACKNOWLEDGMENTS

Special thanks to: Matt Love; Peter Kreisman; Karl Scheuch, retired German Navy Commander (*Fregattenkapitän a. D.*) and S-boat expert; the helpful staffs of the Cologne City Museum (*Kölnisches Stadtmuseum*) and the Dover Museum and Library; my trusted readers and friends for feedback on early versions of this story; Peter Riva, for inspiring me to expand the story; and my wife and reader-editor René again and as always.